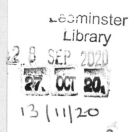

KT-166-347

...ad this year
Daily Mail

'First-rate psychological suspense'
Observer

'The kind of novel words like "unputdownable"
were invented for . . . captivating'
Independent

'A triumph of pacing and suspense'
Woman & Home

'Seriously, amazingly, awesomely brilliant'
CJ Tudor

'The twists are primed and deployed
with a master craftsman's skill'
Sunday Express

'A chilling and uniquely disturbing twenty-first century
twist on the unreliable narrator makes for a compulsive
and deeply thought-provoking psychological thriller'
Cara Hunter

'A completely original psychological thriller
that grabs you and doesn't let go'
K...

'Constantly cranking up the suspense . . .
a thoroughly satisfying read'
Reader's Digest

'A guaranteed best-seller'
Red Magazine

'The most intriguing plot idea I've seen in a good while'
The Spectator

'Genuinely eerie . . . beautifully handled'
USA Today

'Riveting . . . Writing with precision and grace,
Delaney strips away the characters' secrets
until the raw truth of each is revealed'
Publishers Weekly

'A guaranteed best-seller'
Prima

'A masterfully crafted spellbinder . . . guaranteed to astonish'
Booklist

'Superior psychological suspense . . . a
cleverly constructed thriller'
The Bookseller

JP Delaney's first psychological thriller, *The Girl Before*, was an instant *Sunday Times* and *New York Times* bestseller and went on to sell over a million copies worldwide. His next two books, *Believe Me* and *The Perfect Wife*, were also global bestsellers. His fourth psychological thriller, *Playing Nice*, will be published summer 2020.

www.jpdelaney.co.uk

THE
GIRL
BEFORE

JP DELANEY

Quercus

First published in the USA in 2017 by
Ballantine Books
First published in Great Britain in 2017 by
Quercus Editions Ltd

First published in paperback in Great Britain in 2017 by Quercus
This paperback edition published in 2020 by

Quercus Editions Ltd
Carmelite House
50 Victoria Embankment
London EC4Y 0DZ

An Hachette UK company

A CIP catalogue record for this book is available
from the British Library

PB ISBN 978 1 52941 050 1
EB ISBN 978 1 78648 027 9

10 9 8 7 6 5 4 3 2 1

Typeset by CC Book Production
Printed and bound in Great Britain by Clays Ltd, Elcograf S.p.A.

For Ollie and Nicholas

Mr Darkwood, once so interested in romantic love and whatever anyone had to say about it, was now thoroughly sick of the topic. Why did these lovers always repeat themselves? Didn't they ever get tired of hearing themselves talk?

Eve Ottenberg, *The Widow's Opera*

Like all addicts, signature killers work from a script, engaging in repetitive behaviour to the point of obsessiveness.

Robert D. Keppel and William J. Birnes, *Signature Killers*

We may say that the patient does not *remember* anything of what he has forgotten and repressed, but *acts* it out. He reproduces it not as a memory but as an action; he *repeats* it, without, of course, knowing that he is repeating it.

Sigmund Freud, *Remembering, Repeating and Working-Through*

My fascination with letting images repeat and repeat – or in film's case 'run on' – manifests my belief that we spend much of our lives seeing without observing.

Andy Warhol

1. *Please make a list of every possession you consider essential to your life.*

Then: Emma

It's a lovely little flat, the letting agent says with what could almost pass for genuine enthusiasm. Close to the amenities. And you've got that private bit of roof. That could become a sun terrace, subject of course to the freeholder's consent.

Nice, Simon agrees, trying not to catch my eye. I'd known the flat was no good as soon as I saw that six-foot stretch of roof below one of the windows. Si knows it too but he doesn't want to tell the agent, or at least not so soon it'll seem rude. He might even hope that if I listen to the man's stupid patter long enough I'll waver. The agent's Simon's kind of bloke: sharp, laddish, eager. He probably reads the magazine Simon works for. They were exchanging football chat before we even got up the stairs.

And here you've got a decent-size bedroom, the agent's saying. With ample—

It's no good, I interrupt, cutting short the charade. It's not right for us.

The agent raises his eyebrows. You can't be too choosy in this market, he says. This'll be gone by tonight. Five viewings today, and it's not even on our website yet.

It's not secure enough, I say flatly. Shall we go?

There are locks on all the windows, he points out. Plus a Chubb on the door. You could always install a burglar alarm, if security's a particular concern. I don't think the landlord would have any objection.

He's talking across me now, to Simon. *Particular concern.* He might as well have said, *Oh, is the girlfriend a bit of a drama queen?*

I'll wait outside, I say, turning to leave.

Realising he's blundered, the agent adds, If it's the area that's the problem, perhaps you should have a think further west.

We already have, Simon says. It's all out of our budget. Apart from the ones the size of a teabag.

He's trying to keep the frustration out of his voice, but the fact that he needs to riles me even more.

There's a one-bed in Queen's Park, the agent says. A bit grotty, but . . .

We looked at it, Simon says. In the end, we felt it was just a bit too close to that estate.

His tone makes it clear that *we* means *she*.

Or there's a third-floor just come on in Kilburn—

That too. There was a drainpipe next to one of the windows.

The agent looks puzzled.

Someone could have climbed it, Simon explains.

Right. Well, the letting season's only just started. Perhaps if you wait a bit.

The agent has clearly decided we're time-wasters. He too is sidling towards the door. I go and stand outside, on the landing, so he won't come near me.

We've already given notice on our old place, I hear Simon say. We're running out of options. He lowers his voice. Look, mate, we

4

were burgled. Five weeks ago. Two men broke in and threatened Emma with a knife. You can see why she'd be a bit jumpy.

Oh, the agent says. Shit. If someone did that to my girlfriend I don't know what I'd do. Look, this might be a long shot, but . . . His voice trails off.

Yes? Simon says.

Has anyone at the office mentioned One Folgate Street to you?

I don't think so. Has it just come on?

Not exactly, no.

The agent seems unsure whether to pursue this or not.

But it's available? Simon persists.

Technically, yes, the agent says. And it's a fantastic property. Absolutely fantastic. In a different league to this. But the landlord's . . . To say he's *particular* would be putting it mildly.

What area? Simon asks.

Hampstead, the agent says. Well, more like Hendon. But it's really quiet.

Em? Simon calls.

I go back inside. We might as well take a look, I say. We're halfway there now.

The agent nods. I'll stop by the office, he says. See if I can locate the details. It's been a while since I took anyone round, actually. It's not a place that would suit just anyone. But I think it might be right up your street. Sorry, no pun intended.

Now: Jane

'That's the last one.' The estate agent, whose name is Camilla, drums her fingers on the steering wheel of her Smart car. 'So really, it's time to make up our minds.'

I sigh. The flat we've just viewed, in a run-down mansion block off West End Lane, is the only one in my price range. And I'd just about persuaded myself it was all right – ignoring the peeling wallpaper, the faint smell of someone else's cooking seeping up from the flat below, the poky bedroom and the mould spattered across the unventilated bathroom – until I'd heard a bell being rung nearby, an old-fashioned handbell, and the place was suddenly filled with the noise of children. Going to the window, I found myself looking down at a school. I could see into a room being used by a toddler group, the windows hung with cut-outs of paper bunnies and geese. Pain tugged at my insides.

'I think I'll pass on this one,' I managed to say.

'Really?' Camilla seemed surprised. 'Is it the school? The previous tenants said they rather liked the sound of children playing.'

'Though not so much they decided to stay.' I turned away. 'Shall we go?'

Now Camilla leaves a long, tactical silence as she drives us back to her office. Eventually she says, 'If nothing we saw today took your fancy, we might have to think about upping your budget.'

'Unfortunately, my budget can't budge,' I say drily, looking out of the window.

'Then you might have to be a bit less picky,' she says tartly.

'About that last one. There are . . . personal reasons why I can't live next to a school. Not right now.'

I see her eyes going to my stomach, still a little flabby from my pregnancy, and widen as she makes the connection. 'Oh,' she says. Camilla isn't quite as dim as she looks, for which I'm grateful. She doesn't need me to spell it out.

Instead, she seems to come to a decision.

'Look, there is one other place. We're not really meant to show it without the owner's express permission, but occasionally we do anyway. It freaks some people out, but personally I think it's amazing.'

'An amazing property on my budget? We're not talking about a houseboat, are we?'

'God, no. Almost the opposite. A modern building in Hendon. A whole house – only one bedroom, but loads of space. The owner is the architect. He's actually really famous. Do you ever buy clothes at Wanderer?'

'Wanderer . . .' In my previous life, when I had money and a proper, well-paid job, I did sometimes go into the Wanderer shop on Bond Street, a terrifyingly minimalist space where a handful of eye-wateringly expensive dresses were laid out on thick stone slabs like sacrificial virgins, and the sales assistants dressed in black kimonos. 'Occasionally. Why?'

'The Monkford Partnership designs all their stores. He's what they call a techno-minimalist or something. Lots of hidden gadgetry, but otherwise everything's completely bare.' She shoots me a look. 'I should warn you, some people find his style a bit . . . *austere*.'

'I can cope with that.'

'And . . .'

'Yes?' I prompt, when she doesn't go on.

'It's not a straightforward landlord–tenant agreement,' she says hesitantly.

'Meaning?'

'I think,' she says, flicking down her indicator and moving into the left-hand lane, 'we should take a look at the property first, see if you fall in love with it. Then I'll explain the drawbacks.'

Then: Emma

OK, so the house is extraordinary. Amazing, breathtaking, incredible. Words can't do it justice.

The street outside had given no clue. Two rows of big, nondescript houses, with that familiar Victorian red-brick/sash-window combo you see all over north London, marched up the hill towards Cricklewood like a chain of figures cut from newspaper, each one an exact copy of the next. Only the front doors and the little coloured windows above them were different.

At the end, on the corner, was a fence. Beyond it I could see a low, small construction, a compact cube of pale stone. A few horizontal slits of glass, scattered apparently at random, were the only indication that it really was a house and not some giant paperweight.

Wow, Simon says doubtfully. Is this really it?

Certainly is, the agent says cheerfully. One Folgate Street.

He takes us round the side, where a door is fitted into the wall, perfectly flush. There doesn't seem to be a bell – in fact, I can't see a handle or a letter box either; no nameplate, nothing to indicate human occupation at all.

The agent pushes the door, which swings open.

Who lives here now? I ask.

No one at the moment, he says, standing aside for us to go in.

So why wasn't it locked? I say nervously, hanging back.

The agent smirks. It was, he goes. There's a digital key on my smartphone. One app controls everything. All I have to do is switch it from Unoccupied to Occupied. After that, it's all automatic – the house's sensors pick up the code and let me in. If I wear a digital bracelet, I don't even need the phone.

You are *kidding* me, Simon says, awestruck, staring at the door. I almost laugh out loud at his reaction. For Simon, who loves his gadgets, the idea of a house you can control from your phone is like all his best birthday presents rolled into one.

I step into a tiny hall, barely larger than a cupboard. It's too small to stand in comfortably once the agent has followed me, so without waiting to be asked I go on through.

This time it's me who says wow. It really is spectacular. Huge windows, looking on to a tiny garden and a high stone wall, flood the inside with light. It isn't big, but it feels spacious. The walls and floors are all made of the same pale stone. Notches running along the base of each wall give the impression they're floating in the air. And it's *empty*. Not unfurnished – I can see a stone table in a room to one side, some designery-looking, very cool dining chairs, a long, low sofa in a heavy cream fabric – but there's nothing else, nothing for the eye to catch on to. No doors, no cupboards, no pictures, no window frames, no electric sockets that I can see, no light fittings or – I look around, perplexed – even light switches. And although it doesn't feel abandoned or unlived in, there's absolutely no clutter.

Wow, I say again. My voice has an odd, muffled quality. I realise I can't hear anything from the street outside. The ever-present

London background noise of traffic and scaffolding riggers and car alarms has gone.

Most people say that, the agent agrees. Sorry to be a pain, but the landlord insists we remove our shoes. Would you . . . ?

He bends down to unlace his own flashy footwear. We follow suit. And then, as if the stark, bare emptiness of the house has sucked all his patter out of him, he simply pads about in his socks, apparently as dumbstruck as we are, while we look round.

Now: Jane

'It's beautiful,' I say. Inside, the house is as sleek and perfect as an art gallery. 'Just *beautiful*.'

'Isn't it?' Camilla agrees. She cranes her neck to look up at the bare walls, made of some expensive cream-coloured stone, that soar into the void of the roof. The upper floor is reached by the most crazily minimalist staircase I've ever seen. It's like something hewn into a cliff face: floating steps of open, unpolished stone, with no handrail or visible means of support. 'No matter how often I come here, it always takes my breath away. The last time was with a group of architecture students – that's one of the conditions, by the way: you have to open it for visits every six months. But they're always very respectful. It's not like owning a stately home and having tourists drop chewing gum on your carpets.'

'Who lives here now?'

'No one. It's been empty almost a year.'

I look across at the next room, if 'room' is the right word for a free-flowing space that doesn't actually have a doorway, let alone a door. On a long stone table is a bowl of tulips, their blood-red blooms a shocking dash of colour against all that pale stone. 'So where did the flowers come from?' I go and touch the table. No dust. 'And who keeps it so clean?'

'A cleaner comes every week from a specialist firm. That's another condition – you have to keep them on. They do the garden, too.'

I walk over to the window, which reaches right to the floor. 'Garden' is also a bit of a misnomer. It's a yard, really – an enclosed space about twenty feet by fifteen, paved with the same stone as the floor I'm standing on. A small oblong of grass, eerily precise and trimmed as short as a bowling green, butts up against the far wall. There are no flowers. In fact, apart from that tiny patch of grass, there's nothing living, no colour of any kind. A few small circles of grey gravel are the only other feature.

Turning back to the interior, it occurs to me that the whole place just needs some colour, some softness. A few rugs, some humanising touches, and it would be really beautiful, like something out of a style magazine. I feel, for the first time in ages, a small flutter of excitement. Has my luck finally changed?

'Well, I suppose that's only reasonable,' I say. 'Is that all?'

Camilla gives a hesitant smile. 'When I say *one* of the conditions, I mean one of the more straightforward ones. Do you know what a restrictive covenant is?'

I shake my head.

'It's a legal condition that's imposed on a property in perpetuity, something that can't be removed even if the house is sold. Usually they're to do with development rights – whether the house can be used as a place of business, that sort of thing. With this house, the conditions are part of the lease agreement, but because they're also restrictive covenants, they can't ever be negotiated or varied. It's an extraordinarily tight contract.'

'What kind of thing are we talking about?'

'Basically, it's a list of dos and don'ts. Well, don'ts mostly. No alterations of any kind, except by prior agreement. No rugs or carpets. No pictures. No potted plants. No ornaments. No books—'

'No *books*! That's ridiculous!'

'No planting anything in the garden; no curtains—'

'How do you keep the light out if you can't have curtains?'

'The windows are photosensitive. They go dark when the sky does.'

'So no curtains. Anything else?'

'Oh, yes,' Camilla says, ignoring my sarcastic tone. 'There are about two hundred stipulations in all. But it's the final one that causes the most problems.'

Then: Emma

... No lights other than those already here, the agent says. No washing lines. No wastepaper baskets. No smoking. No coasters or placemats. No cushions, no knick-knacks, no flat-pack furniture—

That's *mental*, Si says. What gives him the right?

The IKEA furniture in our current flat took him weeks to assemble, and as a result he regards it with the same personal pride as something hewn from trees and carved by his own hand.

I told you it was a tricky one, the agent shrugs.

I'm looking up at the ceiling. Talking of lights, I say, how do you turn them on?

You don't, the agent says. Ultrasonic motion sensors, coupled with a detector that adjusts the level according to how dark it is outside. It's the same technology that makes your car headlights come on at night. Then you just choose the mood you want from the app. Productive, peaceful, playful, and so on. It even adds extra UV in the winter so you don't get depressed. You know, like those SAD lights.

I can see Simon is so impressed by all this that the right of the architect to ban flat-pack furniture is suddenly no longer an issue.

The heating's underfloor, obviously, the agent continues, sensing he's on a roll. But it draws heat from a borehole directly

15

under the house. And all these windows are triple glazed – the house is so efficient, it actually returns power to the national grid. You'll never pay a fuel bill again.

This is like someone describing porn to Simon. And the security? I say sharply.

All on the same system, the agent says. You can't see it, but there's a burglar alarm built into the outside wall. All the rooms have sensors – the same ones that turn the lights on. And it's smart. It learns who you are and what your usual routine is, but anyone else, it'll check with you to make sure they're authorised.

Em? Simon calls. You have *got* to see this kitchen.

He's wandered into the space to one side, the one with the stone table. At first, I can't even see how he's identified it as a kitchen. A stone counter runs along one wall. At one end is what I suppose could be a tap, a slim steel tube jutting over the stone. A slight depression underneath suggests this might be a sink. At the other end is a row of four small holes. The agent waves his hand over one. Instantly it spouts a fierce, hissing flame.

Ta-da, he goes. The cooker. And actually the architect prefers the word 'refectory' to 'kitchen'. He grins as if to show he realises how stupid this is.

Now that I look more closely, I can see that some of the wall panels have tiny grooves between them. I push one and the stone opens – not with a click, but with an unhurried, pneumatic sigh. Behind it is a very small cupboard.

I'll show you the upstairs, the agent says.

The staircase is a series of open stone slabs, set into the wall. It's not safe for children, obviously, he warns as he leads us up it. Mind how you go.

Let me guess, Simon says. Handrails and stair gates are on the no-no list as well?

And pets, the agent says.

The bedroom is just as sparse as the rest of the house. The bed is built-in – a plinth of pale stone, complete with a rolled-up, futon-style mattress – and the bathroom isn't closed off, just tucked behind another wall. But while the emptiness of the downstairs was dramatic and clinical, up here it feels calm, almost cosy.

It's like a very posh prison cell, Simon comments.

Like I said, it's not to everyone's taste, the agent agrees. But for the right person . . .

Simon presses the wall by the bed and another panel swings open. Inside is a wardrobe. There's barely room for a dozen outfits.

One of the rules is, nothing on the floor at any time, the agent says helpfully. Everything has to be put away.

Simon frowns. How would they even know?

Regular inspections are built into the contract. Plus if any of the rules are broken, the cleaner's obliged to inform the management agency.

No way, Simon says. That's like being back at school. I'm not having someone tell me off for not picking up my dirty shirts.

I realise something: I haven't had a single flashback or panic attack since I stepped inside the house. It's so cut off from the outside world, so *cocooned*, I feel utterly safe. A line from my favourite film floats into my head. *The quietness and the proud look of it. Nothing very bad could happen to you there* . . .

I mean, it's amazing, obviously, Simon goes on. And if it wasn't for all those rules, we'd probably be interested. But we're messy people. Em's side of the bedroom looks like a bomb went off in French Connection.

Well, in that case, the agent says, nodding.

I like it, I say impulsively.

You do? Simon sounds surprised.

It's different, but . . . it sort of makes sense, doesn't it? If you'd built somewhere like this, somewhere incredible, I can see why you'd want it to be lived in properly, the way you'd meant it to be. Otherwise, what would be the point? And it's fantastic. I've never seen anything like it, not even in magazines. We *could* be tidy, couldn't we, if that's the price for living somewhere like this?

Well – great, Simon says uncertainly.

You like it too? I say.

If you like it, I love it, he goes.

No, I say, but do you really? It would be a big change. I wouldn't want us to do it unless you really wanted to.

The agent's watching us, amused to see how this little domestic turns out. But this is always the way it is with us. I have an idea, and then Simon thinks about it and eventually says yes.

You're right, Em, Simon says slowly. It's much better than anywhere else we're going to get. And if it's a fresh start we want – well, this is a whole lot fresher than if we just moved into another standard one-bed flat, isn't it?

He turns to the agent. So how do we take this further?

Ah, the agent says. That's the tricky bit.

Now: Jane

'The final stipulation being – what?'

'Despite all the restrictions, you'd be surprised how many people still want to go for it. But the last hurdle is that the architect himself has right of veto. Effectively, he gets to approve the tenant.'

'In person, you mean?'

Camilla nods. 'If it even gets that far. There's a lengthy application form. And of course you have to sign something to say you've read and understood the rules. If that's successful, you get invited to a face-to-face interview wherever in the world he happens to be. The last few years, that meant Japan – he was building a sky-scraper in Tokyo. But he's back in London now. Usually, though, he doesn't bother with the interview. We just get an email saying the application's been rejected. No explanation.'

'What sort of people get accepted?'

She shrugs. 'Even in the office, we can't see any pattern. Although we have noticed that architecture students never get through. And you certainly don't need to have lived in a place like this before. In fact, I'd say it's a drawback. Other than that, your guess is as good as mine.'

I look around. If I'd built this house, I think, what kind of person would I choose to live in it? How would I judge an application from a prospective tenant?

'Honesty,' I say slowly.

'Sorry?' Camilla's looking at me, puzzled.

'What I take out of this house isn't just that it looks nice. It's how much commitment has gone into it. I mean, it's uncompromising, obviously – even a bit brutal, in some ways. But this is someone who's put everything, every ounce of passion he's got, into creating something that's one hundred per cent as he wants it. It's got – well, it's a pretentious word, but it's got *integrity*. I think he's looking for people who are prepared to be equally honest about the way they live in it.'

Camilla shrugs. 'You may be right.' Her tone suggests she doubts it. 'So, do you want to go for it?'

By nature, I am a careful person. I rarely make decisions without thinking things through: researching the options, weighing the consequences, working out the pros and cons. So I'm slightly taken aback to hear myself saying, 'Yes. Definitely.'

'Good.' Camilla doesn't sound at all surprised, but then who wouldn't want to live in a house like this? 'Come back to the office and I'll find you an application pack.'

Then: Emma

1. Please make a list of every possession you consider essential to your life.

I pick up my biro, then put it down again. A list of everything I want to keep would take all night. But then I think some more, and that word 'essential' seems to float out of the page at me. What, really, is essential? My clothes? Since the break-in, I've virtually been living in the same two pairs of jeans and an old baggy jumper. There are some dresses I'd want to take, obviously. A couple of nice jackets. My shoes and boots. But nothing else I'd really miss. Our photographs? They're all backed up online. My few half-decent pieces of jewellery were taken by the burglars. Our furniture? There isn't a piece that wouldn't look tatty and out of place in One Folgate Street.

It occurs to me that the question has been worded this way deliberately. If I'd been asked to make a list of what I could do without, I'd never have managed it. But by putting the thought in my head that really none of it's important, I find myself wondering if I can't just shed all my things, my *stuff*, like an old skin.

Maybe that's the real point of The Rules, as we've already dubbed them. Maybe it isn't simply that the architect's a control freak who's worried we'll mess up his beautiful house. Maybe it's a kind of experiment. An experiment in living.

Which, I suppose, would make Si and me his guinea pigs. But actually I don't mind that. Actually I *want* to change who I am – who we are – and I know I can't do it without some help.

Especially who *we* are.

Simon and I have been together ever since Saul and Amanda's wedding, fourteen months ago. I knew the two of them from work, but they're a bit older than me and apart from them I didn't know many people there. But Simon was Saul's best man, the wedding was beautiful and romantic, and we hit it off right away. Drinking and talking turned into slow dancing and exchanging phone numbers. And then later we discovered we were staying at the same B & B and, well, one thing led to another. The next day I thought, What have I done? Clearly, this was yet another impulsive one-night stand and I was never going to see him again and would now be left feeling cheap and used. But in fact it was the other way round. Si called the moment he got home, and again the next day, and by the end of the week we were an item, much to the amazement of our friends. Especially *his* friends. He works in a very laddish, boozy environment where having a steady girlfriend is almost a black mark. In the kind of magazine Si writes for, girls are 'lookers' or 'honeys' or 'cuties'. Page after page is filled with pictures of 'B & K', as it's known – 'bra and knickers' – though the articles are mostly about gadgets and technology. If the article is about mobile phones, say, there's a picture of a girl in her underwear, holding one. If the article is about laptops, she'll still be in her undies, but wearing specs and typing on a keyboard. If the article is about underwear, she probably won't be wearing any underwear at all, but holding it up instead as if she's just slipped it off. Whenever the magazine throws a party, the models all turn up dressed pretty much as they appear in the magazine, and then the pictures of the party get splashed all over the magazine too. It isn't my scene in the least, and Simon told me early on that it wasn't his either – one of the reasons he liked me, he said, was because I wasn't anything like those girls, I was 'real'.

There's something about meeting at a wedding that turbocharges the first bit of a relationship. Simon asked me to move in with him just a few weeks after we started going out. That surprised people too – usually it's the girl pushing the guy, either because she wants to get married or just to move on to the next stage. But with us it was always the other way round. Maybe that's because Simon's a bit older than me. He's always said, the moment he saw me he knew I was the one. I liked that about him – the way he knew what he wanted, and what he wanted was me. But it never really occurred to me to ask myself whether this was what I wanted too, whether he meant to me what I clearly meant to him. And recently, what with the burglary and the decision to move out of his old flat and find somewhere new together, I've started to realise it's time to make a decision. Life's too short to spend it in the wrong relationship.

If that's what this is.

I think about that a bit longer, unconsciously chewing the end of my biro until it splinters and bits of sharp plastic fill my mouth. A bad habit I have, along with biting my nails. Perhaps that's something else I'll stop doing in One Folgate Street. Perhaps the house will turn me into a better person. Perhaps it will bring order and discipline to the random chaos of my life. I will become the sort of person who sets goals, makes lists, sees things through.

I turn back to the form. I'm determined to make the answer to the question as short as possible, to prove that I get it, that I'm in tune with what the architect's trying to do.

And then I realise what the right answer is.

I leave the box for the answer completely blank. As blank and empty and perfect as the interior of One Folgate Street.

Later, I give the form to Simon and explain what I've done. He's like, But what about *my* stuff, Em? What about The Collection?

'The Collection' is a motley assortment of NASA memorabilia he's been painstakingly building up for years, mostly in boxes under the bed. Maybe it could go into storage, I suggest, torn between amusement that we're actually debating whether a few bits of eBay tat signed by Buzz Aldrin or Jack Schmitt are going to stop us from living in the most incredible house we've ever seen, and outrage that Simon can seriously think his astronauts take priority over what happened to me. You've always said you wanted it to have a proper home, I say.

A cupboard at Big Yellow wasn't exactly what I had in mind, babe, he goes.

So I'm like, It's only things, Si. And things don't really matter, do they?

And I feel another argument brewing, the familiar rage bubbling to the surface. *Once again*, I want to shout, *you've made me think you're going to do something, and once again when it actually comes to it you're going to try to wriggle out.*

I don't say it, of course. This anger isn't me.

24

Carol, the therapist I've been seeing since the burglary, says being angry is a good sign. It means I'm undefeated or something. Unfortunately, my anger is only ever directed at Simon. That's normal too, apparently. Those who are closest bear the heaviest burden.

OK, OK, Simon says quickly. The Collection goes into storage. But there might be some other things . . .

Already I feel weirdly protective of the lovely blank empty space of my answer. Let's ditch everything, I say impatiently. Let's start again. Like we're going on holiday and the airline charge for baggage, all right?

All right, he says. But I can tell he's only saying it to stop me kicking off. He goes over to the sink and pointedly starts to wash up all the dirty cups and plates I've piled in there. I know he thinks I can't do this, that I'm not disciplined enough to live an uncluttered lifestyle. I attract chaos, he always says. I go over the top. But that's exactly why I want to do this. I want to reinvent myself. And the fact that I'm doing it with someone who thinks he knows me, and thinks I'm not up to it, pisses me off.

I reckon I'll be able to write there, I add. In all that calm. You've been encouraging me to write my book for ages.

He grunts, unconvinced.

Or maybe I'll do a blog, I say.

I consider the idea, examining it from every angle. A blog would be pretty cool, actually. I could call it *Minimalist Me*. *My Minimalist Journey*. Or maybe something even simpler. *Mini Miss*.

Already I'm getting quite excited about this. I think how many followers a blog about minimalism could get. Maybe I'll attract advertisers, give up the day job, turn it into a best-selling lifestyle journal. Emma Matthews, the Princess of Less.

So would you close down the other blogs I set up for you? he asks, and I bridle at the implication I'm not serious about this. It's true that *London Girlfriend* only has eighty-four followers, and *Chick-Lit Chick* a mere eighteen, but I never really had the time to write enough content.

I turn back to the application form. One question down, and already we're fighting. There are another thirty-four questions to go.

Now: Jane

I glance through the application pack. Some of the questions are decidedly strange. I can see how asking what possessions you want to bring or what fixtures and fittings you might change is relevant, but what about:

23. Would you sacrifice yourself to save ten innocent strangers?
24. What about ten thousand strangers?
25. Do fat people make you feel a) sad, or b) annoyed?

I'd been right earlier, I realise, when I used the word 'integrity'. These questions are some form of psychometric test. But then, 'integrity' isn't a word estate agents need very often. No wonder Camilla had looked bemused.

Before I fill it in, I google the Monkford Partnership. The first link is to their own website. I click, and a picture of a blank wall appears. It's a very beautiful wall, made of pale, soft-textured stone, but a little uninformative, even so.

I click again and two words appear:

Works
Contact

When I select *Works*, a list fades on to the screen:

Skyscraper, Tokyo
Monkford Building, London
Wanderer Campus, Seattle
Beach House, Menorca
Chapel, Bruges
The Black House, Inverness
One Folgate Street, London

Clicking on each name brings up more pictures – no words, just images of the buildings. All are utterly minimal. All are built with the same attention to detail, the same high-quality materials, as One Folgate Street. There isn't a single person in the photographs, or anything that even hints at human occupancy. The chapel and the beach house are almost interchangeable: heavy cubes of pale stone and plate glass. Only the view beyond the windows is different.

I go to Wikipedia:

Edward Monkford (b.1980) is a British techno-architect associated with the minimalist aesthetic. In 2005, along with data technologist David Thiel and two others, he formed the Monkford Partnership. Together they have pioneered the development of domotics, intelligent domestic environments in which the house or building becomes an integrated organism with no extraneous or unnecessary elements.[1]

Unusually, the Monkford Partnership accepts only a single commission at a time. Their output to date has thus been intentionally small. They are currently working on their most ambitious project so far: New Austell, an eco-town of 10,000 homes in North Cornwall.[2]

I skim down through lists of awards. The *Architectural Review* called Monkford 'a wayward genius', while *Smithsonian* magazine described him as 'Britain's most influential starchitect . . . A taciturn trailblazer whose work is as unshowy as it is profound.'

I skip to 'Private Life'.

In 2006, when still largely unknown, Monkford married Elizabeth Mancari, a fellow member of the Monkford Partnership. They had one son, Max, in 2007. Mother and child were killed in an accident during the construction of One Folgate Street (2008–2011), which had been intended to serve as the family home, as well as being a showcase for the fledgling partnership's talents.[3] Some commentators[who?] have pointed to this tragedy, and Edward Monkford's subsequent lengthy sabbatical in Japan, as the formative event behind the austere, highly minimalist style that made the partnership's name.

Returning from his sabbatical, Monkford abandoned the original plans for One Folgate Street – at the time, still a building site[4] – and redesigned it from scratch. The resulting house became the recipient of several major awards, including a Stirling Prize from the Royal Institute of British Architects.[5]

I read the words again. So the house started with a death. Two deaths, in fact: a double bereavement. Is that why I felt so at home there? Is there some kind of affinity between those austere spaces and my own sense of loss?

Automatically, I glance at the suitcase by the window. A suitcase full of baby clothes.

My baby died. My baby died and then, three days later, she was born. Even now, it's the unnatural wrongness of it, the horror of that casual inversion of the proper order of things, that hurts almost more than anything.

Dr Gifford, a consultant obstetrician despite being barely older than I am, had been the one to look me in the eye and explain that the baby would have to be born naturally. The risk of infections and other complications, plus the fact that a Caesarean is a major surgical procedure, meant it was hospital policy not to offer one in cases of prenatal mortality. *Offer* – that was the word he used, as if having a baby by Caesarean, even a dead one, was some kind of treat, like a free basket of fruit in a hotel. But they'd induce me with a drip, he said, and make the whole thing as fast and painless as possible.

I thought: but I don't want it to be painless. I want it to hurt, and to have a live baby at the end of it. I found myself wondering if Dr Gifford had children. Yes, I thought. Doctors married young, to other doctors usually, and he was far too nice not to have a family. He would go home that night and describe to his wife, over a pre-dinner beer, how his day had been, using words like 'prenatal mortality' and 'full term' and possibly 'bit grim'. Then his daughter would show him a drawing she'd done at school, and he would kiss her and tell her she was brilliant.

I could tell from the set, strained faces of the medical team as they went about their work that even for them, this was horrible and rare. But whereas for them professionalism could provide some sort of refuge, for me there was only an overwhelming, numbing sense of failure. As they attached the drip with its cargo of hormones to get me started, I could hear the howls of another woman, further down the maternity ward. But that woman would walk out with a baby, not an appointment card to see a bereavement officer. 'Maternity': another strange word, when you thought about it. Would I even *be* a mother, technically, or was there some other term for what I was about to become? I'd already heard them saying 'post-partum' instead of 'post-natal'.

Someone asked about the father and I shook my head. No father to contact, just my friend Mia here, her face white with misery and worry as all our carefully laid birthing plans – Diptyque candles and water pools and an iPod full of Jack Johnson and Bach – were discarded in the sombre rush of medical activity; not even mentioned, as if they'd only ever been part of an illusion that all was safe and well, that I was in control, that childbirth was barely more taxing than a spa treatment or a particularly fierce massage, not a deadly business in which outcomes like this were perfectly possible, even to be expected. One in two hundred, Dr Gifford had said. In a third of cases, no reason was ever found. That I was fit and healthy – before the pregnancy, I'd done Pilates every day, and run at least once a week – made no difference; neither did my age. Some babies simply died. I would be childless, and little Isabel Margaret Cavendish would never have a mother. A life would never happen. As the contractions started, I took a gulp of gas and air and my mind filled with horrors. Images of abominations in Victorian formaldehyde jars swam into my mind. I screamed and clenched my muscles, even though the midwife was telling me it wasn't time yet.

But afterwards – after I had given birth, or given death, or whatever it should be called – everything was strangely peaceful. That was the hormones, apparently – the same cocktail of love and bliss and relief every new mother feels. My daughter was perfect and quiet and I held her in my arms and cooed over her

31

just as any mother would. She smelled of snot and body fluids and sweet new skin. Her warm little fist curled loosely around my finger, like any baby's. I felt . . . I felt *joy*.

The midwife took her away to make casts of her hands and feet for my memory box. It was the first time I'd heard that phrase and she had to explain. I would be given a shoebox containing a snippet of Isabel's hair, the cloth she was swaddled in, some photographs and the plaster casts. Like a little coffin; the mementoes of a person who had never been. When the midwife brought the casts back, they were like a kindergarten project. Pink plaster for the hands, blue for the feet. That's when it finally started to sink in that there would be no art projects, no drawings on the walls, no choosing of schools, no growing out of uniforms. I hadn't only lost a baby. I had lost a child, a teenager, a woman.

Her feet, and all the rest of her, were cold now. As I washed the last bits of plaster off her toes at the tap in my room, I asked if I could take her home with me, just for a while. The midwife looked askance and said that would be a bit strange, wouldn't it? But I could hold her for as long as I wanted, here at the hospital. I said I was ready for them to take her away.

After that, looking at the grey London sky through my tears, it felt as if something had been amputated. Back at home, raging grief gave way to more numbness. When friends spoke to me in shocked, sympathetic tones about my *loss*, I knew of course what they meant, and yet the word also felt deadly accurate. Other women had won – victorious in their gamble with nature, with procreation, with genetics. I had not. I – who had always been so efficient, so high achieving, so successful – had lost. Grief, I discovered, feels not so very different from defeat.

And yet, bizarrely, on the surface, everything was almost back to the way it had been before. Before the brief, civilised liaison with my opposite number in the Geneva office, an affair played out in hotel rooms and bland, efficient restaurants; before the mornings of vomiting and the – initially awful – realisation that we might not have been quite as careful as I'd thought. Before the difficult phone calls and emails and the polite hints from him about 'decisions' and 'arrangements' and 'unfortunate timing', and finally the slow dawning of a different feeling, a feeling that the timing might be right after all, that even if the affair was not going to lead to a long-term relationship, it had given me, unmarried at thirty-four, an opportunity. I had more than enough income for two, and the financial PR firm I worked for prided itself on the generosity of its maternity benefits. Not only would I be able to take off almost a whole year to be with the baby, but I was guaranteed flexible working arrangements when I came back.

My employers were just as helpful after I told them about the stillbirth, offering me unlimited sick leave; they'd already arranged maternity cover, after all. I found myself sitting alone in a flat that had been carefully prepared for a child: the Kuster cot, the top-of-the-range Bugaboo, the hand-painted circus frieze around the spare-bedroom wall. I spent the first month expressing breast milk that I poured down the sink.

Bureaucracy tried to be kind, but, inevitably, wasn't. I discovered that the law makes no special provision for a stillbirth; a woman in my position is required to go and register the death, and the birth, simultaneously – a legal cruelty that still makes me angry whenever I think about it. There was a funeral – again, a legal requirement, though I would have wanted one anyway. It's hard to give a eulogy for a life that didn't happen, but we tried.

Counselling was offered, and accepted, but in my heart I knew it wouldn't make any difference. There was a mountain of grief to be climbed, and no amount of talk would help me up it. I needed to work. When it became clear I actually couldn't go back to my old job for another year – you can't just get rid of someone who's doing maternity cover, apparently; they have rights, just like any other employee – I resigned and started working part-time for a charity that campaigns to improve research about stillbirths. It meant I couldn't afford to go on living where I was, but I would have moved anyway. I could get rid of the cot and the nursery wallpaper, but it would still always be the home where Isabel isn't.

Then: Emma

Something's woken me up.

I know straight away it isn't drunks outside the kebab shop or a fight in the street or a police helicopter overhead because I'm so used to those, they barely register. I lift my head and listen. A thud, then another.

Someone's moving around in our flat.

There've been a few break-ins recently round here, and for a moment I feel my stomach knot with adrenalin. Then I remember. Simon's been out – some work piss-up or other – and I went to bed without waiting up. The sounds suggest he's had too much to drink. I hope he'll have a shower before he comes to bed.

I can tell roughly how late it is by the street noise, or rather the lack of it. No growl of engines accelerating away from the traffic lights. No car doors slamming around the kebab shop. I find my phone and peer at the clock. I don't have my lenses in, but I can see it says 2:41.

Si comes along the corridor, drunk enough not to remember that the floor by the bathroom always creaks.

It's OK, I call out. I'm awake.

His footsteps pause outside the door.

To show I'm not cross I add, I know you're drunk.

Voices, indistinct. Whispering.

Which means he's brought someone home. Some workmate who didn't make the last train back to the suburbs. That's annoying, actually. I've got a busy day tomorrow – *today*, now – and providing breakfast for Simon's hungover colleagues isn't part of the plan. Although, when it actually comes to it, I know Simon will be charming and funny and call me 'babe' and 'beautiful' and tell his mate how I almost became a model and isn't he the luckiest man in the world, and I'll give in and just be late for work. Again.

I'll see you later then, I call out, a bit peeved. They'll probably get the Xbox out.

But the footsteps don't move away.

Annoyed now, I swing my legs out of bed – I'm decent enough for workmates, just, in an old T-shirt and boxers – and pull open the bedroom door.

But I'm not as quick as the figure on the other side, the one in the dark clothing and the balaclava who pushes his shoulder against it, hard and sudden, knocking me backwards. I scream – at least, I think I do: it might just be a gasp, fear and shock paralysing my throat. The kitchen light's on, and I see the flash as he raises the knife. A small knife, such a small one, hardly bigger than a pen.

His eyes stand out against the dark wool of the balaclava. They widen as he takes in the sight of me.

Whoa, he says.

Behind him I see another balaclava, another set of eyes, more anxious this time.

Leave it, bruv, the second one says.

One of the intruders is white, one black, but both are talking the same black street slang.

Chill, the first one says. Sick, innit.

He raises the knife further, until it's directly in front of my face.

Gimme your phone, you stuck-up bitch.

I freeze.

But then I'm too quick for him. I reach behind me. He thinks I'm getting my phone but actually I'm grabbing my own knife, the big meat knife from the kitchen that's on the bedside table. The handle comes into my hand, smooth and heavy, and in one fluid movement I bring it round so that it slides into the bastard's belly, just below the ribs. It goes in easily. No blood, I think, as I pull it out and stab him again. There's no spurt of blood like there is in horror films. That makes it easier. I punch the knife through his arm, then his abdomen, then lower still, somewhere round his balls, twisting it savagely into his groin. As he crumples to the ground, I step over his body to the second figure.

You too, I tell him. You were there, you didn't stop him. You little *prick*. I jam the knife into his mouth, as easy as posting a letter.

And then everything goes blank, and I wake up screaming.

It's normal, Carol says, nodding. It's perfectly normal. In fact, it's a good sign.

Even now, in the calm of the sitting room where Carol does her consultations, I'm shaking. Nearby, someone is mowing a lawn.

How's it good? I say numbly.

Carol nods again. She does this a lot, whenever I say pretty much anything in fact, as if to indicate that she doesn't usually answer her clients' questions, but is going to make an exception, just this once, for me. For someone who is doing such *good work*, making such *excellent progress*, perhaps even *turning a corner*, as she concludes at the end of every session. She was recommended by the police, so she must be good, but to be honest I'd rather they caught the bastards than dished out therapists' cards.

Fantasising you had a knife might be your subconscious indicating that it wants to take control of what happened, she goes.

Really? I say. I tuck my feet under me. Even without shoes, I'm not sure this is strictly allowed, given the pristine state of Carol's sofa, but I reckon I might as well get something for my fifty quid. Is this the same subconscious that's decided I mustn't remember anything that happened after I handed over my phone? I say. Couldn't it just be telling me what a dick I was not to keep a knife by my bed in the first place?

That's one interpretation, Emma, she says. But not a very helpful one, it seems to me. Survivors of assault often blame themselves rather than the attacker. But the attacker is the one who's broken the law, not you.

Look, she adds, I'm not so much concerned about the actual circumstances of what happened to you as the process of recovery. Seen from that perspective, this is a significant step. In these latest flashbacks, you're starting to fight back – blaming your assailants rather than yourself. Refusing to be defined as their victim.

Except I *am* their victim, I say. Nothing changes that.

Am? Carol says quietly. Or *was*?

After a long, significant pause – a 'therapeutic space', as she sometimes calls it, a pretty stupid way of describing what is, after all, just silence – she prompts gently: And Simon? How are things with him?

Trying, I say.

I realise this could be taken two ways, so I add, I mean he's trying his best. Endless cups of tea and sympathy. It's like he feels responsible because he wasn't there. He seems to think he could have beaten them both up and made a citizen's arrest or something. When actually they'd probably have stabbed him. Or tortured him for his PIN numbers.

Carol says mildly, Society has a kind of . . . *construct* of what masculinity is, Emma. When that's undermined, it can leave any man feeling threatened and uncertain.

This time the silence drags on for a whole minute.

Are you managing to eat properly? she adds.

For some reason I've confided in Carol that I used to have an eating disorder. Well, 'used to' is a relative term because, as anyone who's ever had one knows, it never really goes away, and it's when things get shaken up and out of control that it threatens to come back.

Si's making me eat, I say. I'm fine.

I don't tell her that sometimes I dirty a plate and put it in the sink so Simon thinks I've eaten when I haven't, or that sometimes I make myself throw up after we've been out. Some parts of my life are off-limits. Actually, it's one of the things I used to like about Simon, the way he'd look after me when I was ill. The problem is, when I'm not ill, his being all attentive and caring drives me crazy.

I didn't do anything, I say suddenly. When they broke in. That's what I can't understand. I was literally shaking with adrenalin.

It's meant to be fight or flight, isn't it? But I didn't do either. I did *nothing*.

For no particular reason, I'm crying now. I pick up one of Carol's cushions and hold it against myself, hugging it to my chest, as if by squeezing it I can somehow squeeze the life out of the shitty little toerags.

You did do something, she says. You played possum. As an instinct, that's perfectly valid. It's like hares and rabbits – rabbits run, hares crouch. There's no right or wrong response in these situations, no 'what if'. There's just whatever happened.

She leans forward and edges a box of tissues closer to me across the coffee table. Emma, I want to try something, she says when I've finished blowing my nose.

What? I say dully. Not hypnosis. I've told you I won't do that.

She shakes her head. This is something called EMDR, Eye Movement Desensitisation and Retraining. It can seem a slightly strange process at first, but it's actually very straightforward. I'm going to sit beside you and move my fingers from side to side across your field of vision. I want you to track them with your eyes while you relive the traumatic experience in your mind.

What's the point of that? I say doubtfully.

The truth is, she says, we don't know exactly how EMDR works. But it seems to help people work through what happened, to give a sense of perspective. And it's particularly helpful in cases like this, where someone's unable to remember the details of what happened. Are you willing to give it a try?

All right, I shrug.

Carol moves her chair so she's a couple of feet from me and holds up two fingers.

Concentrate on a visual image from the beginning of the break-in, she says. Keep it static for now, though. Like when you pause a film.

She starts to move her fingers from side to side. Obediently, I follow them.

That's it, Emma, she says. And now let the film start. Remember how you felt.

It's hard to concentrate at first, but, as I get used to the movement of her fingers, I can focus enough to replay the night of the break-in in my mind.

A thud in the sitting room.

Footsteps.

Whispers.

Me getting out of bed.

The door crashing open. The knife in front of my face—

Deep breaths, Carol murmurs, just like we practised.

Two, three deep breaths. *Me getting out of bed . . .*

The knife. The intruders. The argument between the two of them, short and urgent, as to whether my presence meant they should get the hell out of there or go ahead and rob the flat anyway. The older one, the one with the knife, gesturing at me.

Skinny bird. What's she gonna do?

Breathe, Emma. Breathe, Carol instructs.

Touching his knife against the base of my throat. *Cos if she does try something, we'll cut her, right?*

No, I say sharply, panicked. I can't do this. I'm sorry.

Carol sits back. You've done very well, Emma. Well done.

I breathe some more, until I've got back my composure. I know from previous sessions it'll be up to me to break the silence now. But I don't want to talk about the burglary any more.

We may have found somewhere else to live, I say.

Oh yes? Carol's voice is as neutral as ever.

Simon's flat's in a really horrible area. Even before I made the crime figures worse. I bet the neighbours hate me. I've probably knocked five per cent off the value of their homes.

I'm sure they don't hate you, Emma, she says.

I put the sleeve of my sweater into my mouth and suck at it – an old habit I seem to have started again. I say, I know moving's giving in. But I can't stay there. The police say with this sort of attacker, there's a chance they'll come back. They get a sense of *ownership*, apparently. Like you're somehow theirs now.

Which you're not, of course, Carol says quietly. You are your own person, Emma. And I *don't* think moving on is giving in. Quite the reverse. It's a sign you're making decisions again. Regaining control. I know it's hard at the moment. But people do come through this kind of trauma. You just have to accept that it takes time.

She glances at the clock. Excellent work, Emma. You've made real progress today. I'll see you next week at the same time, shall I?

Now: Jane

30. *Which statement best describes your most recent personal relation-*
    ship?
    a) *More like friends than lovers*
    b) *Easy and comfortable*
    c) *Soulful and intense*
    d) *Tempestuous and explosive*
    e) *Perfect but short-lived*

The questions on the application form seem to get odder and
odder. To begin with, I try to give each one careful consideration,
but there are so many that, by the end, I'm hardly even thinking
about my answers, I'm just dashing them off on instinct.

They want three recent photographs. I choose one taken at
a friend's wedding, a selfie of me and Mia climbing Snowdon a
couple of years back, and a formal portrait I had done for work.
And then it's done. I write a covering letter; nothing over the
top, just a polite note emphasising how much I like One Folgate
Street and how I will strive to live there with the integrity it
deserves. Even though it's just a few lines, I redraft it half a
dozen times before I'm happy with it. The agent said not to get
my hopes up, that most applicants never get past this stage, but

43

I go to bed really hoping I will. A new beginning. A fresh start. And as I drift off to sleep, another word floats into my head as well. A *rebirth*.

2. *When I'm working on something, I can't relax until it's perfect.*

Agree ☐ ☐ ☐ ☐ ☐ *Disagree*

Then: Emma

A week goes by with no response to our application, then another. I send an email checking they've received it. There's no reply. I'm starting to get pissed off – they made us answer all those stupid questions, choose the photographs, write a letter; the least they could do is write back saying we haven't got it – when finally an email arrives from admin@themonkfordpartnership.com, subject: 'One Folgate Street'. I don't give myself time to get nervous. I open it straight away.

> Please come for an interview at 5pm tomorrow, Tuesday, 16th March, at the Monkford Partnership.

Nothing else. No address, no details, no indication if we're meeting Edward Monkford himself or some underling. But of course the address is easily found online and it doesn't really matter who we're meeting. This is it. We've cleared every hurdle but the last one.

The Monkford Partnership occupies the top floor of a well-known modern building in the City. It's got an address, but most people just call it 'The Hive' because that's what it looks like – a giant stone beehive. Amongst all the boxy glass-and-steel skyscrapers in the Square Mile, it sits on the approach to St Paul's like some weird, pale chrysalis laid by an alien. And from street level it's even stranger. There's no reception desk, just a long wall of pale stone with two slits that must lead to the lifts, because there's a steady stream of people coming in and out. All of them, both men and women, seem to be wearing expensive black suits and open-neck shirts.

I feel my phone buzz. Something's flashed up on the screen:

The Monkford Building. Check in now?

I touch *Accept*.

Welcome, Emma and Simon. Please take lift three and get out at floor fourteen.

I've no idea how the building has identified us. Perhaps there was a cookie embedded in the email. Simon knows about that kind of techy stuff. I show him, hoping it'll excite him, but he just shrugs dismissively. Places like this – rich, moneyed, self-confident – aren't his cup of tea.

There's no one else waiting for our lift, apart from a man who looks even more out of place here than us. His hair is long and grey, unkempt even though it's tied back in a ponytail. He's got a two-day growth of stubble and he's wearing a moth-eaten cardigan and shabby linen trousers. I glance at his feet and see he isn't even wearing shoes, just socks. He's eating some chocolate, a Crunchie bar, very noisily. When the lift doors open, he shuffles inside and takes up a position at the back.

I look around for buttons, but there aren't any. I guess it only goes to the floors it's programmed to.

As we go up, so smoothly there's no sense of movement, I

feel the man's eyes travelling over me. They come to rest on my midriff. And there they stay, as he licks chocolate crumbs off his fingers. Awkwardly, I put my hand where he's looking and find my shirt has ridden up. A small piece of bare stomach is showing just above my trousers.

What's up, Em? Simon says, noticing my discomfort.

Nothing, I say, turning to face him, away from the strange man, surreptitiously tucking my shirt in as I do so.

Changed your mind yet? Simon says quietly.

I don't know, I say. In fact I haven't, but I don't want Si to think I'm not open to a discussion about this.

The lift doors open and the man shuffles off, still eating his Crunchie.

Showtime, Simon says, looking around.

It's another big, sleek space, an open light-filled area running the length of the building. At one end a wall of curved glass overlooks the City – you can see the dome of St Paul's, Lloyds of London, all those other landmark buildings, then Canary Wharf in the distance, the Thames snaking round the Isle of Dogs and off through the endless flat plains to the east. A blonde in a tailored black suit unfolds herself from a leather chair, where she's tapping on an iPad.

Welcome, Emma and Simon, she goes. Please take a seat. Edward will see you shortly.

The iPad must be where all her emails are, because after ten minutes of silence she says, Please follow me.

She pushes open a door. Just from the way it moves, I can tell how heavy it is, how balanced. Inside, a man is standing at a long table, resting on his balled fists, studying some plans. The sheets

49

are so big they only just fit on the table. Glancing at them, I see they aren't printouts but actual drawings. Two or three pencils and a rubber are grouped in one corner, neatly arranged in order of size.

Emma, Simon, the man says, looking up. Would you like some coffee?

OK, so he's attractive. That's the first thing I notice about him. And the second. And the third. His hair is an indeterminate blond, the fair curls cropped close to his head. He's wearing a black pull-over and an open-neck shirt – nothing fancy, but the wool hangs nicely from his wide, lean shoulders – and he has a warm, slightly self-deprecating smile. He looks like a sexy, relaxed schoolteacher, not the strange obsessive I've been picturing.

And Simon clearly clocks all this too, or sees me clock it, because he suddenly strides forward and grasps Edward Monkford's shoulder.

Edward, is it? he goes. Or Eddy? Ed? I'm Simon. Nice to meet you, mate. Swanky place you've got here. This is my girlfriend, Emma.

And I cringe, because this mock-cockney thing is something Simon only ever does with people he feels threatened by. Quickly I say, Coffee would be great.

Two coffees please, Alisha, Edward Monkford says to his assistant, very politely. He gestures me and Simon towards the chairs on the other side of the table.

So tell me, he says when we're all seated, looking straight at me and ignoring Simon, why you want to live at One Folgate Street.

No, not a schoolteacher. A headmaster, or the chairman of the governors. His stare is still friendly, but a little bit fierce too. Which, of course, only makes him more attractive.

We've anticipated this question, or something like it, and I manage to get out the answer we've prepared, something about how much we'll appreciate the opportunity and how we'll try to do the house justice. Next to me, Simon glowers silently. When I've finished, Monkford nods politely. He looks a bit bored.

And I think it will change us, I hear myself say.

For the first time, he looks interested. Change you? How?

We were burgled, I say slowly. Two men. Well, youths really. I can't actually remember what happened, not the details. I'm suffering from some kind of post-traumatic shock.

He nods thoughtfully.

Encouraged, I go on: I don't want to be the person who just stood there and let them get away with it. I want to be someone who makes decisions. Who fights back. And I think the house will help. I mean, we're not the sort of people who would normally live that way. All those rules. But we'd like to give it a go.

Again, the silence stretches on. Mentally, I'm kicking myself. How can what happened to me possibly be relevant? How can the house make me a different person?

The ice-cool blonde brings the coffees. I jump up to take one and in my haste and nervousness I somehow manage to spill the cup, the whole cup, over the drawings.

Jesus, Emma, Simon hisses, jumping up too. Look what you're doing.

I'm so sorry, I say miserably, as the brown river slowly engulfs the designs. God, I'm *so* sorry.

The assistant rushes out to get cloths. I can see this opportunity slipping away. That dramatic blank list of possessions, all those hopeful lies I put in the questionnaire – they'll all count for nothing now. The last thing this man wants is a clumsy coffee-spilling oaf messing up his beautiful house.

To my surprise, Monkford only laughs. They were terrible drawings, he says. I should have binned them weeks ago. You've saved me the bother.

The assistant returns with J-cloths and rushes around, dabbing and wiping.

Alisha, you're making it worse, Monkford says sharply. Let me.

He bundles up the drawings so the coffee's contained on the inside, like a giant nappy. Dispose of that, he says, handing it to her.

Mate, I'm so sorry, Simon goes.

For the first time, Monkford looks directly at him.

Never apologise for someone you love, he says quietly. It makes you look like a prick.

Simon's so stunned, he says nothing. I can only gawp, astonished. Nothing in Edward Monkford's manner so far has suggested he would say anything so personal. And Simon has punched people for less – far less. But Monkford only turns back to me and says easily, Well, I'll let you know. Thank you for coming, Emma.

There's a brief pause before he adds, And you, Simon.

Now: Jane

I wait in a reception area on the fourteenth floor of the Hive, watching two men argue in a glass-walled meeting room. One, I'm pretty sure, is Edward Monkford. The same fairish curls framing a lean, ascetic face as in a photo I found on the internet; the same black cashmere pullover and white open-necked shirt. He's handsome – not eye-catchingly so, but he has an air of confidence and charm, with a nice lopsided smile. The other man is shouting at him, although the glass is so thick I can't make out the words – it's as quiet as a laboratory up here. Something about the gestures the man's making, and his swarthiness, makes me think he could be Russian.

The woman standing to one side, occasionally adding an interjection of her own, could definitely be an oligarch's wife. Much younger than her husband, dressed in gaudy Versace prints, her sleek hair dyed an expensive shade of blonde. Her husband ignores her, but Monkford occasionally turns politely in her direction. When the man finally stops shouting, Monkford calmly says a few words and shakes his head. The man explodes again, even more angrily.

The immaculate brunette who checked me in comes over. 'I'm

afraid Edward's still in a meeting. Can I get you anything? Some water?'

'I'm fine, thank you.' I nod at the dumbshow in front of me. 'That meeting, I take it?'

She follows my gaze. 'They're wasting their time. He won't change it.'

'What are they arguing about?'

'The client commissioned a house when he was in a previous marriage. Now his new wife wants an Aga. To make it more cosy, she says.'

'And the Monkford Partnership doesn't do cosy?'

'That's not the point. If it wasn't agreed as part of the original brief, Edward won't make alterations. Not unless it's something *he's* unhappy with. He once spent three months rebuilding the roof of a summerhouse to make it four feet lower.'

'What's it like, working for a perfectionist?' I say. But I've clearly crossed a line, because she just gives me a cool smile and moves away.

I continue to watch the argument – or rather, the rant, because Edward Monkford takes almost no part in it. He allows the other man's anger to wash over him like waves over a rock, his expression one of polite interest, no more. Eventually, the door is thrown open and the client storms out, still muttering, his wife teetering after him on her high heels. Monkford strolls out last. I smooth down my dress and stand up. After much consideration, I've gone for Prada – navy blue, pleated, hemline just below the knee; nothing too showy.

'Jane Cavendish,' the receptionist reminds him.

He turns to look at me. Just for a moment he seems surprised

– startled, even, as if I'm not quite what he'd expected. Then the moment passes and he extends his hand. 'Jane. Of course. We'll go in here.'

I would sleep with this man. I've barely said more than hello to him, but I have nevertheless registered that something, some part of me quite beyond my conscious control, has made a judgement. He holds the meeting-room door open for me and somehow even this simple, everyday courtesy seems charged with significance.

We sit opposite each other, across a long glass table dominated by an architectural model of a small town. His gaze travels across my face. When I'd decided he wasn't much more than reasonably good-looking, that was before I'd seen him up close. His eyes, in particular, are striking; pale blue, their corners etched with lines, even though I know he's only in his thirties. Laughter lines, my grandmother used to call them. But on Edward Monkford, they give his face a fierce, almost hawk-like intensity.

'Did you win?' I ask, when he doesn't say anything.

He seems to shake himself. 'Win what?'

'That argument.'

'Oh, that.' He shrugs and smiles, and his face instantly softens. 'My buildings make demands of people, Jane. I believe they're not intolerable, and in any case, the rewards are far greater than the demands. In one sense, I suppose, that's why you're here.'

'It is?'

He nods. 'David, my technology partner, talks about something called UX – that's tech-speak for User Experience. As you'll be aware, having seen the terms and conditions of the lease, we gather information from One Folgate Street and use it to refine the user experience for our other clients.'

I'd actually skimmed most of the conditions document, which ran to about twenty pages of tiny print. 'What kind of information?'

He shrugs again. His shoulders under the sweater are broad but lean. 'Metadata, mostly. Which rooms you use most often, that kind of thing. And from time to time, we'll ask you to redo the questionnaire, to see how your answers are changing.'

'I can live with that.' I stop, aware that might sound presumptuous. 'If I get the chance, I mean.'

'Good.' Edward Monkford reaches down to where some coffee cups and a bowl of sugar cubes in paper wrappers sit on a tray. Absent-mindedly, he rearranges the sugar in a stack, aligning the edges until it forms a perfect square, like a Rubik's Cube. Then he turns the cups so the handles all point in the same direction. 'I might even ask you to meet some of our clients, to help us convince them that living without an Aga and a cabinet of sports trophies won't be the end of their world.' Another smile touches the corners of his eyes, and I feel myself going a little weak at the knees. This isn't like me, I think, followed by: Is it mutual? I give him a tiny, encouraging smile in return.

A pause. 'So, Jane. Is there anything you'd like to ask *me*?'

I think. 'You built One Folgate Street for yourself?'

'Yes.' He doesn't elaborate.

'So where do *you* live?'

'In hotels, mostly. Near whatever project I'm working on. They're perfectly bearable, so long as you put all the loose cushions in a wardrobe.' He smiles again, but I sense he isn't joking.

'Don't you mind not having a home of your own?'

He shrugs. 'It means I can focus on my work.' Something about the way he says it doesn't invite any more questions.

A man comes into the room – barging in clumsily, banging the door against its stopper, already talking nineteen to the dozen. 'Ed, we need to talk about bandwidth. The idiots are trying to scrimp on the fibre optics. They don't understand that in a hundred years' time, copper wiring will seem as outdated as lead water-pipes are today—'

The speaker is a scruffy, heavily built individual, an erratic growth of stubble covering his fleshy, jowly face. His hair, which is greyer than his stubble, is tied up in a ponytail. Despite the air conditioning, he's wearing shorts and flip-flops.

Monkford doesn't seem perturbed by the interruption. 'David, this is Jane Cavendish. She's applied to live at One Folgate Street.'

So this must be David Thiel, the technology partner. His eyes, set so deep in his face I can barely make out their expression, turn to me incuriously, then swivel back to Monkford. 'Really, the only solution is for the town to have its own satellite. We need to rethink everything—'

'A dedicated satellite? That's an interesting notion,' Monkford says thoughtfully. He glances at me. 'I'm afraid you'll have to excuse us, Jane.'

'Of course.' As I stand up, David Thiel's eyes drop down towards my bare legs. Monkford sees it too, and a frown crosses his face. I get the feeling he's about to say something, but then he restrains himself.

'Thank you for seeing me,' I add politely.

'I'll be in touch soon,' he says.

Then: Emma

And then, the very next day, there's an email:

Your application is approved.

I can't believe it – not least because the email contains nothing else: no explanation about when we can move in, or what their bank details are, or what we're supposed to do next. I call the agent, Mark. I'm getting to know him quite well now I'm doing all this stuff for the application, and he isn't actually as bad as I first thought.

He sounds genuinely pleased when I tell him we've got it. Since it's empty, he says, you can move in this weekend if you want. There's some paperwork to sign, and I'll need to talk you through installing the app on your phones. That's about it, really.

That's about it, really. It's just sinking in that we've done it. We're going to live in one of the most amazing houses in London. Us. Me and Simon. Everything's going to be different now.

3. You are involved in a traffic accident that you know is your fault. The other driver is confused and seems to think she caused the crash. Do you tell the police it was her fault or yours?

☐ Her fault

☐ Your fault

Now: Jane

I am sitting in the spare, empty austerity of One Folgate Street, utterly content.

My gaze takes in the pristine blankness of the garden. I've discovered now why there aren't any flowers. The garden is modelled on what the internet tells me are *karesansui*, the formal meditative gardens of Buddhist temples. The shapes are symbolic: mountain, water, sky. It's a garden for contemplating, not for growing things.

Edward Monkford spent a year in Japan, after his wife and son died. That's what made me think to search for it.

Even the internet is different here. Once Camilla had downloaded the app to my phone and laptop, and handed me the special bracelet that triggers One Folgate Street's sensors, she connected to the wi-fi and typed in a password. Since then, whenever I turn on a device I'm met not by Google or Safari, but by a blank page and the word *Housekeeper*. There are just three tabs: *Home*, *Search* and *Cloud*. 'Home' brings up the current status for One Folgate Street's lighting, heating, and so on. There are four different settings to choose from: productive, peaceful, playful and purposeful. 'Search' takes me to the internet. 'Cloud' is my backup and storage.

Every day, Housekeeper suggests what clothes I should wear, based on the weather outside, my appointments and what's currently at the laundry. If I'm eating in, it knows what's in the fridge, how I might cook it and how many calories it will add to my daily total. Meanwhile, the 'Search' function filters out adverts, pop-ups offering me a flatter belly, distressing news stories, top tens, gossip about minor celebrities, spam and cookies. There are no bookmarks, no history, no saved data. I am wiped clean every time I close the screen. It's strangely liberating.

Sometimes, I pour myself a glass of wine and simply walk around, touching things, acclimatising myself to the cool, expensive textures, adjusting the precise position of a chair or vase. Of course I was already familiar with that saying by Mies van der Rohe, 'Less is more', but I hadn't appreciated just how *sensual* less could be, how rich and voluptuous. The few pieces of furniture are design classics: Hans Wegner dining chairs in pale oak, white Nicolle stools, a sleek Lissoni sofa. And the house comes with a number of simple but luxurious lesser props: thick white towels, bed sheets made of high-thread-count linen, hand-blown wine glasses with thermometer-thin stems. Every touch is a small surprise, a quiet appreciation of quality.

I feel like a character in a film. Amongst so much good taste, the house somehow makes me walk more elegantly, stand in a more considered way, place myself within each vista for maximum effect. There's no one to see me, of course, but One Folgate Street itself seems almost to become my audience, filling the sparse spaces with quiet, cinematic scores from Housekeeper's automated playlist.

Your application is approved. That was all the email said. I'd been reading bad news into the fact that the meeting was so short, but it seems Edward Monkford is inclined to brevity in all things. And I'm sure I wasn't imagining that unspoken undercurrent, that tiny jolt you get when an attraction is reciprocated. Well, he knows where I am, I think. The waiting itself feels charged and sensual, a kind of silent foreplay.

And then there are the flowers. On the day I moved in, they were lying on the doorstep – a huge bouquet of lilies, still wrapped in plastic. No note, nothing to indicate whether this is something he does for all his new tenants or a special gesture just for me. I sent him a polite thank you anyway.

Two days later, another, identical bouquet arrived. And after a week, a third – exactly the same arrangement of lilies, left in exactly the same place beside the front door. Every corner of One Folgate Street is filled with their heavy scent. But, really, this is getting to be too much.

When I find the fourth identical bouquet, I decide enough's enough. There's a florist's name printed on the cellophane wrapper. I call them and ask if it's possible to change the order for something else.

The woman on the other end comes back sounding puzzled. 'I can't find any order for One Folgate Street.'

'It may be under Edward Monkford? Or the Monkford Partnership?'

'There's nothing like that. Nothing in your area, in fact. We're based in Hammersmith – we wouldn't deliver so far north.'

'I see,' I say, perplexed.

Next day, when yet more lilies arrive, I pick them up, intending to throw them in the bin.

And that's when I see it – a card, the first time one's been left, on which someone has written, *Emma, I will love you forever. Sleep well, my darling.*

Then: Emma

It's just as wonderful as we hoped. Well, as I hoped. Simon goes along with everything, but I can tell he's still got reservations. Or perhaps he doesn't like feeling beholden to the architect for letting us live here cheaply.

But even Simon is pretty amazed by a showerhead the size of a dinner plate that simply turns itself on when the cubicle door is opened, identifies each of us from the waterproof bracelet we've been given to wear, and remembers the different water temperatures we like. We wake on our first morning with the light in the bedroom slowly fading up – an electronic sunrise, the street noises muffled to silence by the thick walls and the glass – and I realise I've had my best night's sleep in years.

Unpacking, of course, takes no time at all. One Folgate Street already has lots of nice things, so our old stuff simply joins The Collection in storage.

Sometimes I just sit on the stairs with a mug of coffee, my knees tucked under my chin, drinking in how nice it all is. Don't spill the coffee, babe, Simon calls when he sees me. It's become a standing joke. We've decided it must be because I spilled the coffee that we got the house.

We don't ever mention Monkford calling Simon a prick, or Simon's non-reaction.

Happy? Simon asks, coming to sit next to me on the stairs.

Happy, I agree. Buuuut . . .

You want to move out, he goes. Had enough already. I knew it.

It's my birthday next week.

Is it, babe? I hadn't remembered.

He's joking, of course. Simon always goes way over the top for things like Valentine's and my birthday.

Why don't we get a few people round?

A party, you mean?

I nod. On Saturday.

Simon looks worried. Are we even allowed parties here?

It won't get messy, I say. Not like last time.

I say this because the last time we threw a party, the council sent a noise-abatement officer round.

Well, OK then, he says doubtfully. Saturday it is.

By nine p.m. on Saturday, the house is packed. I've put candles all the way up the stairs and outside in the garden and dimmed the lighting right down. The fact Housekeeper doesn't have a 'party' setting does make me a bit worried at first. But I've checked The Rules and 'No parties' isn't on the list. Maybe they just forgot, but hey, a list is a list.

Of course, our friends can't believe it when they walk through the door, though there are plenty of jokes about where's all the furniture and why haven't we unpacked yet. Simon's in his element – he always likes to be the envy of his mates, to have the most exclusive watch or the latest app or the coolest phone, and now he has the best place to live. I can see him adjusting to this new version of himself, proudly demonstrating the cooker, the automatic entry system, the way the electric sockets are just three tiny slits in a stone wall, how even the drawers built under the bed are different on the man's side and the woman's.

I'd thought about inviting Edward Monkford, but Simon persuaded me not to. Now, as Kylie's 'Can't Get You Out of My Head' ripples through the crowd, I realise he was right – Monkford would loathe all this noise and mayhem and dancing; he'd probably make up another rule on the spot and throw everyone out. Just for a moment, I imagine that happening – Edward Monkford turning up uninvited, turning off the music and telling everyone to get out – and it actually feels rather good. Which is stupid, because after all it's my party.

Simon goes past, his hands full of bottles, and leans in to kiss me. You look great, birthday girl, he says. Is that a new dress?

I've had it for ages, I lie. He kisses me again. Get a room, you two, Saul shouts over the music as Amanda pulls him into the knot of dancers.

There's a lot of booze, a little bit of drugs, plenty of music and shouting. People spill into the tiny garden to smoke and get yelled at by the neighbours. But by three in the morning everyone's starting to drift away. Saul spends twenty minutes trying to persuade Simon and me to come on to a club, but despite having done a couple of lines I'm knackered and Simon says he's too drunk, and eventually Amanda takes Saul home.

Come to bed, Em, Simon says when they've gone.

In a minute, I say. I'm too tired to move.

You smell gorgeous, gorgeous, he says, nuzzling my neck. Let's go to bed.

Si, I say hesitantly.

What? he says.

I don't think I want to have sex tonight, I say. Sorry.

We haven't since the break-in. We haven't really talked about it. It's just one of those things.

You said everything would be different here, he says softly.

It will, I say. Just not yet.

Of course, he says. There's no hurry, Em. No hurry at all.

Later, as we lie beside each other in the darkness, he says quietly, Remember how we christened Belfort Gardens?

It had been a silly challenge we'd set ourselves: to make love in every room before we'd been there a week.

He doesn't say anything else. The silence lengthens, and eventually I fall asleep.

Now: Jane

I invite some friends to lunch – a little house-warming gathering. Mia and Richard bring their children, Freddie and Martha, and Beth and Pete bring Sam. I've known Mia since Cambridge; she's my oldest and closest friend. Certainly I know things her own husband doesn't, such as that in Ibiza shortly before their wedding, she slept with another man and almost called it off, or that she contemplated having a termination with Martha because her post-natal depression with Freddie had been so bad.

Much as I love these people, I shouldn't have invited them together. I only did it because of the novelty of having enough space, but the fact is, however tactful my friends try to be, sooner or later they start talking about their children. Richard and Pete patrol after their toddlers as if jerked along by invisible reins, fearful of the stone floor, those lethal stairs, the floor-to-ceiling glass windows that a running child might not even see, while the girls pour huge glasses of white wine and moan quietly but with a kind of battle-weary pride about how boring their lives have become: 'God, last week I fell asleep watching the *Six O'Clock News*!' 'That's nothing – I'd crashed by CBeebies!' Martha regurgitates her lunch over the stone table, while Sam manages to smear the plate-glass windows with fingers previously dipped in chocolate mousse. I find myself thinking there are advantages to not having a child. A part of me just wants them all to go so I can tidy up.

And then there's a funny little moment with Mia. She's helping me get the salad ready when she calls out, 'J, where do you keep the African spoons?'

'Oh – I donated them to the charity shop.'

She gives me a strange look. '*I* gave you those.'

'Yes, I know.' Mia went to do voluntary work in an African orphanage once, and she brought me back two hand-carved salad spoons, made by the kids. 'Sorry. I decided they didn't quite make the cut. D'you mind?'

'I suppose not,' she says with a slightly put-out expression on her face. Clearly she does mind. But pretty soon lunch is ready and she forgets about it.

'So, J, how's your social life?' Beth asks, pouring herself a second glass of wine. She offers me the bottle, but I shake my head.

'The usual drought,' I say. For years, this has been my allotted role within the group: to provide them with vicarious stories of sexual disasters that make them feel they haven't completely left all that behind, while simultaneously reassuring them that they're much better off as they are.

'What about your architect?' Mia says. 'Anything come of him?'

'Ooh, I didn't know about the architect,' Beth says. 'Tell.'

'She fancies the man who built this house. Don't you, J?'

Pete has taken Sam outside. The child is squatting next to the patch of grass, scattering it with tiny fistfuls of gravel. I wonder if it would be spinsterish to ask him to stop. 'I haven't done anything about it, though,' I say.

'Well, don't hang around,' Beth says. 'Grab him before it's too late.' She stops, horrified at herself. 'Shit, I didn't mean . . .'

Grief and anguish rip at my heart, but I say calmly, 'It's OK, I know what you meant. Anyway, my biological clock seems to have set itself to snooze for the time being.'

'Sorry, anyway. That was unbelievably tactless of me.'

'I wondered if that was him outside,' Mia says. 'Your architect, I mean.'

I frown. 'What are you talking about?'

'When I got Martha's penguin from the car just now, there was a man with flowers coming to your front door.'

'What sort of flowers?' I say slowly.

'Lilies. Jane?'

I'm already hurrying to the door. The flower mystery has been nagging at me ever since I found that strange note. As I pull the door open, the bouquet has already been laid on the step and he's almost back at the road. 'Wait!' I call after him. 'Wait a moment, will you?'

He turns. He's about my age, maybe a couple of years older, his dark hair prematurely flecked with grey. His face looks drawn and his gaze is strangely intense. 'Yes?'

'Who are you?' I gesture at the bouquet. 'Why do you keep bringing me flowers? My name isn't Emma.'

'The flowers aren't for you, obviously,' he says disgustedly. 'I only keep replacing them because you keep taking them. That's why I left a note – so you'd finally get it into your thick skull that they're not there to brighten up your designer kitchen.' He stops. 'It's her birthday tomorrow. That is, it would have been.'

Finally, I realise. They're not a gift, they're a memorial gesture.

Like the ones people leave at the scene of a fatal accident. Mentally, I kick myself for being so wrapped up in thinking about Edward Monkford, I hadn't even considered that possibility.

'I'm so sorry,' I say. 'Did she . . . Was it near here?'

'In that house.' He gestures behind me, at One Folgate Street, and I feel a shiver go down my spine. 'She died in there.'

'How?' Realising that might sound intrusive, I add, 'I mean, it's none of my business—'

'It depends who you ask,' he interrupts.

'What do you mean?'

He looks straight at me. His eyes are haggard. 'She was murdered. The coroner recorded an open verdict, but everyone – even the police – knew she'd been killed. First he poisoned her mind, then he killed her.'

For a moment I wonder if this is all nonsense, if this man is simply deranged. But he seems too sincere, too ordinary for that.

'Who did? Who killed her?'

But he only shakes his head and turns away, back towards his car.

Then: Emma

It's the morning after the party and we're still asleep when my phone goes. It's a new phone to replace the one stolen in the burglary and it takes me a while to wake up with the unfamiliar ringtone. My head's groggy from the night before, but even so I notice how the light in the bedroom comes up in perfect sync with the sound of the phone, the windows gradually shedding their dimness.

Emma Matthews? a female voice says.

Yes? I say, my voice a bit hoarse from last night.

It's Sergeant Willan, she goes, your liaison officer. I'm outside your flat with one of my colleagues. We've been ringing the bell. Can we come in?

I'd forgotten to tell the police we were moving. We're not at that address any more, I say. We're in Hendon. One Folgate Street.

Hang on, Sergeant Willan says. She must have put the phone against her chest to speak to someone, because her voice goes muffled. Then she comes back on.

We'll be there in twenty minutes, Emma. There's been an important development in your case.

*

By the time they arrive we've cleared away most of the party debris. There are some unfortunate red-wine stains on the stone floor we'll have to deal with later, and One Folgate Street isn't looking its best, but Sergeant Willan seems pretty amazed.

Bit different from your last place, she comments, looking around.

I spent all last night trying to explain The Rules to our friends, and I don't really have the energy to do it again. We got it cheap, I say, in exchange for looking after it.

You said there was news, Simon says impatiently. Have you caught them, then?

We believe so, yes, the older police officer says. He's already introduced himself as Detective Inspector Clarke. His voice is low and calm and he has the stocky build and ruddy cheeks of a farmer. I like him immediately.

Two men were apprehended on Friday night carrying out a burglary very similar in method to the one you suffered, he says. When we went to an address in Lewisham we recovered a number of items listed on our database as stolen.

That's fantastic, Simon says, elated. He glances at me. Isn't it, Emma?

Brilliant, I say.

There's a pause.

Now that there's a strong possibility of a trial, Emma, we need to ask you some more questions, Sergeant Willan says. Perhaps you'd prefer to do this in private.

That's all right, Simon says. It's great you've actually got the bastards. We'll help any way we can, won't we, Em?

The sergeant's still looking at me. Emma? Would you rather do this without Simon present?

Put like that, how can I say yes? In any case, there is nowhere private in One Folgate Street. The rooms all flow into each other, even the bedroom and the bathroom.

Here is fine, I say. Will I have to go to court? To give evidence, I mean?

A glance passes between the two of them. It depends whether they plead guilty, Sergeant Willan says. We're hoping the evidence is so strong they don't see any point in fighting it.

A pause, then she says, Emma, we recovered a number of mobile phones at that address we mentioned. One of them we've identified as yours.

Suddenly I have a very bad feeling about this. *Breathe*, I tell myself.

Some of the phones had photographs and videos on them, she continues. Photographs of women in sexual situations.

I wait. I know what's coming now, but it seems easier to say nothing, to let the words pass over me as if they aren't real.

Emma, we found evidence on your phone indicating that a man matching the description of one of the men we arrested used it to film himself engaging in a sexual act with you, she says. Can you tell us anything about that?

I sense Simon's head swivelling towards me. I don't look in his direction. The silence stretches out like a thread of molten glass, getting thinner and thinner, until eventually it has to snap.

Yes, I say at last. My voice has shrunk to nothing. I can hardly hear myself, only the hammering in my ears. But I know I have to say something now, that I can't simply blot it out.

I take a deep breath. He said he'd send the film out, I say. To everyone. Every name in my contacts. He made me . . . do *that* to him. What you saw. And he used my own phone to film it.

I stop. It's like looking over a cliff edge. He had a knife, I say.

Take your time, Emma. I know how hard this must be, Sergeant Willan says gently.

I can't bear to look at Simon, but I force myself to go on. He said if I told anyone – the police, my boyfriend – he'd know and send out the film. And that phone was a work phone, it's got everyone stored on it. My boss. My whole company. My family.

There's something else . . . I'm afraid we have to ask, DI Clarke says apologetically. Is there any possibility this man could have left any DNA behind? On the bed, perhaps? Or the clothes you were wearing?

I shake my head.

You understand the question, don't you, Emma? Sergeant Willan says. We're asking if Deon Nelson ejaculated.

Out of the corner of my eye I see Simon clench his fists.

He held my nose, I say in a tiny voice. He held my nose and made me swallow. He said it all had to go, every bit, to stop the police getting any DNA. So I knew there was no point. No point in telling you. I'm sorry.

Now I do manage to look at Simon. I'm sorry, I repeat.

There's another long silence.

In your previous statement, Emma, DI Clarke says gently, you told us you couldn't remember exactly what happened during the break-in. Just so we understand, can you explain in your own words why you said that to us?

I wanted to forget it had happened, I say. I didn't want to admit I was too scared to tell anyone. I was ashamed.

I start to cry now. I didn't want to have to tell Simon, I say.

There's a crash. Simon has thrown his coffee cup at the wall. Shards of white pottery and brown liquid explode across the pale stone. Simon, wait, I say desperately. But he's already gone.

Drying my eyes on my sleeve, I say, Will you be able to use this? To convict him, I mean?

Once again, they exchange glances. It's a difficult situation, Sergeant Willan says. Juries expect DNA evidence these days. And it's impossible to identify the suspect absolutely from the video – he's careful never to show his face, or the knife.

She pauses. Plus we're obliged to disclose to the defence that you initially said you couldn't remember. They may try to spin that, I'm afraid.

You said there were other phones, I say dully. Won't those women be able to give evidence?

We suspect he did to others exactly what he did to you, DI Clarke says. Offenders – particularly sexual offenders – tend to develop a pattern over time. They repeat what works and discard what doesn't. They even get a kick out of repeating themselves – turning what they do into a kind of ritual. But unfortunately, we haven't been able to trace those other victims yet.

You mean, none of them reported it, I say, seeing the implication. His threat worked and they kept quiet.

It looks that way, DI Clarke says. Emma, I understand why you didn't tell anyone before. But it's important we get an accurate account of what happened. Will you come into the station and update your previous statement for us?

I nod miserably. He picks up his jacket. Thank you for being honest with us, he says kindly. I know how difficult this must be.

But understand this: according to the law, any kind of forced sex, including forced oral sex, is rape. And that's what we're going to charge this man with.

Simon's gone over an hour. I spend the time picking up bits of broken mug and scrubbing the wall clean. Like a whiteboard, I think. Except that what's been written here can't be erased.

When he does come back, I scrutinise his face, trying to work out his mood. His eyes are red and it looks like he's been crying.

I'm sorry, I say miserably.

Why, Em? he says quietly. Why didn't you tell me?

I thought you'd be angry.

You mean, you thought I wouldn't be sympathetic? He looks bewildered as well as upset. You thought I wouldn't *care*?

I don't know, I say. I didn't want to think about it. I was . . . I was ashamed. It was so much easier just to pretend it didn't happen. And I was scared.

Jesus, Em, he shouts. I know I can be a bit of an idiot sometimes but do you really think I wouldn't *care*?

No . . . I messed up, I say miserably. I couldn't talk to you about it. I'm sorry.

It's like Monkford said. Deep down, you think I'm a prick.

What does Monkford have to do with it?

He gestures at the floor, the beautiful stone walls, the dramatic double-height void. That's why we're here, isn't it? I'm not good enough for you. Our old flat wasn't good enough.

This isn't about you, I say dully. And anyway, I don't think that.

Suddenly he shakes his head and I can see his anger's gone as quickly as it arrived. He says, If only you'd told me.

The police think he may get off, I say. I reckon I may as well get all the bad news out now.

He's like, *What?*

They didn't actually say so. But because I've changed my evidence, and no other women have come forward, they clearly think he might get away with it. They said maybe there's no point in pursuing it.

Oh no, he says, balling his fists and banging them down on the stone table. I promise you this, Emma. If that creep gets acquitted, I'm going to kill him myself. And I know his name now. Deon Nelson.

Now: Jane

When my friends have gone, I go to my laptop and type in *One Folgate Street*. Then I add *death* and, finally, *Emma*.

There are no matches. But I'm learning that Housekeeper doesn't work quite the same way Google does. Where Google throws thousands, even millions, of results at you, Housekeeper likes to select one perfect match and nothing else. Mostly, it's a relief not to be bombarded with alternatives. But when you don't quite know what you're looking for, it's not so good.

The next day is Monday, one of my days to work at Still Hope, the charity. It's run out of three crowded rooms in King's Cross – the contrast with the stark, austere beauty of One Folgate Street couldn't be more pronounced. I have a desk there, or rather half a desk, because I share it with Tessa, another part-timer. And a creaking old desktop computer.

I type the same search terms into Google. Most of the results are about Edward Monkford. Irritatingly, an architectural journalist who also had the first name Emma once wrote a piece about him titled 'The Death of Clutter', so there are about five hundred links to that. On the sixth page of results, though, I find it. An archived piece from a local paper.

INQUEST INTO HENDON DEATH RECORDS OPEN VERDICT

The inquest into the death of Emma Matthews, 26, who was found dead at her rented home in Folgate Street, South Hendon, last July, has concluded with an open verdict, despite a six-month adjournment to allow the police more time to make inquiries.

Detective Inspector James Clarke said, 'We had a number of potential leads, which at one point did lead to an arrest. However, it was felt by the Crown Prosecution Service that there was insufficient evidence to show Emma died unlawfully. We will, of course, continue to investigate this unexplained fatality to the very best of our abilities.'

The house, designed by leading international architect Edward Monkford, was described by the coroner in his summing-up as 'a health-and-safety nightmare'. The inquest had previously heard that Emma's body was found at the bottom of an open, uncarpeted staircase.

Local residents fought a protracted battle in 2010 to try to prevent the house from being built, with permission only finally granted by the Mayor's office. A neighbour, Maggie Evans, said yesterday, 'We warned the planners time and again something like this would happen. The best thing now would be if they pulled it down and built something more in keeping.'

The Monkford Partnership, which was not represented at the inquest, declined to comment yesterday.

Not two deaths, I think, but three. First Monkford's own family, then this. One Folgate Street is an even more tragic place than I'd realised.

I picture a young woman's body lying at the bottom of those sleek stone stairs, blood spreading across the floor from a shattered skull. The coroner was right, of course: the open staircase is ridiculously dangerous. And why, once that had been proved in the most horrific way possible, hadn't Edward Monkford done something to make it safer – wall it in with glass, say, or put up some kind of rail?

But of course, I already know the answer. *My buildings make demands of people, Jane. I believe they're not intolerable.* No doubt somewhere in the terms and conditions, there's a clause saying tenants use the staircase at their own risk.

'Jane?' It's Abby, the office manager. I look up. 'There's someone here to see you.' She looks a little flustered, a touch of pink in her cheeks. 'He says his name's Edward Monkford. I must say, he's *very* good-looking. He's waiting downstairs.'

He's standing in the tiny waiting area, dressed almost identically to the last time we met. Black cashmere pullover, white open-necked shirt, black trousers. The only concession to the chilly weather is a scarf looped around his neck in the French style, like a slipknot.

'Hello,' I say, although what I really want to say is, *What on earth are you doing here?*

He'd been examining the Still Hope posters on the walls, but when he hears my voice he turns to me. 'It makes sense now,' he says softly.

'What does?'

He gestures at one of the posters. 'You lost a child too.'

I shrug. 'I did, yes.'

He doesn't say 'I'm sorry' or any of those other platitudes people mutter when they don't really know what to say. He just nods.

'I'd like to have coffee with you, Jane. I can't stop thinking about you. But if it's too soon, just say so and I'll go away.'

There are so many assumptions, so many questions and revelations in those three brief sentences that I can't quite process them all. But the first thought flashing through my brain is, I wasn't mistaken. It *was* mutual.

And the second, even more certain, is, *Good*.

'So that was Cambridge. But there aren't many career openings for History of Art graduates. The fact is, I'd never really thought about what I wanted to do afterwards. There was an internship at Sotheby's that failed to turn into a job, then I worked in a couple of galleries – I was called something like "senior art consultant", but really I was just a glorified receptionist. Then I just sort of drifted into PR. To begin with I worked in the West End, on media accounts, but I never felt very comfortable with that whole Soho scene. I liked the City, where the clients are more buttoned down. If I'm honest, I quite liked the money as well. But the work was interesting. Our clients were big financial institutions – for them, PR was all about keeping their name out of the papers, not getting it in. I'm talking too much.'

Edward Monkford smiles and shakes his head. 'I like listening to you.'

'And you?' I prompt. 'Did you always want to be an architect?'

A shrug of the lean shoulders. 'I spent some time working for the family business – a printing firm. I hated it. A friend of my father's was building a holiday home in Scotland and was struggling with the local architect. I persuaded him to let me do it for the same budget. I learned on the job. Are we going to go to bed together?'

The change of tack is so abrupt my mouth falls open.

'Human relationships, like human lives, tend to accumulate the unnecessary,' he says softly. 'Valentine's cards, romantic gestures, special dates, meaningless endearments – all the boredom and inertia of timid, conventional relationships that have run their course before they've even begun. But what if we strip all that away? There's a kind of purity to a relationship unencumbered by convention, a sense of simplicity and freedom. I find that exhilarating – two people coming together with no agenda other than the present. And when I want something, I pursue it. But I want to be very clear with you what it is I'm suggesting.'

He means no-ties sex, I realise. Many of the men who have asked me out in the past, I'm sure, wanted me for that rather than love – Isabel's father among them. But few have had the confidence to spell it out so matter-of-factly. And although a part of me is a little bit disappointed – I quite *like* the occasional romantic gesture – another part can't help being intrigued.

'Which bed did you have in mind?' I say.

The answer, of course, is the bed at One Folgate Street. And if my dealings with Edward Monkford thus far might have led me to believe he'd be an ungenerous or a reticent lover – would a minimalist need to fold up his trousers before sex? Would someone who disdains soft furnishings and patterned cushions also be squeamish about bodily fluids and other signs of passion? – I am pleasantly surprised to find the reality is very different. Nor was his reference to an unencumbered relationship a euphemism for one dedicated solely to the man's pleasure. In bed, Edward is considerate, generous, and by no means inclined to brevity. Only when my own senses are blurred by orgasm does he finally permit himself to let go, his hips bucking and locking as he shudders inside me, saying my name out loud, over and over.

Jane. Jane. Jane.

Almost, I think later, like someone trying to imprint it on his mind.

Afterwards, as we're lying together, I recall the article I was reading earlier. 'There's a man who's been leaving flowers outside the front door. He said they were for Emma, who died here. It was something to do with the staircase, wasn't it?'

His hand, which is idly stroking up and down my back, doesn't pause in its movements. 'That's right. Is he being a nuisance?'

'Hardly. Besides, if he's lost someone he cared about . . .'

He's silent a moment. 'He blames me – he's convinced himself the house was responsible, somehow. But the post-mortem showed she'd been drinking. And the shower was on when they found her. She must have been running downstairs with wet feet.'

I frown. Running seems such an unlikely thing to do in the calm of One Folgate Street. 'Running away from someone, you mean?'

He shrugs. 'Or hurrying to meet them at the door.'

'The article said the police made an arrest. It didn't say who. But whoever it was, they had to let him go.'

'Did they?' His pale eyes are inscrutable. 'I don't remember all the details. I was away, working on a commission, at the time.'

'And he talked about someone, a man, poisoning her mind . . .'

Edward glances at his watch and sits up. 'I'm so sorry, Jane. I completely forgot – I'm due at a site inspection.'

'Don't you have time for some food?' I say, disappointed he's leaving so soon.

He shakes his head. 'Thank you. But I'm late as it is. I'll call you.' He's already reaching for his clothes.

4. *I have no time for people who don't strive to better themselves.*

Agree ☐☐☐☐☐ Disagree

Then: Emma

The fact is, Brian says belligerently, we can't possibly write a mission statement until we've decided what our values are. He looks around the meeting room as if challenging anyone to disagree.

We're in Room 7b – a glass-walled box, identical to 7a and 7c. Someone has written the purpose of the meeting on a flip chart. *Company mission statement.* There are still torn-off pages from a previous meeting stuck to the glass. One says, *24-hour response? Emergency warehouse capability?* It looks a lot more exciting than what we're doing.

For over a year now I've been angling to move into marketing. I suspect the fact I'm here today, though, probably has more to do with my being a friend of Amanda's, and therefore of Saul's, than with Brian actually wanting me – Saul being quite high up on the financial side. I try to nod energetically whenever Brian looks in my direction. Somehow I'd thought marketing would be more glamorous than this.

Is someone going to act as scribe? Leona asks, looking at me. I take the hint and jump up to stand next to the flip chart, marker pen in hand, the eager new girl. At the top of the page I write *VALUES*.

Energy, someone suggests. Obediently, I write it down.

Positivity, someone else says.

Other voices chip in. Caring. Dynamism. Reliability.

Charles says, Emma, you haven't written down 'Dynamism'.

Dynamism was his suggestion. Isn't it the same as 'Energy'? I ask. Brian frowns. I write down *Dynamism* anyway.

I think we should ask ourselves, What exactly is the higher purpose of Flow? Leona says, looking around self-importantly. What is the unique contribution we at Flow can make to people's lives?

There's a long silence. Delivering bottled water? I suggest. I say this because Flow's business is to supply the big bottles of water that slot into office water coolers. Brian frowns again, and I resolve to keep my mouth shut.

Water's essential. Water is *life*, Charles says. Write that down, Emma.

Meekly, I obey.

I read somewhere, Leona adds, that we're all mostly water. So water is, quite literally, a big part of us.

Hydration, Brian says thoughtfully. Several people nod, including me.

The door opens and Saul sticks his head in. Ah, the creative geniuses of marketing hard at work, he says genially. How're you getting on?

Brian grunts. Mission statement hell.

Saul glances at the flip chart. It's pretty straightforward, isn't it? To save people the bother of running a tap, and charge them a crazy premium for it.

Sod off, you, Brian says with a laugh. You're not helping.

All right, Emma? Saul says cheerily as he obliges. He winks. I see Leona's head swivel towards me. She clearly didn't know I had friends in management.

I write down *Mostly water* and *Hydration*.

When the meeting is finally over – apparently Flow's mission and higher purpose is *To make more water-cooler moments happen, every day and everywhere*, an insight all present agree is suitably creative and brilliant – I go back to my desk and wait until the office empties for lunch before I dial a number.

The Monkford Partnership, a well-bred female voice says.

Edward Monkford, please, I say.

Silence. The Monkford Partnership doesn't go in for recorded music. Then: Edward here.

Mr Monkford, it's Emma. From One Folgate Street—

Call me Edward.

Edward, I need to ask you something about our contract.

I know I should be going through Mark, the agent, about this sort of thing. But I have a feeling he'd only tell Simon.

I'm afraid the rules are non-negotiable, Emma, Edward Monkford says sternly.

I don't have a problem with the rules, I assure him. Quite the opposite. And I don't want to leave One Folgate Street.

A pause. Why would you need to?

That contract Simon and I signed . . . What would happen if one of us stopped living there? And the other one wanted to stay?

Are you and Simon no longer together? I'm sorry to hear that, Emma.

It's a . . . theoretical enquiry at the moment. I'm just wondering what the situation would be, that's all.

My head is pounding. Just thinking about leaving Simon gives me a strange feeling, like vertigo. Is it the break-in that's done this? Is it talking to Carol? Or is it One Folgate Street itself, those powerful empty spaces in which, suddenly, everything seems so much clearer?

Edward Monkford considers. Technically, he says, you'd be in breach of contract. But I imagine you could sign a deed of variation to say you take on all the responsibilities yourself. Any competent solicitor could draw one up in ten minutes. Would you still be able to afford the rent?

I don't know, I say truthfully. One Folgate Street might cost a preposterously small amount for somewhere so amazing, but it's still more than I can afford on my tiny salary.

Well, I'm sure we can come to some arrangement.

That's really kind of you, I say. And now I feel even more disloyal, because Simon, if he were listening to this conversation, would say that I phoned Edward Monkford rather than the agent because this was precisely the outcome I was hoping for.

Simon gets back to One Folgate Street about an hour after me. What's all this? he says.

I'm cooking, I say, flashing him a smile. Your favourite. Beef Wellington.

Wow, he says, amazed, looking round the kitchen. Admittedly, it's a bit of a mess, but at least he can see what an effort I've made. How long has this taken? he asks.

I did the shopping at lunchtime and I left work on time to get it all ready, I say proudly.

As soon as I'd put the phone down on Edward Monkford, I'd felt terrible. What was I thinking? Simon has tried so hard, and really I've behaved like a monster these past few weeks. I've decided I'm going to make it up to him, starting tonight.

I've got wine too, I tell him. Simon's eyes widen when he sees I'm already a third of the way down the bottle, but he doesn't say anything. Oh, and olives, and crisps, and many other nibbly things, I add.

I'll have a shower, he says.

By the time he comes down again, showered and changed, the beef is in the oven and I'm a little pissed. He hands me a wrapped-up parcel. I know it isn't till tomorrow, babe, he goes, but I want you to have this now. Happy birthday, Em.

I can tell from the shape it's a teapot, but it's only when I get the paper off that I see it's not just any teapot, but a beautiful art deco one with a peacock-feather design, like something from a 1930s ocean liner. I gasp. It's gorgeous, I say.

I found it on Etsy, he says proudly. Do you recognise it? It's the one Audrey Hepburn uses in *Breakfast at Tiffany's*. Your favourite film. I had it shipped over from an antiques shop in America.

You're incredible, I say. I put it down and go and sit in his lap. I love you, I murmur, kissing his ear.

I haven't said it for too long. Neither of us has. I slip a hand between his thighs.

What's got into *you*? he says, amused.

Nothing, I say. Maybe you need to get into me. Or one bit of you, anyway.

I wriggle in his lap and feel him starting to get hard. You've been so patient, I whisper in his ear. I slip down until I'm kneeling between his legs. I'd been planning to do this later, after supper, but there's no time like the present, and the wine is helping. I pull down his zipper and take out his cock. Looking up, I give him what I hope is a slutty, inviting smile, then slide my lips over the head.

For a minute or so he lets me. But I can feel him getting softer, not harder. I redouble my efforts, but that only makes things worse. When I look up again, his eyes are tightly closed and his fists clenched, as if he's desperately willing himself to get an erection.

Mmm, I murmur, to encourage him. Mmmmmm.

At the sound of my voice his eyes fly open and he pushes me away. Jesus, Emma, he says. He stands up, pushing his cock back inside his trousers. Jesus, he repeats.

What's wrong? I say numbly.

He stares down at me. There's a strange expression on his face. Deon Nelson, he says.

What about him?

How can you do to me what you did to that . . . that *bastard*?

Now it's my turn to stare. Don't be ridiculous, I say.

You let him come in your mouth, he says.

I flinch as if I've been hit. I didn't *let* him, I say. He made me. How can you say that? How dare you?

I get up. My mood's changed again, from euphoria to abject misery. We should eat the beef, I say.

Wait, he goes. There's something I've got to tell you.

He looks so miserable that I think, This is it. He's breaking up with me.

The police came to see me today, he says. About a . . . discrepancy in my evidence.

What do you mean, 'discrepancy'?

He walks to the window. It's gone dark, but he stares out as if he can see something.

After the break-in, he says, I gave the police a statement. I told them I'd been in a pub.

I know, I say. The Portland, wasn't it?

It turns out it wasn't the Portland, he says. They checked. The Portland doesn't have a late licence. So they looked at my credit-card records.

It seems a lot of work, just to check which bar Simon was in. Why? I ask.

They said if they hadn't, Nelson's solicitor might claim they weren't doing their job.

He pauses.

I wasn't in a pub that night, Emma. I was in a club. A lap-dancing club.

So you're telling me, I say slowly, that all the time I was being . . . being *raped* by that monster, you were looking at naked women?

It was a group of us, Em. Saul and some of the boys. It wasn't my idea. I didn't even enjoy it.

How much did you spend?

He looks bewildered. What does that have to do with anything?

How much did you spend? I shout. My voice echoes off the stone walls. I hadn't even realised until now that One Folgate Street has an echo. It's like the house is joining in, shouting at him too.

He sighs. I dunno. Three hundred quid.

Jesus, I say.

The police reckon it's all bound to come out in court, he says.

It's just sinking in what this means. Not just that Simon's capable of spending money he hasn't got staring at naked women he can't fuck just because his mates drag him there. Not just that he thinks I'm somehow soiled because of what that man did to me. But what it could mean for the case against Deon Nelson. The defence will say that our relationship is fucked up, that we lie to each other as well as to the police.

They're going to say I consented that night, and that was why I didn't report it.

I try to make it to the sink, but the sick – all that red wine, the black olives, nibbly things for our special night in – tumbles out of my mouth, a torrent of hot, bitter vomit.

Get out, I say, when I've finished throwing up. Just get out. Take your things and go.

I've been sleepwalking through life, letting this weak, feeble man pretend he loves me. It's time to end it. Go, I repeat.

Em, he says, pleadingly. Em, this isn't you. You're only talking like this because of everything that's happened. We love each other. We'll get over it. Don't say something you'll regret tomorrow.

I won't regret it tomorrow, I say. I won't ever regret it. We're breaking up, Simon. It hasn't been working for ages. I don't want to be with you any more and I've finally found the courage to say it.

Now: Jane

'He said *what*?'

'He said there's an exhilarating purity to the unencumbered relationship. I mean, I may be paraphrasing slightly, but that was the gist.'

Mia looks appalled. 'Is this guy for real?'

'Well, that's the point. He's just so . . . different from anyone else I've ever been with.'

'You're sure you're not getting Stockholm syndrome or whatever it's called?' Mia looks around at the pale empty spaces of One Folgate Street. 'Living here . . . It must be a bit like being stuck inside his head. Maybe he's brainwashed you.'

I laugh. 'I think I'd have found Edward interesting even if I didn't live in one of his buildings.'

'And you? What does he see in you, my love? Other than the unencumbered fuck or whatever he called it?'

'I don't know.' I sigh. 'In any case, I don't suppose there's much chance of finding out now.'

I tell her how Edward left my bed so abruptly, and she frowns. 'It sounds like he's got serious issues, J. Maybe avoid this one?'

'Everyone has issues,' I say lightly. 'Even me.'

'Two damaged people don't make a whole. What *you* need

right now is someone nice and solid. Someone who'll take care of you.'

'Sadly, I don't think "nice and solid" is my type.'

Mia doesn't comment on that. 'And there's been no contact since?'

I shake my head. 'I haven't called him.' I don't mention the pointedly casual email I sent the next day, the one that didn't get a response.

'Well, that *is* unencumbered.' She's silent a moment. 'And flower man? Any more from him?'

'No. But Edward said the death was an accident. The poor girl fell down the stairs, apparently. That is, the police did consider foul play, but they couldn't make it stick.'

Mia stares at me. '*These* stairs?'

'Yes.'

'And foul play – what the hell's *that* about? Doesn't that freak you out? To know you're living in a crime scene?'

'Not really,' I say. 'I mean, it's a tragedy, of course. But, like I said, probably not a crime scene at all. And lots of houses have had someone die in them.'

'Not like that. And you living here all alone . . .'

'I don't get scared. It's a very calm house.' And I have held a dead baby in my arms, I think. The death of a total stranger, several years ago, is hardly going to bother me.

'What was her name?' Mia's pulling out her iPad.

'Emma Matthews. Why?'

'Aren't you curious?' She taps at the screen. 'Oh my God.'

'What?'

Silently, she shows me. On her screen is a picture of a woman in her mid-twenties. She's rather pretty – slim and dark-haired. She seems familiar, somehow.

'And?' I say.

'Can't you see it?' Mia demands.

I scrutinise the picture again. 'See what?'

'J, she looks just like you. Or rather, *you* look just like *her*.'

I suppose it's true, in a way. The young woman and I both have the same unusual colouring – brown hair, blue eyes and very pale skin. She's thinner than me, younger and, if I'm honest, better looking, and she uses more make-up – two dramatic splashes of black mascara – but there's a definite resemblance.

'Not just facially,' Mia adds. 'You see the way she's standing? Good posture. You stand exactly like that.'

'Do I?'

'You know you do. Still think he doesn't have issues?'

'It could be a coincidence,' I say at last. 'After all, there's no reason to think Edward was even in a relationship with this girl. How many millions of women in the world have brown hair and blue eyes?'

'Did he know what you looked like before you moved in?'

'Yes,' I admit. 'There was the interview.' And, even before that, the request for three photographs. It didn't occur to me at the time, but why would a landlord need to see photographs of his tenants?

Mia's eyes widen as something else occurs to her. 'And the wife? What was *her* name?'

'Mia, no . . .' I say weakly. I'm pretty sure this has gone far enough. But she's already tapping at her screen.

'Elizabeth Monkford, maiden name Elizabeth Mancari,' she

says after a while. 'Now let's do an image search . . .' She scrolls rapidly through pictures. 'That can't be her . . . Wrong nationality . . . Gotcha.' She gives a low whistle of surprise.

'What is it?'

She turns the screen towards me. 'Not so unencumbered after all,' she says quietly.

The image shows a dark-haired young woman sitting at some kind of architect's easel, smiling up at the camera. It's quite grainy, but even so I can tell that she bears a strong resemblance to Emma Matthews. And therefore also, I suppose, to me.

Then: Emma

Telling Simon and the police I was lying about not remembering the rape was bad enough, but telling Carol is almost worse. To my relief she's very nice about it.

You're not the guilty party in any of this, Emma, she says. Sometimes we're simply not ready to face up to the truth.

To my surprise, though, it isn't Deon Nelson and his horrible threats she homes in on during our session, but Simon. She wants to know how he's taken the break-up, whether he's been in contact since – which, of course, he has, constantly, though I'm not replying to his messages any more – and what I'm going to do about it.

So where does this leave you, Emma? she says at last. What do you want to happen next?

I don't know, I shrug.

Well, let me put it this way: is this separation final?

Simon thinks not, I admit. We've broken up before, but he always begs and begs until eventually it just seems easier to let him come back. This time it's different, though. I've got rid of all my old things – all that useless stuff. I think it's given me the strength to get rid of him too.

But a human relationship is very different to stuff, she says.

I look at her sharply. Do you think I'm doing the wrong thing?

She doesn't reply for a few moments. One of the curious aspects of a traumatic experience like the one you've been through, she says at last, is how it sometimes results in a softening of your existing boundaries. Sometimes the changes are temporary, but sometimes the person finds they actually quite like this new aspect of their personality, and it becomes a part of them. Whether that's a good thing or not isn't for me to say, Emma. Only you can make that judgement.

After therapy, I have an appointment with the solicitor who's drawn up the deed of variation on the tenancy. Edward Monkford was right: I went to a local firm and it turned out they could do one for fifty pounds. The only catch, the solicitor I spoke to said, was that Simon might have to sign it too. For another fifty pounds, he agreed to look through all the paperwork to see.

Today, the same solicitor tells me he's never seen an agreement like it. Whoever drew this up meant it to be completely watertight, he says. To be on the safe side, you should really ask Simon to sign as well.

I doubt Simon will sign anything that formalises us splitting up, but I take the documents anyway. As he finds me an envelope the solicitor says chattily, I looked the property up in the council archive, by the way. It's rather fascinating.

Oh? I go. Why's that?

It seems One Folgate Street has a somewhat tragic history, he says. The original house was destroyed by a German bomb during the war. All the occupants were killed – an entire family. There were no surviving relatives, so the council issued a compulsory purchase order to get the remains knocked down. After that, the plot remained derelict until it was bought by this architect chap. His original plans were for a much more conventional building – some of the neighbours wrote to the council afterwards, complaining they'd effectively been duped. Things got quite heated, from the look of it.

But it went ahead, I say, not really interested in the house's past.

Indeed. And then, to add insult to injury, he applied for permission to bury someone there. Two people, actually.

Bury someone? I repeat, puzzled. Is that even legal?

The solicitor nods. So long as the Environment Agency raises no objection and there are no local by-laws against it, the council's more or less obliged to grant permission. The only requirement is that the names of the deceased and their location have to be marked on the plans, for obvious reasons. Here they are.

He produces a stapled photocopy and unfolds a plan from the back. Final resting place of Mrs Elizabeth Domenica Monkford and Maximilian Monkford, he reads out loud.

He slips it into the envelope alongside the other documents and hands it to me. There. You can keep that, if you like.

Now: Jane

When Mia's gone, I go to my own laptop and type in *Elizabeth Mancari*, meaning to take another look without Mia hovering over my shoulder. But Housekeeper doesn't bring up any of the pictures she found.

It's true what I said to Mia: in the short time I've lived here, I've never found One Folgate Street a frightening place. But now, the silence and the emptiness seem to take on a more sinister hue. Ridiculous, of course – like being scared after a ghost story. All the same I select the brightest light setting and go round checking for . . . what? Not intruders, obviously. But for some reason, the house no longer feels quite so protective.

It feels like I'm being watched.

I shake the feeling away. Even when I first moved in, I remind myself, it felt like a film set. I enjoyed the sensation then. All that's happened since is some stupid, abortive sex with Edward Monkford and the discovery that he likes a certain type of woman.

Lying at the bottom of the stairs with her skull smashed in. Without quite meaning to, I go and stare at the spot. Is that a faint outline of a bloodstain, long since scrubbed clean? But of course I don't even know there *was* any blood.

I look up. Above me, at the top of the stairs, I see something: a chink of light that hasn't been there before.

I go up the stairs cautiously, my eyes fixed on it. As I get nearer, it takes on the outline of a small door, no more than five feet high – a hidden panel in the wall, similar in construction to the concealed cupboards in the bedroom and kitchen. I hadn't even realised it was there.

'Hello?' I call out. There's no reply.

I reach out and push the door all the way open. Inside is a deep, tall cupboard, full of a cleaner's bits and pieces: mops, squeegees, a Hoover, a floor polisher, even an extendable ladder. I relax. I should have realised there'd be somewhere like this in One Folgate Street. The cleaner – a middle-aged Japanese lady who speaks almost no English and who resists all my attempts at interaction during her weekly visits – must have left it ajar.

The cupboard looks as if it's designed to give access to the house's other services too. One wall is covered with wiring. Computer cables snake off into One Folgate Street's innards, through a hatchway in the roof.

I pick my way around the cleaning products and push my head up through the hatch. By the light of my phone, I can see a kind of crawl space running the length of the house, its floor thick with more cables. It opens into what looks like a bigger, attic-like space above the bedroom. At the far end, I can just make out some water pipes.

It occurs to me I may have just found a solution to something that's been bothering me. I couldn't bring myself to send Isabel's unworn clothes and other things to Oxfam along with my books, but unpacking them and putting them neatly away in One Folgate

Street's cupboards seemed wrong too. The suitcase has been sitting in the bedroom ever since I moved in, waiting to be found a home. I go and get it, then push it along the crawl space until I reach the attic. It can stay up here, out of the way.

The light from my phone isn't very strong, and it's only when I feel something soft under my feet that I look down and see a sleeping bag, pushed between two rafters. It has clearly been here a long time – it's covered with dust and dirt. I lift it up, and something falls out. A pair of girlish pyjama bottoms, printed with a pattern of tiny apples. I feel around inside the bag, but there's nothing else, except for some balled-up socks, right at the bottom. And a business card, very scrunched up – *Carol Younson. Accredited Psychotherapist.*

Turning, I see a few other things scattered around: some empty tins of supermarket tuna, candle stubs, an empty bottle of perfume, a plastic bottle of energy drink.

Strange. Strange and inexplicable. I have no way of knowing if the sleeping bag belonged to Emma Matthews – it may have been some other tenant's. And if it *was* Emma's, I'll clearly never know what nameless fear caused her to leave that beautiful, sleek bedroom and sleep up here instead.

My phone rings, very loud in the confined space. I pull it out.

'Jane, it's Edward,' a familiar voice says.

Then: Emma

I try to get Simon to meet me somewhere neutral, like a pub. But although he says he'll sign the papers, he point-blank refuses to do it anywhere but One Folgate Street.

I need to come round anyway, he goes. I left some of my things when I moved out.

Reluctantly I say, All right then.

I put the lighting on the brightest setting and pull on some scruffy jeans and my least glamorous old shirt. I'm just tidying the kitchen – it's extraordinary how, even with so little, clutter builds up – when I hear a sound behind me. I jump.

Hello, Em, he says.

Christ, you gave me a shock, I say furiously. How did you get in?

I'm just keeping the key code till I've got my stuff, he says. Don't worry, I'll delete it after that.

Well, OK, I say reluctantly. I make a mental note to ask Mark, the agent, how to block the code from this end.

How have you been? Simon asks.

I'm fine, I say. I know I ought to ask how he is too, but I can already see he's not good. His skin's got the pale, blotchy look he gets when he's drinking too much, and he's had an over-severe haircut.

Here's the agreement, I say, handing it to him. And a pen. I've already signed it.

Hey! Hey! Aren't we even going to have a drink together first?

I'm like, I don't think that's a good idea, Si. But I realise from the way he smirks he's already had one.

This is all wrong, he says when he's read the document through.

It was drawn up by a solicitor, I say.

I mean, what we're doing is all wrong. We love each other, Em. We've had our problems but deep down we do love each other.

Please don't be difficult, Simon.

Difficult? he goes. That's a bit rich, isn't it? When I'm the one who's been thrown out with nowhere to live. If I didn't know you were going to take me back eventually I'd be really upset.

I'm not going to take you back, I say.

Yes you are.

No I'm not, I say.

But I *am* back, aren't I? Here I am.

Just to get your things.

Or to come back here where my things are.

Simon, you need to go now, I say, starting to get angry.

He leans against the counter. Only when we've had a drink and a proper discussion, he announces.

For fuck's sake, I shout. Can't you behave like an adult for once?

Em, Em, he wheedles. Don't get upset. All I'm saying is, I love you and I don't want to lose you.

Like this is the way, I snap back.

Ah! he says. So there *might* be a way?

I'm torn. If I say there might be a chance of us getting back together at some point in the future, perhaps he'll go without any fuss. The old Emma would have said yes. But the new Emma's stronger than that.

No, I say firmly. There is no prospect whatsoever of us being a couple again, Simon.

He comes towards me and puts his hands on my shoulders. I can smell the drink on his breath. I love you, Em, he repeats.

Don't, I say, struggling.

I can't just stop loving you, he says. His eyes are a little crazy.

A phone rings. I glance around. My phone is flashing and beeping, shaking itself towards the edge of the counter.

Let me go, I say, pushing at his chest.

This time he does let me go. I snatch up the phone. Yes?

Emma, it's Edward. I just wanted to check that you managed to resolve the contractual issues we spoke about. Edward Monkford's voice is formal and polite.

Yes, thanks. Simon's actually here right now, about to sign the paperwork.

I can't help adding, At least, I hope he is.

There's a short silence. Put him on, will you? Edward says.

I watch Simon's face darken as Edward speaks to him. The conversation lasts about a minute and in all that time Simon barely says a word, just the occasional Uh-huh and Mmmn.

Here, he says sulkily, handing the phone back to me.

Simon's going to sign the papers now, Emma, Edward's voice says, and then he's going to leave. I'm coming round to check he's really gone, but also because I want to take you to bed. Don't tell Simon that, of course.

He hangs up. I look at the phone, gobsmacked. Did I really just hear that? But I know I did.

What did he say to you? I ask Simon.

I wouldn't have hurt you, he says sadly, not answering my question. I would never hurt you. Not deliberately. I can't help loving you, Em. And I *will* win you back. You'll see.

How long will Edward Monkford be? Do I even have time for a shower? I look at the interior of One Folgate Street and realise there are about a dozen rule violations in full view – stuff on the floor, things on the counters, a copy of the *Metro* on the stone table, the recycling bin overflowing on to the floor – not to mention that the bedroom looks like a bomb's hit it and I never scrubbed away all the wine stains after the party. I do a speedy shower, then quickly tidy up, selecting clothes as I go, a simple skirt and shirt. I hesitate over perfume, but decide that's a bit much. A part of me still thinks Edward might be joking or that I misheard him.

Though I hope I didn't.

My phone buzzes again. It's Housekeeper, telling me someone's at the door. I press for video and it shows Edward. He's carrying flowers and a bottle of wine.

So I wasn't mistaken. I press *Accept* to let him in.

By the time I get to the stairs, he's already at the bottom, watching me hungrily. You can't hurry down that staircase: it forces you to step carefully, formally, one foot at a time. Even before I reach him I'm dizzy with anticipation.

Hello, I say nervously.

He reaches out and tucks a stray lock of hair behind my left ear. It's still wet from the shower and it feels cold against my neck. His fingers brush my earlobe and I jump.

It's all right, he says quietly. It's all right.

His fingers travel under my chin and gently tilt my head up.

Emma, he says. I can't stop thinking about you. But if it's too soon, just say so and I'll go away.

He undoes the top two buttons of my shirt. I'm not wearing a bra.

You're shaking, he says.

I was raped.

I hadn't meant to blurt it out like that. I just want him to understand that this means something to me, that he's special.

Instantly, his face clouds. By Simon? he says furiously.

No. He'd never . . . By one of the burglars. The ones I told you about.

Then this *is* too soon, he says.

He slides his hand out from my shirt and does it up again. I feel like a child being dressed for school.

I just wanted you to know. In case . . . We can still go to bed if you like, I say timidly.

No we can't, he says. Not today. Today you're coming with me.

5 a) *You have a choice between saving Michelangelo's statue of David or a starving street child. Which do you choose?*

☐ *The statue*

☐ *The child*

Now: Jane

'Stop here,' Edward says to the cab driver. We're in the middle of the City. On every side, modern constructions of glass and steel tower over us, with the tops of the Shard and the Cheese Grater just visible beyond them. Edward sees me looking up at them as he pays the cabbie. 'Trophy buildings,' he says dismissively. 'We're going in here.'

He steers me towards a small, plain parish church I'd hardly noticed, tucked away amongst all these strutting, modernist behemoths. The interior is lovely – quite plain, almost square, but flooded with light from huge windows high in the walls. The walls are the same pale cream as One Folgate Street. The sun throws a lattice across the floor from the lead in the clear glass. Apart from the two of us, it's deserted.

'This is my favourite building in London,' he says softly. 'Look.'

I follow his gaze upwards, and my breath is taken away. Over our heads is a vast dome. Its pale void dominates the tiny church, floating on the slimmest of pillars over the entire central section. The altar, or what I assume must be the altar, is directly underneath: a massive circular slab of stone, five feet across, positioned in the very centre of the church.

'Before the Great Fire of London, there were two sorts of

churches.' He doesn't whisper, I notice. 'Dark, gloomy Gothic ones that had been built the same way since England was Catholic, crammed with arches and ornaments and stained glass, and the plain, undecorated meeting houses of the Puritans. After the fire, the men who rebuilt London saw an opportunity to create a new kind of architecture – places where everyone could worship, no matter what their religious affiliation. So they deliberately adopted this stripped-back, uncluttered style. But they knew they had to replace the Gothic gloom with something.'

He points at the floor, to the lattice of sunlight that makes the stone glow as if lit from within. 'Light,' he says. 'The Enlighten-ment was literally all about light.'

'Who was the architect?'

'Christopher Wren. The tourists flock to St Paul's, but this is his masterpiece.'

'It's beautiful,' I say truthfully.

When Edward called me earlier, there'd been no reference to the suddenness with which he'd left my bed a week ago, no small talk. Just, 'I'd like to show you some buildings, Jane. Do you want to come?'

'Yes,' I'd said without hesitation.

It isn't that I've decided to ignore Mia's warnings completely. But if anything they've only made me more curious about this man. And I'm reassured by the fact that he's brought me here today. Why would he do that, if he was only attracted to me because of a fleeting physical resemblance to his dead wife? I have to embrace the parameters he's set for us, I've decided – to take each moment as it comes, and not burden our relationship with over-thinking or expectation.

From St Stephen's we go to John Soane's house in Lincoln's Inn Fields. A notice says it's closed to the public today, but Edward rings the bell and greets the curator by name. After some friendly discussion, we're invited to come in and wander as we please. The tiny house is stuffed with artefacts and curiosities, everything from fragments of Greek sculpture to mummified cats. I'm surprised Edward likes it, but he says mildly, 'Just because I build in one particular style doesn't mean I don't appreciate others, Jane. Excellence is what matters. Excellence and originality.'

From a chest in the library he pulls out an architectural drawing of a small neoclassical temple. 'This is particularly good.'

'What is it?'

'The mausoleum he built for his dead wife.'

I take the drawing and pretend to study it, but actually I'm thinking about that word *mausoleum*.

I'm still considering the implications as we get a taxi back to One Folgate Street. As we approach, I look at the house with new eyes, making connections with the buildings we've seen.

At the door, he holds back. 'Do you want me to come in?'

'Of course.'

'I don't want to seem as if I'm taking that part for granted. You do understand, don't you, that this works two ways?'

'That's sweet of you. But I really do want you to come in.'

Then: Emma

Where are we going? I say, as Edward hails a cab.

Walbrook, he says, as much to the driver as me. Then: I want to show you some buildings.

Despite all my questions, he refuses to say more until we pull up in the middle of the City. We're surrounded by huge modern skyscrapers, and I wonder which one we're going to. But instead he steers me towards a church. It seems out of place here in the middle of all these gleaming banks.

The interior is nice, if a bit unexciting. There's a big dome overhead, with the altar directly underneath – a great big slab of rock, plonked in the middle of the floor. It makes me think of pagan circles and sacrifices.

Before the Great Fire, there were two sorts of churches, he says. Dark Gothic ones, and the plain meeting-houses where the Puritans worshipped. After the fire, the men who rebuilt London saw an opportunity to create a new style, a hybrid. But they knew they had to replace all that Gothic gloom with something.

He points at the floor, where the big clear-glass windows throw a criss-cross pattern of shadow and sunlight.

Light, he says. The Enlightenment was literally all about light.

While he walks around looking at things, I clamber up on to

the altar rock. I fold my legs under me and arch backwards until my head touches stone. Then I do a few more poses: the bridge, the upward bow, the lying hero. I did yoga for about six months and I've still got all the moves.

What are you doing? Edward's voice says.

Offering myself for ritual sacrifice.

That altarpiece is by Henry Moore, he says disapprovingly. He sourced the stone from the same quarry Michelangelo used.

I bet he had sex on it.

I think it's time to go, Edward says. I'd hate to be banned from this particular church.

We get a taxi to the British Museum. He speaks to someone at the admissions desk, a red rope is lifted, and somehow we're in a part of the museum reserved for academics. An assistant unlocks a cabinet and leaves us to it.

Put these on, Edward says, handing me some white cotton gloves and pulling on a pair himself. Then he reaches into the cabinet and takes something out.

This is a ritual mask made by the Olmec people – the first civilisation in America to build cities. They were wiped out three thousand years ago.

He hands it to me. I take it, scared I'll drop it. The eyes seem almost alive.

It's amazing, I say. In truth, it isn't really my kind of thing and this isn't my kind of place, any more than the church was, but I'm happy to be here with him.

He nods, satisfied. I make it a rule to only ever look at one thing in a museum, he says as we retrace our steps. Any more, and you can't appreciate what you're seeing.

So that's why I don't like museums, I say. I've just been doing them all wrong.

He laughs.

By now I'm getting hungry, and we go to a Japanese restaurant he knows. I'll order for us both, he announces. Something simple, like *katsu*. English people get scared by real Japanese food.

Not me, I say. I'll eat anything.

He raises his eyebrows. Is that a challenge, Miss Matthews?

If you like.

He starts me off with some raw sushi – octopus, sea urchin, various kinds of shrimp.

I'm well within my comfort zone here, I tell him.

Hmm, he says. He speaks to the chef in a fluent torrent of Japanese, clearly letting him in on the joke, and the chef grins at the prospect of serving the little *gaijin* girl something she won't be able to handle. Soon a plate is brought over with a pile of white gristle on it.

Try some, Edward says.

What are they?

They're called *shirako*.

Experimentally I put a couple in my mouth. They burst between my teeth, oozing a briny, creamy goo.

Not bad, I say, swallowing, although actually they're pretty gross.

They're the fish's sperm sacs, he says. In Japan, they're considered a delicacy.

Great. But I think I prefer the human kind. So what's next?

The chef's speciality.

The waitress brings over a platter containing a whole fish. With a shock, I realise it's still alive. Only just, admittedly – it's lying on its side, feebly raising and lowering its tail, its mouth working as if it's trying to say something. The whole of the topmost side has been cut into thin slices. For a moment I almost baulk. But then I just close my eyes and go for it.

The second mouthful, I keep my eyes open.

You're an adventurous eater, he says grudgingly.

Not just eater, I come back at him.

There's something you should know, Emma.

He looks serious, so I put down my chopsticks and pay attention.

I don't do conventional relationships, he says, any more than I do conventional houses.

OK. So what *do* you do?

Human relationships, like human lives, tend to accumulate the unnecessary. Valentine's cards, romantic gestures, special dates, meaningless endearments . . . What if we strip all that away? There's a kind of purity to a relationship unencumbered by convention, a sense of simplicity and freedom. But it can only work if both parties are very clear about what it is they're doing.

I'll make a mental note not to expect a Valentine's card, I say.

And when it's no longer perfect, we'll both move on, with no regrets. Agreed?

How long will that be?

Does it matter?

Not really.

I sometimes think all marriages would be better if divorce was obligatory after a certain time, he muses. Say three years. People would appreciate each other much more.

Edward, I say, if I agree to this, are we going to go to bed?

We don't have to go to bed at all. If bed is difficult for you, I mean.

You don't think I'm soiled goods, do you?

What do you mean?

Some men . . . My voice trails off. But this needs to be said. I take a shaky breath. After Simon found out about the rape, I say, he didn't want to have sex. He couldn't.

My God, Edward says. But you? You're quite sure it's not too soon?

Impulsively, I reach for his hand under the table and put it under my skirt. He looks surprised but goes with it. I almost laugh out loud. Made you look, made you stare. Made you feel my underwear.

I pull his hand deeper into my crotch, feeling his knuckles slide over my knickers.

It's *definitely* not too soon, I tell him.

I keep hold of his wrist, moving against it, rubbing myself on him. He pushes my knickers to one side and slides a finger inside me. My knees come up and rattle the table, like a medium at a seance. I stare into his eyes. He looks transfixed.

We'd better go, he says. But he doesn't take his hand away.

Now: Jane

After we make love, I'm drowsy and sated. Edward props himself up on one elbow, examining me minutely, his free hand exploring my skin. When he gets to the stretch marks from Isabel I feel self-conscious and try to roll away, but he stops me.

'Don't. You're beautiful, Jane. Every bit of you is beautiful.'

His questing fingers encounter a scar under my left breast. 'What's this?'

'Childhood accident. I came off my bike.'

He nods as if this is acceptable and continues down to my belly button. 'Like the mouth of a knotted balloon,' he says, spreading it apart. His fingers follow the soft pathway of hair downwards. 'You don't wax,' he observes.

'No. Should I? My last . . . Vittorio liked me this way. There's so little of it, he said.'

Edward considers. 'You should make it symmetrical, at least.'

Suddenly this seems hilariously funny. 'Are you asking me to declutter my pubes, Edward?' I splutter.

He puts his head on one side. 'Yes, I suppose I am. What's so amusing?'

'Nothing. I will try to minimise my body hair for you.'

'Thank you.' He plants a kiss on my belly, like a tiny flag. 'I'm going to take a shower.'

I hear the hiss of water behind the stone partition that separates off the bathroom. From the way the sound changes, I can picture his body moving in and out of the spray, his sleek, hard torso turning this way and that. Idly, I wonder how the sensor recognises him, whether he has some special privileges still registered on the system, or if there's simply some universal, generic setting for visitors.

The water stops. When he hasn't reappeared after several minutes, I sit up. There's a rubbing sound coming from the direction of the bathroom.

I follow the noise around the partition. Edward, a white towel wrapped around his waist, is crouched in the shower, polishing the stone walls with a cloth.

'This is a hard-water area, Jane,' he says without looking up. 'If you're not careful, you'll get limescale building up on the stone. It's already noticeable. Really, you should dry the shower off every time you use it.'

'Edward . . .'

'What?'

'Isn't that a bit . . . well, *obsessive*?'

'No,' he says. 'It's whatever the opposite of lazy is.' He considers. 'Meticulous, perhaps.'

'Isn't life simply too short to dry showers after you use them?'

'Or perhaps,' he says reasonably, 'life is simply too short to live it less perfectly than it could be lived.' He stands up. 'You haven't done an assessment yet, have you?'

'Assessment?'

'With Housekeeper. It's currently set to monthly intervals, I think. I'll adjust it so you do one tomorrow.' He pauses. 'I'm sure you're doing fine, Jane. But having the numbers will help you improve still further.'

Next morning, I wake up happy and a little stiff. Edward's already gone. I go downstairs to get a coffee before my shower and find a message from Housekeeper on my laptop screen.

Jane, please score the following statements on a scale of 1–5, where 1 is 'Strongly Agree' and 5 is 'Strongly Disagree'.

I sometimes make mistakes
I am easily disappointed
I become anxious over unimportant things

There are dozens more. Leaving them for later, I make my coffee and take it upstairs. I step into the shower, waiting for the luxurious cascade of warmth. Nothing happens.

I wave my arm, the one with the digital bracelet on, but there's still nothing. A power cut? I try to remember if there's a fuse box in the cleaner's cupboard. But it can't be that; there was power downstairs, or Housekeeper wouldn't have been working.

Then I realise what it must be. 'Damn you, Edward,' I say aloud. 'I wanted a bloody shower.'

Sure enough, when I go to look at Housekeeper more closely,

I see the words *Some house facilities have been disabled until the assessment is completed.*

At least it let me have coffee. I settle down to answer the questions.

Then: Emma

The sex is good.

Good, but not spectacular.

I get the feeling he's holding back, trying to be a gentleman. When actually a gentleman is the last person I want to share my bed with. I want him to be the selfish alpha male he's so clearly capable of being.

Still, there's plenty to work with.

Afterwards I sit at the stone table in a robe, watching him cook us a stir-fry. He puts on an apron before he starts, a strangely feminine gesture for such a masculine man. But once the ingredients are prepped and he gets going it's all concentration and precision, fire and energy, tossing the ingredients up in the air and catching them again like a big sloppy pancake. Within minutes the meal is ready. I'm ravenous.

Have you always had relationships like this? I say as we eat.

Like what?

Whatever this is. Unencumbered. Semi-detached.

For a long while, yes. It's not that I have anything against conventional relationships, you understand. It's just that my lifestyle doesn't really allow for them. So I made a conscious decision to adjust to shorter ones. I've found when you do that, the relationships can actually be better: more intense, a sprint instead of a marathon. You appreciate the other person more, knowing it's not going to last.

How long do they usually last?

Until one of us decides to call it off, he says without smiling. This only works if both parties want the same thing. And don't think that by 'unencumbered' I mean without commitment or effort. It's just a different sort of commitment, a different sort of effort. Some of the most perfect relationships I've had lasted no more than a week, some several years. The duration really doesn't matter. Only the quality.

Tell me about one that lasted several years, I say.

I never talk about my previous lovers, he says firmly. Just as I'll never talk to others about you. Anyway, it's my turn now. How do you organise your spices?

My spices?

Yes. It's been bothering me ever since I tried to find the cumin just now. They're clearly not arranged alphabetically or by use-by date. Is it by flavour profile? Or by continent?

You're joking, right?

He looks at me. You mean they're *random*?

Completely random.

Wow, he says. I think he's being ironic. But sometimes with Edward it's hard to be sure.

When he leaves, he tells me it has been a wonderful evening.

5 b) Now you have a choice between donating a small sum to a local museum that's fundraising for an important artwork, or sending it to tackle hunger in Africa. Which do you choose?

☐ The museum

☐ Hunger

Now: Jane

'I admire how the work unfolds rigorously, with a variety of different typologies,' a man wearing a corduroy jacket announces, waving his champagne flute at the glass-and-steel roof in big, sweeping gestures.

'. . . a fusion of non-Cartesian infrastructure and social functionality . . .' a woman says earnestly.

'Lines of desire implied and then denied . . .'

Apart from the jargon, I decide, topping-out parties aren't so very different from the gallery openings I went to when I worked in the art world: a lot of people in black, a lot of champagne, a lot of hipster beards and expensive Scandinavian spectacles. Tonight, the occasion is the inauguration of a new concert hall by David Chipperfield. I'm gradually becoming familiar with the names of the best-known British architects: Norman Foster, the late Zaha Hadid, John Pawson, Richard Rogers. Many will be present this evening, Edward has told me. Later, there'll be a fireworks-and-laser show, visible through the glass roof, which will be seen as far away as Kent.

I wander through the crowd, champagne glass in hand, eavesdropping. I'm wandering because, although Edward has invited me to accompany him, I'm determined not to be an encumbrance.

In any case, it isn't hard to fall into conversation when I want to. The crowd is mostly male, very confident, slightly drunk. More than one person has stopped me and said, 'Do I know you?' 'Where do you work?' Or, simply, 'Hello.'

Seeing Edward looking in my direction, I head back towards him. He turns away from the group he's with. 'Thank God,' he says quietly. 'If I have to listen to one more speech about the importance of programmatic requirements, I think I'll go mad.' He looks at me appreciatively. 'Has anyone told you you're the most beautiful woman in this room?'

'Several people, actually.' I'm wearing a backless Helmut Lang dress, thigh length, cut loose behind so that it moves when I do, coupled with some simple scalloped flats from Chloé. 'Though not in so many words.'

He laughs. 'Come over here.'

I follow him behind a low wall. He puts his champagne glass on it, then runs his hand down my hip.

'You're wearing knickers,' he observes.

'Yes.'

'I think you should take them off. They spoil the line. Don't worry, no one will see.'

For a moment, I freeze. Then I glance around. No one's looking our way. As unobtrusively as I can, I slip out of my panties. When I reach down to pick them up, he puts a hand on my arm.

'Wait.'

His right hand lifts the hem of the dress. 'No one will see,' he repeats.

The hand slides up my thigh, then reaches between my legs. I'm shocked. 'Edward, I—'

'Don't move,' he says softly.

His fingers slide back and forth, barely making contact. I feel myself angling against him, craving more pressure. This isn't me, I think. I don't do things like this. He circles my clitoris, two, three times, then, without warning, one finger gently slides inside me.

He pauses to take the glass from my hand and set it down next to his, then suddenly he has two hands on me – one from the back, two fingers sliding in and out; one from the front, delving and circling. The noise of the party seems to dim. Breathless, I leave the whole question of whether someone might spot us to him. He's in charge now. Despite the unlikely setting, waves of pleasure start to wash over me.

'Do you want to find somewhere private?' I whisper.

'No,' he says simply. His fingers increase their tempo, utterly confident. I feel a climax building. My knees sag and his hands take more of my weight. And then I'm there, juddering and shaking around him. Fireworks flash and flicker – real fireworks, the laser show that can be seen as far as Kent, I realise as I come back to reality. That's what they're all applauding, thank God. Not me.

My legs are still shaking as he withdraws his hands and says, 'Excuse me, Jane. There are some people over there I have to talk to.'

He strides over to someone who I'm pretty sure is Britain's most eminent architect, a member of the House of Lords, and, with an easy smile, offers him his hand. The same hand that, seconds ago, was inside me.

*

I'm still reeling as the party starts to break up. Did we really just do that? Did I really just have an orgasm in a room full of people? Is that who I am, now? He takes me to a Japanese restaurant nearby, the sort that has a sushi counter in the middle with a chef standing behind it. The other customers are all Asian businessmen in dark suits. The chef greets Edward as if he knows him well, bowing and speaking in Japanese. Edward replies in the same language.

'I've told him to choose what to serve us,' he says to me as we sit down at a table. 'It's a mark of respect to trust the *itamae*'s judgement.'

'Your Japanese seems very fluent.'

'I did a building in Tokyo recently.'

'Yes, I know.' His Japanese skyscraper is an elegant, sensuous helix, a giant drill bit piercing the clouds. 'Was that your first time there?'

I know it wasn't, of course. I watch as he rearranges his chopsticks so they're exactly parallel to each other.

'I spent a year there after the death of my wife and child,' he says quietly, and I feel a thrill of excitement at this first tiny glimpse of self-revelation, of intimacy. 'It wasn't just the place I felt at home in. It was the culture: the emphasis on self-discipline and restraint. In our society, austerity is associated with deprivation and poverty. In Japan, they consider it the highest form of beauty – what they call *shibui*.'

A waitress brings two bowls of soup. The bowls are made of painted bamboo, so light and small they fit into the hand. 'These bowls, for example,' he says, picking one up. 'They're old and they don't quite match. That's *shibui*.'

I take a mouthful of soup. Something wriggles against my tongue – a strange, flickering sensation.

'They're alive, by the way,' he adds.

'What are?' I say, startled.

'The broth contains tiny shrimp. *Shirouo* – the newborns. The chef throws them in at the very last minute. It's considered a great delicacy.' He gestures at the sushi counter, where the chef bows to us again. 'Chef Atara's speciality is *ikizukuri*, live seafood. I hope that's all right.'

The waitress brings another dish and places it on the table between us. On it is a red snapper, its brilliant copper-coloured scales very bright against the strips of white radish. One side of the fish has been sliced neatly into sashimi, all the way down to the backbone. But the creature itself is still alive, its tail curling up like a scorpion's before flapping feebly down again, the mouth gulping, the eye rolling in alarm.

'Oh my God,' I say, aghast.

'Try some. It's delicious, I assure you.' He reaches out and takes a slice of the pale flesh between his chopsticks.

'Edward, I can't eat this.'

'No matter. I'll order you something else.' He gestures to the waitress, who's at our side in moments. But the broth in my stomach is suddenly threatening to come back up. *Newborns.* The word starts to hammer in my head.

'Jane. Are you all right?' He's looking at me, concerned.

'I'm not – I'm not—'

One of the strange things about grief is the way it ambushes you when you least expect it. Suddenly, I'm back in the maternity unit, holding Isabel, frantically tucking her swaddling cloth around her head like a shawl to keep the last precious remnants of body warmth – *my* body warmth – from escaping, trying to postpone the moment when her little limbs go cold. I'm looking at her eyes, her tiny closed eyes with their sweet pouchy eyelids, wondering what colour they are, whether they're blue like mine or dark like her father's—

I blink, and the memory's gone, but the dull leaden weight of failure and despair has coshed me once again and I sob suddenly into my wrist.

'Oh my God.' Edward smacks his forehead. 'The *shirouo*. How could I be so stupid?' He speaks to the waitress in an urgent stream of Japanese, pointing at me and ordering more food. But there's no time for that now, no time for anything at all. Already I'm bolting for the door.

Then: Emma

Thank you for coming, Emma, DI Clarke says. One sugar, yes?

The detective inspector's office is a tiny cubbyhole filled with paperwork and files. There's a framed photograph, quite an old one, showing him in the front row of a rugby team, holding a ridiculously large trophy. The mug of instant coffee he hands me has a picture of Garfield on it, which seems too cheerful for a police station.

That's all right, I say nervously. What's it about?

DI Clarke takes a mouthful of his own coffee and sets the mug down on the desk next to a plate of biscuits, which he pushes towards me.

The two men charged in connection with your case have both pleaded not guilty and made bail applications. Regarding the accomplice, Grant Lewis, there's not a lot we can do about that. But the one who raped you, Deon Nelson, may be a different matter.

Right, I say, although I don't really see why he's called me in to explain this. It's bad news they're pleading not guilty, of course, but couldn't he have told me over the phone?

As the victim, DI Clarke continues, you're entitled to make a Victim Personal Statement – what the press sometimes calls an

137

impact statement. You can tell the bail hearing how the crime affected you, how you feel about the prospect of Nelson being free until his trial begins.

I nod. How do I feel? I don't really feel anything. So long as he goes to prison in the end, that's all that matters.

Seeing my lack of enthusiasm, DI Clarke says gently, The thing is, Emma, Nelson is a clever and violent individual. I personally would feel much more comfortable if he were to stay behind bars right now.

He wouldn't risk doing it again while he was out on bail, though, would he? I say. Then I see what DI Clarke's getting at.

You think I could be in danger, I say, staring at him. That he might try to stop me giving evidence.

I don't want you getting alarmed, Emma. Thankfully, instances of witness intimidation are very rare. But in cases like this, where the whole thing basically hangs on one person's evidence, it's better to be safe than sorry.

What do you want me to do?

Write a VPS for the bail hearing. We can give you some pointers, but the more personal it is, the better.

He pauses. I should remind you, though, that once your statement's been read to the court it becomes a legal document. The defence will be entitled to cross-examine you on it when it comes to the trial.

Who would read it out?

Well, it could be the prosecution lawyer, or a police officer for that matter. But these things are always more powerful if they come directly from the victim. Even judges are only human. And I think you'll make a very strong impression.

Just for a moment, DI Clarke's face softens and he almost seems to go a little misty-eyed. Then he clears his throat. We'll make an application for Special Measures. That means you can be screened from Nelson during the hearing. You won't have to look at him when you read your statement and he won't be able to see you.

But he'll *be* there, I say. Listening.

DI Clarke nods.

And what will happen if the judge disagrees, and he does get bail? Isn't there a chance I'll have made things worse?

We'll make sure you're safe, DI Clarke says reassuringly. It's fortunate, after all, that you've moved address. He doesn't know where you live.

He fixes me with his kindly, careful gaze. So, Emma. Will you write a VPS and read it to the court?

This is why I'm here, I realise. He knew if he'd just called me, I might have said no.

Well, if you think it'll help, I hear myself say.

Good girl, he says.

Coming from anyone else that would sound patronising, but his relief is so evident I don't mind.

The hearing'll be on Thursday, he adds.

So soon?

He's got a very persistent lawyer, unfortunately. All at the tax-payer's expense, of course.

DI Clarke stands up. I'll get someone to find you an empty interview room. You can start drafting it now.

Now: Jane

A few days after the restaurant episode, two packages arrive. One is a large, thin box bearing the distinctive *W* of Wanderer in Bond Street. The other's smaller – about the size of a paperback. I lift the bigger one on to the stone table. Despite its size, it weighs almost nothing.

Inside, cocooned in tissue paper, is a dress. It drapes over my arm, the black fabric flowing silkily to either side. I can tell immediately how sensual and caressing it's going to feel against my skin.

I take it upstairs and try it on. I barely have to do more than lift my arms and the fabric falls into place around my body. When I turn, the material moves with me, almost playfully. Examining the weave, I see it's cut along the diagonal.

It needs a necklace, I find myself thinking. And, immediately, I guess what's in the smaller package.

There's a card, written in a beautiful, almost calligraphic hand. *Jane – forgive me for being an insensitive fool. Edward.* And a clamshell case that opens to reveal, nestled in the velvet interior, a three-row collar of pearls. The pearls aren't large, but their appearance is distinctive – pale cream in colour, and not quite round, with an opalescent shimmer deep in the nacre.

The exact same colour as the walls of One Folgate Street.

The necklace looks small – *too* small, I think, when I first put it on; it's tight against my throat and, for a moment, I feel constricted by the lack of give, so different from the flowing, sensuous dress. But then I look at myself in the mirror and the combination is stunning.

I put my hair up with one hand to see what it looks like. Yes, like that, tumbling to the side. I take a selfie to send Mia.

Edward should see this too, I think. I forward the picture to him as well. *Nothing to forgive. But thank you.*

He replies less than a minute later. *Good. Because I'm two minutes away and closing.*

I walk downstairs and stand in front of the plate-glass window, facing the door, positioning myself for maximum effect. Waiting for my lover.

He takes me over the stone table, still in the dress and the pearl collar – urgent, direct, without preamble or small talk.

I've never had a relationship like this before. I've never made love anywhere but a bed before. I've been told I'm self-contained and aloof; and, by one man, sexually dull. And yet, somehow, here I am. Doing this.

Afterwards, it's as if he comes out of a kind of trance, and the urbane, thoughtful Edward is back in charge. He cooks us some pasta, the sauce nothing more than some green olive oil from an unlabelled bottle, a smear of fresh goat's cheese and plenty of ground pepper. The oil is called '*lacrima*', he tells me: the first precious tears that rise to the surface when the olives are washed before pressing. He has some sent over from Tuscany every harvest. The pepper is from Tellicherry, on the Malabar Coast. 'Though sometimes I use Kampot peppercorns from Cambodia. They're milder, but more aromatic.'

Sex and good, simple food. Somehow it feels like the height of sophistication.

When the pasta has been devoured, he loads the dishwasher and cleans the pans. Only then does he take a document from a leather case. 'I brought your metrics. I thought you'd like to know how you're doing.'

'Did I pass?'

He doesn't smile. 'Well, your aggregate is eighty.'

'What should it be?'

'There's no real benchmark. But we'd be hoping to see it come down to a fifty or even lower, over time.'

I can't help feeling criticised. 'So what am I doing wrong?'

He scans the document, which I now see consists of rows of numbers, like a spreadsheet. 'You could do a bit more exercise. A couple of sessions a week should be enough. You've lost some weight since you've been here, but you could probably do with losing a bit more. Your stress levels are generally in the acceptable range – your speech rate tends to go up when you're on the phone, but that's not uncommon. You're drinking hardly any alcohol, which is good. Temperature, respiration and kidney function are all fine. Your REM sleep is adequate and you're spending a healthy amount of time in bed. Most important of all, you have a more positive outlook on life. You have an increasingly high level of personal integrity, you're more disciplined and you're managing to keep the limescale off the shower.' He smiles to show that the last bit, at least, is a joke, but I'm breathless with indignation.

'You know all that about me!'

'Of course. If you'd read the terms and conditions properly, none of this would come as a surprise.'

My anger evaporates as I realise that this was, after all, what I signed up to – the only reason I'm able to afford One Folgate Street in the first place.

'This is the future, Jane,' he adds. 'Health and wellbeing monitored by your domestic environment. If there were any major issues, Housekeeper would pick them up long before it occurred to you to see a doctor. These stats allow you to take control of your life.'

'What if people don't want to be spied on?'

'They won't be. We only have this specific data on you because we're still in the beta stage. For future users, we'll only ever see general trends, not data relating to individuals.' He stands up. 'Work on it,' he says kindly. 'See if you get used to it. If you can't . . . well, that's useful feedback too, and we'll see how we can change the system to make it more acceptable. But I think you'll soon start to see how beneficial it is.'

Then: Emma

I'm still staring at the notes I've made for my VPS, wondering how to begin, when my phone goes. I glance at the screen. *Edward.*

Hello, Emma. Did you get my message? He sounds amused, even cheerful.

What message?

The one I left at your office.

I'm not at work, I say. I'm at a police station.

Is everything all right?

Not really, I say. I glance down at my notes. DI Clarke told me to group the main points under some headings. *WHAT HE DID. HOW I FELT AT THE TIME. THE EFFECT ON MY RELATIONSHIP. HOW I FEEL NOW.* I stare at what I've written. *Disgusted. Terrified. Ashamed. Dirty.* Just words. Somehow I never imagined it would come to this.

It's not really all right at all, I say.

Which police station?

West Hampstead.

I'll be there in ten minutes.

He rings off. And immediately I feel better, much better, because what I want more than anything right now is for someone strong and decisive, someone like Edward, to come and pick up my life and rearrange all the pieces for me and somehow make everything work.

Emma. Oh, Emma, he says.

We're in a café off West End Lane. I've been crying. Occasionally other people shoot us suspicious looks – *Who is that girl? What has that man done to make her cry like that?* – but Edward ignores them. One hand gently covers mine for reassurance.

It's a terrible thing to think about something as horrible as this, but I feel special. Edward's concern is totally different to Simon's insecure fury.

Edward picks up the draft of my statement. May I? he asks. I nod and he reads it, frowning occasionally.

What was the message? I say.

Oh, that. Just a small gift. Well, two gifts, actually.

He lifts a bag that's been sitting beside him. On it is a big, bold *W* logo.

For me? I say, amazed.

He nods. I was going to ask you to accompany me to something very tedious. So I thought the least I could do was to get you something to wear. But you won't be in the mood now.

I reach into the bag and take out a clamshell case.

You can open it if you want, he says mildly.

Inside the case is a necklace. And not just any necklace. I've always wanted a pearl choker like Audrey Hepburn's in *Breakfast at Tiffany's*. And here it is. Not quite identical – there are three strings, not five, and no front cluster – but already I can see how it will fit around my neck like a collar, high and tight.

It's beautiful, I say.

I reach for the larger box but he stops me. Perhaps not here, he says.

What was the occasion? The one you were going to take me to?

Some architectural award ceremony. Very dull.

Have you won?

I believe so, yes.

I smile at him, suddenly happy. I'll go home and change, I say.

I'll come with you, he says. He gets to his feet and whispers in my ear, Because I know that as soon as I see you in that dress, I'm going to want to fuck you in it.

Now: Jane

I wake to find Edward gone. This must be what it's like to have an affair with a married man, I think. The thought gives me some comfort. In France, for example, where people are more relaxed about these things, perhaps our relationship would be considered perfectly normal.

Mia, of course, is convinced it's going to be another disaster, that he'll never change, that anyone who's managed to be self-contained for so long can never be anything else. When I demur, she tuts exasperatedly. 'J, you have this schoolgirl fantasy that you're going to be the one to melt his ice-cold heart. When the truth is, he's simply going to break yours.'

But my heart has already been broken by Isabel, I reflect, and Edward's irregular incursions into my life mean it's easy not to let Mia see just how serious it's getting with him.

And it turns out that Edward's right: there *is* something perfect about two people who come together without expectations or demands. I don't have to hear the details of his day, or worry about which one of us is going to take the rubbish out. There are no joint schedules to negotiate, no domestic routines to slip into. We never spend long enough together to get bored.

Yesterday he gave me my first orgasm before he'd even taken

off his clothes. That's something he likes, I've noticed: to stay fully dressed while he peels my clothes off – everything but the necklace – and reduce me to a quivering wreck with fingers and tongue. As if it's not enough for him to retain control: I have to lose it too. Only then does he feel comfortable letting go himself.

That feels like an interesting insight about him and I'm still mulling it over as I come downstairs. There's a small pile of damp post on the doorstep. I've asked Edward why there's no letterbox here – it seems a strange oversight in what is, generally, such a well-thought-out house – and he told me that when One Folgate Street was built, David Thiel was predicting that email would have replaced physical letters altogether within a decade.

I glance through them. They're mostly political circulars to do with the upcoming local elections. I doubt I'll even register to vote. Rows about the local library and the frequency of refuse collections have little relevance to my life at One Folgate Street. A couple of the letters are addressed to Ms Emma Matthews. They're clearly junk, but I put them aside to send on to Camilla, the estate agent.

The last letter is addressed to me. The outside looks so bland that at first I assume it's just more junk mail. Then I see the logo of the Hospital Trust and my heart skips a beat.

Dear Ms Cavendish,
Post-mortem results: Isabel Margaret Cavendish (deceased)

I agreed to a post-mortem because it seemed right to try to get some answers. Dr Gifford told me when I went for my follow-up appointment that it hadn't revealed anything. That was a month ago. The letter must have been stuck in the system ever since.

I sit down, my head swimming, and go through it twice, trying to understand the medical jargon. It starts with a brief history of my pregnancy. There's a reference to the time, a week before they realised something was wrong, when I'd had back pain and taken myself to the maternity unit for a check-up. They'd done some tests, listened to the baby's heartbeat, then sent me home to have a hot bath. I'd felt Isabel kicking quite actively after that, so I'd been reassured. The letter makes it clear that *correct procedures were followed on that occasion, including a symphysis–fundal height assessment in accordance with NICE guidelines*. Then there's a description of my subsequent visit, when they discovered Isabel's heart had stopped. And finally, the post-mortem itself. Lots of figures that mean nothing to me – platelet counts and other blood work, followed by the comment, *Liver: normal.*

At the thought of some pathologist patiently removing her tiny little liver, my throat constricts. But there's more:

```
Kidneys: normal.
Lungs: normal.
Heart: normal.
```

I skip down to the summary.

```
While an exact diagnosis is not possible at this stage,
signs of placental thrombosis may point to a partial placenta
abruptio, leading to death by asphyxiation.
```

Placenta abruptio. It sounds like a Harry Potter spell, not something that could kill my baby. Dr Gifford's name at the bottom of the page swims glassily as the tears spring to my eyes and I start crying again, great gulping snotty sobs I can't control. It's all too much to take in and in any case I don't understand most of the words.

Tessa, the woman I share a desk with at the office, has a background in midwifery. I decide to take the letter to work so she can talk me through it.

Tessa reads the letter carefully, giving me the occasional concerned look. She knows, of course, that I had a stillbirth; many of the women who volunteer at Still Hope have a similar personal reason for doing so.

'Do you know what it all means?' she says when she's finished. I shake my head.

'Well, placenta abruptio is a ruptured placenta. Effectively, they're saying the foetus stopped getting nutrients and oxygen before you went in.'

'Nice of them to use English,' I say.

'Yes. Well, there may be a reason for that.'

Something about her voice makes me look at her.

'When you went in with back pain,' she says slowly, 'what happened, exactly?'

'Well . . .' I think back. 'They clearly thought I was being over-anxious – first-time mother and all that. But they were very nice about it. I don't actually remember being given all those tests they talk about—'

'A symphysis–fundal height assessment is just medical-speak

for measuring the bump with a tape measure,' she interrupts. 'And while it's true that it's a NICE guideline to do one at every prenatal visit, it's certainly not going to show up a failing placenta. Did they do a cardiotocograph?'

'The heart-monitor thing? Yes, the nurse did that.'

'Who did she show the trace to?'

I try to remember. 'I think she phoned Dr Gifford and read the results to him. Or, at any rate, told him they were normal.'

'Any other scans? Regular ultrasound? Doppler?' Tessa's voice has taken on a grim tone.

I shake my head. 'They told me to go home, have a hot bath and try not to worry. And I felt Isabel kicking later, so I realised they were right.'

'Who's "they"?'

'Well – the nurse, I suppose.'

'Did she speak to anyone else? A senior midwife? Registrar?'

'Not that I recall. Tessa, what is this?'

'It's just that this letter reads to me like a carefully-worded attempt to give you the impression there was no medical negligence involved in Isabel's death,' she says bluntly.

I gape at her. 'Negligence? How?'

'If you start from the position that the death of a perfectly viable baby is a death that should have been avoided, then usually you find one of two things has caused it. First, a mismanaged birth. That obviously wasn't the case here. But the second most common cause of stillbirth is an overworked midwife or junior doctor failing to read a CTG trace correctly. In your case, the consultant should have reviewed the results himself and – given the back pain you reported, which can be an indication of problems with the placenta – ordered a Doppler scan.' I know about Doppler scans; one of Still Hope's campaign goals is for every expectant mother to receive one as a matter of course. It will cost about fifteen pounds per baby and the fact that the NHS currently doesn't do them unless a senior doctor specifically requests it is one of the reasons why stillbirth rates in the UK are among the worst in Europe. 'I'm afraid the kicking you felt after you went home may have been distress, not a sign everything was all right. We've got form with this Trust. They're consistently understaffed, particularly at consultant level. Dr Gifford's name comes up again and again. He basically has way too high a workload.'

The words are barely sinking in. But he was so nice, I think.

'Of course, you can argue that's not his fault,' she adds. 'But it's only by going after the senior doctor and proving they failed the patient that we'll ever get the Trust to increase their staffing ratios.'

I remember Dr Gifford telling me, even as he broke the news that Isabel was dead, that in the majority of cases no cause was ever found. Was he trying to cover up for his team's mistakes, even then? 'What should I do?'

She hands the letter back to me. 'Write back asking for a copy of all the medical records. We'll get them reviewed by an expert, but if it looks as if the hospital are covering up incompetence, we should think about litigation.'

Then: Emma

And this year's *Architects' Journal* Award for Innovation goes to . . .

The presenter pauses dramatically and opens his envelope. The Monkford Partnership, he announces.

Our table, made up of Partnership staff, cheers. Images of buildings flash on to the screens. Edward gets up and makes his way to the stage, politely acknowledging a few well-wishers as he does so.

This is nothing like the parties at Simon's magazine, I'm thinking. No models in bras and knickers, anyway.

When Edward has the award in his hands he steps towards the microphone. I may have to put this in a cupboard, he says, looking down at the Perspex blob doubtfully. Laughter. The minimalist has proved he can make fun of himself! But then he turns serious.

Someone once said that the difference between a good architect and a great one is that the good architect gives in to every temptation, and the great one does not.

He pauses. There's silence around the huge room. They seem genuinely interested.

As architects, he says, we're obsessed with aesthetics, with creating buildings that are pleasing to the eye. But if we accept that the real function of architecture is to help people resist temptation, then perhaps architecture . . .

He falters, almost as if he's thinking out loud.

. . . Perhaps architecture isn't really about buildings at all. We accept that town planning is a kind of architecture, after all. Motorway networks, airports – these too, at a stretch. But what about technology? What about that invisible city in which we all stroll, or lurk, or play: the internet? What about the frameworks of our lives, the rules and laws that govern us, our aspirations and our baser desires? Are these not also structures, in a way?

There's another pause before he continues, Earlier today, I was speaking to someone. A young woman who was attacked in her home. Her space was violated. Her possessions were stolen. Her whole attitude to her surroundings has been coloured – I might almost say distorted – by that simple, tragic fact.

He doesn't look at me, but I feel as if every person in the room must know who he means.

Isn't the real function of architecture to make such a thing impossible? he asks. To punish the perpetrator, heal the victim, change the future? As architects, why should we stop at our buildings' walls?

Silence. The audience seems quite baffled now.

The Monkford Partnership is known as a practice that works on a small scale, with wealthy clients, he says. But I see now that our future lies not in building beautiful havens from the ugliness in society, but in building a different kind of society.

He raises the award. Thank you for this honour.

The applause is polite, but looking around, I see people are smiling and rolling their eyes at each other.

And I clap too, harder than anyone, because the man up there, my lover, doesn't care whether they laugh at him or not.

That night, I ask about his wife.

I keep the dress on while we make love, but afterwards I hang it carefully in the tiny cupboard behind the wall panel before slipping, naked except for the necklace, into the warm space beside him.

The solicitor told me your family are buried here, I say tentatively.

How—? Oh, he goes. The Land Registry plans.

He's silent for so long I think that's all the answer I'm going to get.

It was her idea, he says at last. She'd read about *hitobashira* and said that was what she wanted, if she died before me. Under the threshold of one of our own buildings. Of course, we never imagined . . .

Hitobashira?

It means 'human pillar' in Japanese. It's said to bring the house good luck.

You don't mind me talking about her?

Look at me, he says with sudden seriousness, and I turn my head so I can see into his eyes.

Elizabeth was perfect in her own way, he says gently. But she's in the past now. And this is perfect too. What's happening right now, with us. You're perfect, Emma. We don't need to talk about her again.

*

The next morning, after he's gone, I look his wife up on the internet. But Housekeeper can't find anything.

What was the Japanese word he used? *Hitobashira*. I try a search for that.

I frown. According to the internet, *hitobashira* doesn't refer to burying dead people under buildings. It's about burying the living.

> The custom of sacrificing a human being as part of the erection of a new house or fortress is very old. Foundation stones and beams were laid in human blood the world over, and this abominable custom was practised but a few centuries ago in Europe. In the well-known Maori tradition of Taraia, we are told that he had his own child buried alive beneath a post of his new house.

I jump to another article.

> The foundation sacrifice must be in keeping with the importance of the building to be erected. An ordinary tent or house can be bought off with an animal, or a rich man's house with a slave; but a sacred structure, such as a temple or a bridge, needs a sacrifice of special worth, perhaps involving serious pain or anguish to the one making it.

For one mad moment, I wonder if this is what Edward can mean: that he made a sacrifice of his own wife and son. And then I find another article that makes more sense.

> Today, the echo of such practices lives on in innumerable folk customs around the world: sending off a ship with a bottle of champagne, burying

a piece of silver under a doorpost, or topping out a skyscraper with the bough of an evergreen. In other parts, an animal heart is buried, while Henry Purcell chose to be interred 'under the organ' at Westminster Abbey. In many societies, notably in the Far East, the dead are marked with a building constructed in their honour – a practice not so very different, perhaps, from the naming of a Carnegie Hall or a Rockefeller Plaza after some noted philanthropist.

Phew. I go back to bed, burrowing my nose into the pillows for any trace of him – his smell, his shape still outlined in the sheets. His words come back to me. *This is perfect.* I drift back to sleep with a smile on my face.

Now: Jane

'What you experienced when you walked through the front door – into a small, almost claustrophobic hallway, before entering the flowing spaces of the house itself – is a classic architectural device of compression and release. It's a good example of the way Edward Monkford's houses, though seemingly revolutionary, are based on traditional techniques. But more importantly, it marks him out as an architect whose primary purpose is to affect the way the user *feels*.'

The guide walks towards the kitchen, the gaggle of half a dozen visitors following him obediently. 'Users have reported that in a refectory area such as this, for example, with its visual emphasis on austerity and restraint, they find themselves eating less than they did previously.'

Camilla told me before I moved in that I'd be required to open One Folgate Street to visitors occasionally. Back then, it hadn't seemed a great hardship, but as the first open day approached I found myself dreading it more and more. It wouldn't just be the house that was on show, I felt, but me. For days now I've tidied and cleaned, careful not to infringe even the smallest rule.

'Architects and their clients have long sought to create

buildings with a sense of purpose,' the guide continues. 'Banks look imposing and solid partly because the men who commissioned them wanted to instil confidence in potential depositors. Courtrooms seek to impose respect for law and order. Palaces were designed to impress and humble those who entered them. But today, some architects are using new developments in technology and psychology to go far beyond that.'

The guide is very young, with an overly fashionable beard, but I sense from his air of authority he's probably some kind of lecturer. Not all the visitors look as if they're students, though. Some could be tourists or curious neighbours.

'You probably aren't aware of it, but you're currently swimming in a complex soup of ultrasonics – mood-enhancing waveforms. That technology is only in its infancy, but it has far-reaching implications. Imagine a hospital where the structure itself becomes part of the healing process, or a home for dementia sufferers that actually helps them to remember. This house might be simple, but its ambition is extraordinary.'

He turns and leads the way towards the staircase. 'Please follow me in single file, taking special care on the steps.'

I stay downstairs. I can hear the guide's voice explaining how the lighting in the bedroom reinforces the users' circadian rhythms. Only when they come down again do I slip upstairs myself, for privacy.

With a shock, I realise one of the group is still in my bedroom. He's opened the cupboard and, although he has his back to me, I'm fairly sure he's looking through my clothes.

'What the hell are you doing?' I demand.

He turns round. He's one of the ones I'd taken for a tourist. His eyes, behind rimless spectacles, are pale and calm.

'I'm seeing how you fold your things.' His voice is slightly accented. Danish, perhaps, or Norwegian. About thirty years old, wearing a slightly military-looking anorak. Fair, receding hair.

'How dare you!' I explode. 'Those are private.'

'No one who lives in this house should expect privacy. You signed that away, remember?'

'Who are you?' He sounds too well informed for a tourist.

'I applied,' he says. 'I applied to live here. Seven times, actually. I would be perfect for it. But he chose you instead.' He turns back to the cupboard and starts to unfold and refold my T-shirts, as fast and neat as a shop assistant. 'What does Edward see in you? Sex, I suppose. Women are his weakness.' I am breathless with anger, but the realisation that this man standing in my bedroom is almost certainly deranged has paralysed me. 'He's inspired by monasteries and religious communities, but he forgets that women were excluded from those places for a reason.' He picks up a skirt and folds it in three deft movements. 'Really, you should leave. It would be much better for Edward if you went. Like the others.'

'What others? What are you talking about?'

He gives me a smile of almost childish sweetness. 'Oh, hasn't he told you? The ones before. None of them last, you see. That's the whole point.'

'He was crazy,' I say. 'Terrifying. And the way he spoke – it was as if he knew you.'

Edward sighs. 'I suppose he does, in a way. Or, at least, he thinks he does. Because he knows the work.'

We're sitting in the refectory area. Edward has brought wine, something exquisite and Italian. But I'm still a little shaky and, in any case, I haven't really been drinking since I moved to One Folgate Street. 'Who is he?'

'At the office, they call him my stalker.' He smiles. 'That's a joke, of course. He's actually quite harmless. Jorgen something. He dropped out of an architecture degree with mental health problems and became slightly obsessed with my buildings. It's not uncommon. Barragán, Corbusier, Foster – they've all had disturbed individuals fixated on them, thinking they have some special connection.'

'Have you told the police?'

He shrugs. 'What would be the point?'

'But Edward, don't you see what this means? When Emma Matthews died, did anyone ever check to see if this Jorgen person was around?'

He gives me a wary look. 'You're not still on about that, are you?'

'It happened right here. Of course I think about it.'

'Have you been talking to the boyfriend again?' Something about the way he says it suggests he wouldn't be pleased if I had.

I shake my head. 'He hasn't been back.'

'Good. And believe me, Jorgen wouldn't hurt anyone.' He takes another mouthful of wine, then bends down to kiss me. His lips are sweet and bloody with grape.

'Edward . . .' I say, pulling away.

'Yes?'

'Were Emma and you lovers?'

'Does it make a difference?'

'No,' I say. Of course, I mean yes.

'We had a brief affair,' he says at last. 'It was over long before she died.'

'Was it . . .' I don't know how to ask this. 'Was it like this?'

He comes very close to me, holding my head in both hands and fixing me with his gaze. 'Listen to me, Jane. Emma was a fascinating person,' he says. 'But she's in the past now. What's happening right now, with us – this is perfect. We don't need to talk about her again.'

Despite his words, there's an itch of curiosity I can't quite satisfy.

Because I know that, when I know more about the women he's loved, I'll understand him better.

I will tunnel beneath the walls he's erected around himself, the strange invisible labyrinth that keeps me at a distance.

Next morning, after he's gone, I hunt out the card I found in Emma's sleeping bag. *Carol Younson. Accredited Psychotherapist.* There's a web address as well as a phone number. I'm about to look it up on my laptop when I recall what the crazy man in my bedroom said. *No one who lives in this house should expect privacy. You signed that away, remember?*

I take my phone and walk to the extreme corner of the sitting room, where I pick up a faint trace of a neighbour's unsecured Wi-Fi – just enough for me to connect to Carol Younson's website. She has a diploma in something called integrative psychotherapy, and her specialisms are listed as post-traumatic stress, rape counselling and bereavement.

I call the number.

'Hello,' I say when a woman answers. 'I recently suffered a bereavement. I was wondering if I could come and see you about it.'

6. *A person close to you confesses in confidence that they ran someone over while drunk. As a result, they have given up drinking for good. Would you feel obliged to report it to the police?*

   ☐ Report

   ☐ Don't report

Then: Emma

Watching Edward getting ready to cook is like watching a surgeon preparing to operate, everything neatly laid out in its correct place before he even starts. Today he's brought two lobsters, still alive, their big boxing-glove claws cuffed with cable ties. I ask for a job and am given a daikon, a heavy Japanese radish, to grate.

He's cheerful tonight. I'm hoping it's from being with me, but then he says he's had some good news.

That speech I made at the *AJ* awards, Emma. Someone who heard it has asked us to submit designs for a competition.

Is it a big one?

Very. If we win, we'll be building a whole new town. It's a chance to do what I was talking about, to design more than just buildings. A new kind of community, perhaps.

A whole town like this? I say, looking at the stark minimalism of One Folgate Street.

Why not?

I just can't believe most people would want to live like this, I say.

I don't tell him that whenever he comes to the house I still rush around frantically pushing dirty clothes into cupboards, scraping half-eaten plates of food into the bin and hiding magazines and newspapers under the sofa cushions.

You're the proof it can work, he says. An ordinary person who's been changed by architecture.

I've been changed by *you*, I say. And I don't think even you can have sex with an entire town.

He's brought some Japanese tea to go with the lobster. The leaves come in a tiny paper wrap, like an origami puzzle. From the Uji region, he says. The tea's name is Gyokuro, which means 'jewel dew'. I try to pronounce it and he corrects me several times before giving up in pretend disgust.

His reaction when I produce my art-deco teapot, however, is anything but pretend.

What on earth is *that*? he says, frowning at it.

It was my birthday present from Simon. Don't you like it?

I suppose it'll do the job.

He leaves the tea to infuse while he deals with the lobsters. Taking a knife, he slips the blade under the armoured helmets. Moments later there's a cracking sound as he twists the heads away. The legs continue to twitch as he gets to work on the tails, slicing them down each side. The meat slides out easily, a fat column of pale gristle. A few more movements and he's removed the brown skin, rinsing the tails again under cold water before cutting them into sashimi. A dipping sauce made from lemon juice, soy and rice vinegar is the final touch. The whole assembly only takes a few minutes.

We eat with chopsticks, then one thing leads to another and we end up in bed. I almost always come before him and tonight is no exception – by design, I suspect; our lovemaking is as carefully thought out as everything else he does.

I wonder what would happen if I could make him lose control, what revelations or hidden truths lie beyond this rigid self-restraint. One day, I think, I'll find out.

Afterwards, as I'm drifting off, I hear him murmur, You're mine now, Emma. You know that, don't you? Mine.

Mmmm, I say sleepily. Yours.

I wake to find him no longer beside me. Padding to the top of the stairs, I see he's down in the kitchen, tidying up.

Still hungry, I set off to join him. I'm halfway down when I see him pick up Simon's teapot and carefully pour the remains of the tea into the sink. Then there's a crash and the teapot's in pieces all over the floor.

I must make a sound because he looks up. I'm so sorry, Emma, he says calmly. He holds up his hands. I should have dried these first.

I go to help but he stops me. Not in bare feet. You'll cut yourself.

Of course I'll replace it, he adds. There's a good one by Marimekko Hennika. Or the Bauhaus is still very fine.

I go into the kitchen anyway, crouching down and picking up the broken pieces. It doesn't matter, I say. It's only a teapot.

Well, exactly, he says reasonably. It's only a teapot.

And I feel a strange little thrill of satisfaction, of being owned. *You're mine.*

Now: Jane

Carol Younson is based in a quiet, leafy street in Queen's Park. When she opens the door she gives me an odd, almost startled look, then quickly recovers and ushers me through to a sitting room. Directing me to the sofa, she explains this will just be an exploratory session to see if she can help me. If we decide to go ahead, we'll meet at the same time each week.

'So,' she says when these preliminaries are out of the way. 'What brings you to therapy at this time, Jane?'

'Well, several things,' I say. 'The stillbirth I mentioned on the phone, primarily.'

Carol nods. 'Talking about our feelings of grief gives us a way to sort through them, to begin the process of separating the necessary emotions from the destructive ones. Anything else?'

'I think you may have treated someone I have a connection with. I'd like to know what was troubling her.'

Carol Younson shakes her head. 'I can't ever discuss my other clients.'

'It might be different in this case. You see, she's dead. Her name was Emma Matthews.'

I can't be mistaken – the look in Carol Younson's eyes is

definitely shock. Then she says, 'I still can't tell you what Emma and I talked about. A client's right to confidentiality doesn't end at her death.'

'Is it true that I look a bit like her?'

She hesitates for a moment before nodding. 'Yes. I noticed it as soon as I opened the door. You're a relative, I take it? Her sister? I'm sorry.'

I shake my head. 'We never met.'

She looks puzzled. 'Then what's the connection, if you don't mind my asking?'

'I live in the same house as her – the house where she died.' Now it's my turn to hesitate. 'And I'm having a relationship with the same man.'

'Simon Wakefield?' she says slowly. 'Her boyfriend?'

'No – although I have met him, when he came to leave some flowers. The man I'm talking about is the architect who built the house.'

Carol stares at me. 'Let me make sure I've got this straight. You're living in One Folgate Street, just as Emma did. And you're Edward Monkford's lover. Just as Emma was.'

'That's right.' Edward had talked about his relationship with Emma as if it had been little more than a brief affair, but I decide not to lead the witness.

'In that case, I will tell you what Emma and I discussed in therapy, Jane,' she says quietly.

'Despite what you said just now?' I say, rather surprised to have won so easily.

'Yes. You see, there is one special circumstance in which we're allowed to break our professional duty of confidentiality.' She pauses. 'Where it can do no harm to the client, but may prevent harm from coming to someone else.'

'I don't understand,' I say. 'What harm? And to who?'

'I'm talking about you, Jane,' she says. 'I believe you may be in danger.'

Then: Emma

Deon Nelson stole my happiness, I say. He shattered my life and made me afraid of every man I meet. He made me feel ashamed of my own body.

I pause and take a drink from a glass of water. The courtroom is very quiet. Up on the bench the two magistrates, a man and a woman, watch me unblinkingly. It's very hot, the room window-less and beige, the lawyers perspiring a little under their wigs.

Two screens have been rigged up so I can't be seen from the dock. I can sense Deon Nelson's presence behind them. But I don't feel scared. Quite the opposite. The bastard's going to prison.

I've been crying but now I raise my voice, making sure the whole courtroom can hear me. I had to move because I thought he might come back, I say. I suffered flashbacks and memory loss and I started seeing a counsellor. My relationship with my boyfriend broke down.

Nelson's lawyer, a short, trim woman wearing an elegant little power suit under her black gown, looks up, suddenly thoughtful, and makes a note.

How do I feel about the prospect of Deon Nelson getting bail? I say. I feel sickened. Having been threatened at knifepoint by him, having been robbed and raped by him in the most humiliating way possible, I know what he's capable of. The idea that he could be free to walk the streets terrifies me. I would feel intimidated just knowing he was out there.

This last point is something DI Clarke has hinted I should include in my impact statement. It's all very well for Nelson's lawyer to argue that her client has no intention of approaching me. If I feel threatened by the very fact of his freedom, there's a risk I might withdraw my testimony and the trial would collapse. Right now, I'm the most important person in this courtroom.

Both magistrates are still looking at me. The public gallery, too, is silent. Before I started I was nervous, but now I feel powerful and in control.

Deon Nelson didn't just rape me, I say. He made me live with the fear that he was going to send the film of what he'd done to everyone I know. Threats and intimidation are how he works. I hope the justice system will treat his bail application accordingly.

Bravo, a little voice inside my head says.

Thank you, Miss Matthews. We will certainly take your views into very serious consideration, the male magistrate says kindly. Feel free to take a moment to sit down in the witness box, if you wish. Then, when you are feeling well enough, you may go.

There's silence in the courtroom as I gather up my things. Nelson's barrister is already on her feet, waiting to approach the bench.

Now: Jane

'What do you mean, "danger"?' I'm smiling at the ludicrousness of what she's just said, but Carol Younson, I can see, is deadly serious. 'Not from Edward, surely.'

'Emma told me . . .' Carol stops and frowns, as if breaking this taboo doesn't come easily to her. 'As a therapist, I spend most of my time unpicking unconscious patterns of behaviour. When someone asks me, "Why are all men like *that*?", my answer is, "Why are all the men *you* choose like that?". Freud talks about something he called "repetition compulsion". That is, a pattern in which someone acts out the same sexual psychodrama over and over again, with different people allotted the same unchanging roles. At a subconscious or even a conscious level, they're hoping to rewrite the outcome, to perfect whatever it was that went wrong before. Inevitably, though, the same flaws and imperfections they themselves bring to the relationship destroy it, in exactly the same way.'

'How does this relate to Emma and me?' I say, although I've already started to guess.

'In any relationship, there are two repetition compulsions at work – his and hers. Their interaction may be benign. Or it may be destructive – horribly destructive. Emma had low self-esteem that was lowered still further when she was sexually assaulted. Like many rape victims, she blamed herself – quite wrongly, of course. In Edward Monkford, she found someone who would give her the abuse she at some level craved.'

'Wait a minute,' I say, shocked. 'Edward – an *abuser*? Have you met him?'

Carol shakes her head. 'I'm going by what I gleaned from Emma. Which, by the way, was no easy matter. She was always reluctant to be open with me – a classic sign of low self-esteem.'

'It simply isn't possible,' I say flatly. 'I do know Edward. He'd never hit anyone.'

'Not all abuse is physical,' Carol says quietly. 'The need for absolute control is another kind of ill treatment.'

Absolute control. The words hit me like a slap. Because I can see that, viewed a certain way, they fit.

'Edward's behaviour seemed reasonable enough to Emma so long as she colluded with it – that is, so long as she allowed him to control her,' Carol continues. 'There were things that should have served as warning signs: the strange set-up with the house, the way he made even small decisions for her, or separated her from her friends and family – all the classic behaviours of the narcissistic sociopath. But the real problems started when she tried to break away from him.'

Sociopath. I know professionals don't use that term quite the same way it's used in movies and TV dramas, but even so, I can't help remembering what Emma's previous boyfriend – Simon Wakefield, Carol had called him – said that time outside the house. *First he poisoned her mind. Then he killed her . . .*

'Does any of what I'm describing sound familiar, Jane?' she prompts.

I don't answer her directly. 'What happened to Emma? After all this other stuff, I mean?'

'Eventually – with my help – she started to realise how destructive the relationship with Edward Monkford had become. She broke up with him, but it left her depressed and withdrawn – paranoid, even.' She pauses. 'That was when she broke off all contact with me.'

'Hang on,' I say, puzzled. 'How do you know he killed her, then?'

Carol Younson frowns. 'I didn't say he *killed* her, Jane.'

'Oh,' I say, relieved. 'So what *are* you saying?'

'Her depression, her paranoia, the negative feelings and low self-esteem the relationship had fostered – to my mind, these were undoubtedly contributory factors.'

'You think it was *suicide*?'

'That was my professional opinion, yes. I think Emma threw herself down the stairs at a time when she was suffering from extreme depression.'

I'm silent, thinking.

'Tell me about your own relationship with Edward,' Carol suggests.

'Well, that's the strange thing. From the sound of it, there aren't really many similarities. It started not long after I'd moved in. He made it very clear that he wanted me. But also that he wasn't offering a conventional relationship. He said—'

'Wait,' Carol interrupts. 'I'm just going to get something.'

She leaves the room briefly and comes back with a red notebook. 'The notes from my sessions with Emma,' she explains, leafing through the pages. 'You were saying?'

'He said there's a kind of purity—'

'"To the unencumbered affair",' Carol finishes for me.

'Yes.' I stare at her. 'Those were his exact words.' Words he'd previously spoken to someone else, it would appear.

'From what Emma told me, Edward is an extreme, almost obsessive perfectionist,' Carol says. 'Would you agree with that?'

I nod reluctantly.

'But of course our previous relationships can't ever be perfected, no matter how many times we act them out. Each successive failure simply reinforces the maladaptive behaviour. In other words, the pattern becomes more pronounced over time. As well as more desperate.'

'Can't a person change?'

'Oddly enough, Emma asked me the exact same question.' Carol thinks for a moment. 'Sometimes, yes. But it's a painful and difficult process, even with the help of a good therapist. And it's narcissistic to believe that *we're* going to be the one to change another person's fundamental nature. The only person you can ever really change is yourself.'

'You say I'm in danger of going the same way as her,' I object. 'But from what you describe, she was nothing like me.'

'Perhaps. But you've told me that you suffered a stillbirth. It's striking, isn't it, that you were both in some way damaged when he met you. Sociopaths are attracted to the vulnerable.'

'Why did Emma stop seeing you?'

A look of regret crosses Carol's face. 'I don't know. If she'd only stayed in therapy, perhaps she'd still be alive today.'

'She had your card with her. I found her sleeping bag in the attic at One Folgate Street, along with some cans of food. It looked like she'd been sleeping up there. She must have been planning to call you.'

She nods slowly. 'I suppose that's something. Thank you.'

'But I don't think you're right about everything else. If Emma was depressed, it was because the affair with Edward was over, not because he was controlling her. And if she killed herself . . . well, that's horribly sad, but it's hardly his fault. As you said yourself, we all have to take responsibility for our own actions.'

Carol only smiles sadly and shakes her head. I get the impression she's heard something similar before, perhaps even from Emma.

Suddenly I've had enough of this room, with its soft furnishings and its clutter, its cushions and tissues and psychobabble. I stand. 'Thank you for seeing me. It's been interesting. But I don't think I want to talk to you about my daughter after all. Or about Edward. I won't be coming back.'

Then: Emma

I can't go to the public gallery after reading my impact statement because of the Special Measures. So I hang around outside the court, waiting. It's not long before DI Clarke and Sergeant Willan rush out, looking troubled. With them is the lawyer for the prosecution, Mr Broome.

Emma, come this way, Sergeant Willan goes.

Why? What's going on? I say as they whisk me off to another part of the lobby. I look back at the courtroom doors just as Nelson's lawyer emerges. With her is a dark-skinned youth in a suit. He turns in my direction, and I see a flash of recognition in his eyes. Then his lawyer says something and he turns back to her.

Emma, the magistrates have granted bail, Sergeant Willan is saying. I'm sorry.

What? I say, bewildered. Why?

The magistrates agreed with Mrs Fields – the defence counsel – that there were some difficulties with our case.

'Difficulties'? What does that mean? I say. From another door, the one leading to the public gallery, Simon appears. He makes a beeline for me.

Procedural difficulties, DI Clarke says grimly. Around the issue of identification, principally.

No DNA, you mean?

And no fingerprints, the barrister says.

DI Clarke doesn't look at him. At the time, of course, there was no allegation of rape. It was classified as a break-in. A decision was made by the duty officer not to dust for prints.

He sighs. And then later, we should probably have got Nelson into a line-up. But since you'd told us he was wearing a balaclava, there didn't seem much point. Unfortunately, a clever lawyer can use that sort of thing to imply the police have been jumping to conclusions.

But if that's the problem, why don't I do a line-up now? I say.

Clarke and the lawyer exchange glances. It might help, when it comes to trial, the lawyer says thoughtfully.

This is very important, Emma, DI Clarke says. Have you at any point during the proceedings today caught sight of the defendant?

I shake my head. After all, I don't know for sure that *was* Nelson I saw. And even if it was, why should he get off just because the police are such a shambles?

I think we should consider it, the lawyer says, nodding.

Emma? Simon calls, desperate to break into the conversation. Emma, I know you meant it.

Meant what? I say.

That it was only because of that bastard we split up.

What? No, I say, shaking my head. That was for the court, Si. I didn't . . . I'm not going back.

Emma, Edward's voice says, calm and authoritative behind us. I turn to him gratefully. Well done, he says. You were brilliant. He enfolds me in his arms and I see Simon's horror as he realises what this means.

Jesus, he whispers. Jesus, Emma. You can't be.

Can't what, Simon? I say defiantly. Can't choose who I go out with?

The police officers and Broome, aware they're present at some personal drama, look down and shuffle their feet. As usual, Edward takes charge.

Come with me, he says. He puts his arm round me and steers me away. I glance back once and see Simon staring after us, mute with misery and anger.

Now: Jane

At the weekend, Edward takes me to the British Museum, where an assistant unlocks a cabinet and leaves us alone to examine a small prehistoric sculpture. The carving has been smoothed by time, but it's still recognisably two lovers, entwined.

'It's eleven thousand years old – the oldest depiction of sex in the world,' Edward says. 'From a civilisation known as the Natufians – the first people to create communities.'

It's hard to concentrate. I can't stop thinking about the fact that he spoke the exact same words to Emma as he did to me. Some of Carol's other comments I can disregard, given that she never met Edward, but the hard evidence of her notebook is more difficult to ignore.

But then, I think, we're all guilty of dropping into the same familiar phrases, the same linguistic shortcuts. We all tell the same anecdotes to different people, sometimes even the same people, often in the same words. Who doesn't repeat themselves sometimes? Aren't 'repetition compulsion' and 'acting out' just fancy terms for being creatures of habit?

Then Edward passes me the carving to hold, and immediately all my attention is focused on that. I find myself thinking how incredible it is that people have been making love for so many millennia; but of course it's one of the few constants of mankind's history. The same act, repeated through the generations.

Afterwards, I ask if we can go and see the Elgin Marbles, but Edward doesn't want to. 'The public galleries will be full of tourists. Besides, I make it a rule only to look at one thing in a museum. Any more and your brain gets overloaded.' He starts to walk back the way we came.

Carol Younson's words come back to me. *Edward's behaviour seemed reasonable enough to Emma so long as she colluded with it – that is, so long as she allowed him to control her . . .*

I stop dead. 'Edward, I really want to see them.'

He looks at me, puzzled. 'All right. But not now. I'll make an arrangement with the director – we can come back when the museum's closed—'

'Now,' I say. 'It has to be now.' I'm aware I sound childish and stressed. An assistant looks up from a desk and frowns.

Edward shrugs. 'Very well.'

He leads me through another door into the public part of the museum. People ebb and surge round the exhibits like fish feeding on coral. Edward sets off at a normal walking pace, cutting through them without a sideways glance.

'In here,' he says.

This room is even busier, packed with schoolkids holding clipboards and chattering away in French. Then there are the culture zombies nodding along to their audio guides; the couples clutching at each other's hands who drift around the room like dragnets; the buggy pushers, the backpackers, the selfie-takers. And beyond all that, behind a metal rail, some plinths bearing a few fragments of battered sculpture and the famous frieze.

It's hopeless. I try to look properly, but the magic I felt holding that tiny millennia-old carving in my hands is nowhere to be found.

'You were right,' I say miserably. 'This is hideous.'

He smiles. 'They're unexciting at the best of times. If it wasn't for the fuss about ownership, nobody would give them a second glance. Even the building they came from – the Parthenon – is as dull as ditchwater. Ironically, it was built as a symbol of the power of the Greek empire. So it's only appropriate that another greedy empire should have pinched bits of it. Shall we go?'

We drop by his office to pick up a leather holdall, then a fishmonger's, where Edward has pre-ordered the ingredients for a stew. The man is apologetic: one of the fish on Edward's list was hake, but he's had to substitute monkfish. 'Same price of course, sir, although we normally charge more for the monk.'

Edward shakes his head. 'The recipe requires hake.'

'What can I do, sir?' The fishmonger spreads his hands. 'If they don't catch it, we can't sell it.'

'Are you telling me,' Edward says slowly, 'that there was no hake *at all* at Billingsgate this morning?'

'Only for silly money.'

'Then why didn't you pay it?'

The man's smile is faltering. 'Monkfish is better, sir.'

'I ordered hake,' Edward says. 'You've let me down. I won't be coming back.' He turns on his heel and walks out. The fishmonger shrugs and goes back to the fish he was filleting, but not before he's given me a curious look. I feel my cheeks burning.

Edward's waiting in the street. 'Let's go,' he says, raising his arm for a cab. One immediately does a U-turn and pulls up next to us. This is a peculiar gift he has, I've noticed: taxi drivers always seem to have their eyes out for him.

I haven't seen him angry before and I don't know how long his mood will last. But he calmly starts talking about something else, as if the altercation never happened.

If Carol was right, and he's a sociopath, wouldn't he be ranting and raving now? It's yet more evidence, I decide, that she was wrong about him.

He glances across at me. 'I have a feeling you aren't listening, Jane. Is everything all right?'

'Oh – sorry. I was miles away.' I must try not to let my conversation with the therapist get in the way of the here and now, I decide. I indicate the holdall. 'Where are you going?'

'I thought I might move in with you.'

For a moment I think I can't have heard him right. 'Move in?'

'If you'll have me, of course.'

I'm stunned. 'Edward . . .'

'It's too soon?'

'I've never lived with anyone before.'

'Because you've never met the right person,' he says reasonably. 'I understand, Jane, because I think in some ways we're quite alike. You're self-contained – private and a little bit aloof. It's one of the many things I love about you.'

'It is?' I say, although I'm actually thinking, Am I aloof? And did Edward really just say 'love'?

'Don't you see? We're perfect for each other.' He touches my hand. 'We have the same approach to life. You make me happy. And I think I can make you happy too.'

'I'm happy now,' I say. 'Edward, you've already made me happy.' And I smile at him, because it's true.

Then: Emma

Next time Edward comes round, he brings a leather holdall, along with some fish for a stew.

The secret's in the rouille, he tells me as he assembles everything on the counter. So many people skimp on the saffron.

I have no idea what rouille or saffron even are. Are you going somewhere? I say, looking at the holdall.

In a way. Or rather, coming somewhere. If you'll have me, of course.

You want to keep a few things here? I say, surprised.

No, he says, amused. This is all I own.

The bag is as beautiful as everything else he possesses, the leather as soft and polished as a horse's saddle. Under the handle is a discreet label, embossed with the words *Swaine Adeney, luggage makers. By Royal Appointment.* I open it. Inside, everything is as beautifully packed as the engine of a car. I take out the contents one by one, describing them as I go.

Half a dozen Comme des Garçons shirts, all white, very well ironed and folded, I might add. Two silk ties from Maison Charvet. A MacBook Air. A leather-bound Fiorentina notebook. A steel propelling pencil. A Hasselblad digital camera. A rolled cotton sleeve containing . . . let's see . . . three Japanese knives.

Don't touch those, he warns. They're razor sharp.

I roll the knives up again and put them to one side. A washbag. Two black cashmere pullovers. Two pairs of black trousers. Eight pairs of black socks. Eight pairs of black boxer shorts. Is that really it?

Well, I do have a few things at the office. A suit and so on.

How do you manage with so little?

What else do I need? You haven't answered my question, Emma.

It's so sudden, I say, although on the inside I'm somersaulting with joy.

You can throw me out any time you want.

Why would I want to? It's you who'll get tired of *me*.

I'll never get tired of you, Emma, he says seriously. In you I think I've finally found the perfect woman.

But why? I ask.

I mean, I don't really get it. I thought we were just having an unencumbered affair or whatever he called it.

Because you never ask questions, he says reasonably. He turns back to the fish. Pass me those knives now, will you?

Edward!

He pretends to sigh. Oh, all right. Because there's something about you, something vibrant and alive, that makes me feel alive as well. Because you're impulsive and extrovert and all the things I'm not. Because you're different to all the other women I've ever known. Because you've rekindled my desire to live. Because you're all I need. Is that enough explanation for you?

It'll do for now, I say, unable to keep the smile off my face.

7. *Your friend shows you a piece of work she's done. She's clearly proud of it, but it isn't very good. Do you:*

☐ *Give her an honest, dispassionate critique*

☐ *Suggest one small improvement to see if she welcomes it*

☐ *Change the subject*

☐ *Make vague encouraging noises*

☐ *Tell her she's done really well*

Now: Jane

'I have a feeling that what you really want is an apology,' the hospital's mediator says. She's a middle-aged woman with a grey woollen cardigan and a careful, sympathetic manner. 'Is that correct, Jane? Would an acknowledgement by the Trust of everything you've been through help you achieve some closure for your loss?'

On the other side of the table sits a haggard-looking Dr Gifford, flanked by a hospital administrator and a solicitor. The mediator, Linda, sits at the end, as if to emphasise her neutrality. Tessa is next to me.

Dimly, I manage to grasp that within the space of a single sentence, Linda has already downgraded the offered apology into an acknowledgement of my suffering. A bit like one of those sly politician's apologies, when they say they're sorry if other people are upset.

Tessa puts a warning hand on my arm to indicate that she'll take this one. 'An *admission*,' she says, emphasising the word fractionally, 'by the Trust that avoidable errors were indeed made, and that these contributed to Isabel's death, would of course be welcome. As a first step.'

Linda sighs, though whether out of professional empathy or because she's realised she's got a tricky one on her hands here isn't clear. 'The hospital's position – correct me if I'm wrong, Derek – is that they would much prefer precious public funds to be spent on treating patients, rather than on litigation and lawyers' fees.' She turns to the administrator, who nods obligingly.

'Well, quite,' Tessa says reasonably. 'But if you'd ordered Doppler scans for every expectant mother in the first place, we wouldn't be sitting here today. Instead, someone looked at the figures and calculated that it would be cheaper to pay lawyers' fees and compensation in the small but statistically significant number of cases where it would have made a difference. And until organisations like Still Hope succeed in making that callous, inhumane approach *so* expensive, and *so* time-consuming, that the numbers no longer add up, the situation will continue.'

Round one to Tessa, I think.

Derek the administrator speaks. 'If we have to suspend Mr Gifford, which we'll be forced to do if this becomes a formal SUI, his job will be covered by a locum and more patients will be denied the care of an experienced and respected consultant.'

SUI. That's a Serious Untoward Incident. Slowly and painfully, I'm becoming familiar with the jargon. Intermittent auscultation. CTG monitoring. Partograms. The difference between staffing ratios at the birthing centre, where I was, and the labour ward proper, where I should have been.

This meeting was called by the hospital almost as soon as Tessa made a formal request for my medical records. Clearly they'd been waiting to see if their bland, reassuring letter worked. That in itself – the realisation that they'd attempted to brush me off, and that if it hadn't been for Tessa they'd have succeeded – makes me almost as furious as the waste of Isabel's life.

'The thing is,' Tessa had explained to me on our way to the meeting, 'if it did come to compensation, this could be an expensive case for them.'

'Why?' I know how much payouts for babies who shouldn't have died are – almost laughably tiny.

'The actual compensation might not be much, but then there's loss of earnings. You had a well-paid job. If Isabel hadn't died, you'd have taken your maternity leave and gone back to it, yes?'

'I suppose so. But . . .'

'And now you're working for a stillbirth charity for minimum wage. If we add in the salary you've foregone, that's a hefty sum.'

'But that was my choice.'

'A choice you wouldn't have made had circumstances been different. Don't go easy on the hospital, Jane. The more you cost them, the more likely they are to change.'

She's magnificent, I realise. Strange how you can think you know someone, and not really know them at all. In the Still Hope offices, sharing a desk, I'd seen a funny, lively woman with an easy laugh and a penchant for office gossip. Here in this dingy meeting room I see a seasoned warrior, evading the Trust's parries with practised ease.

'It sounds to me,' she says now, 'as if you're trying to morally blackmail Ms Cavendish by telling her other babies will die if she pursues her case. That's duly noted. But a more responsible position would be to increase staffing levels, not reduce them, at least until the outcome of the SUI review is clear.'

The faces opposite look at us stonily.

Finally, Dr Gifford speaks. 'Ms Cavendish . . . Jane. I just want to say, first, that I am truly sorry for your loss. And second, I want to apologise for the mistakes that were made. Opportunities to intervene were missed. I can't tell you whether Isabel would be alive today if we'd spotted the problems sooner. But she would certainly have had a better chance.' He's speaking to the surface of the table, choosing his words, but now he looks up and meets my gaze. His eyes are bloodshot with fatigue. 'I was the senior doctor on call. I take full responsibility.'

There's a long silence. Derek the administrator throws his hands up in the air, as if to say, *That's torn it*. It's Linda who says, carefully, 'Well, I think we'll all want a period of time to reflect on that. As well as on all the other good points that have been made today.'

'It was harrowing,' I tell Edward later. 'But not in the way I'd expected. I suddenly realised that if I go ahead with this I'm going to destroy a man's career, when what happened isn't remotely his fault. I think he's a genuinely nice person.'

'Perhaps if he wasn't so nice, and his staff were more frightened of him, the midwife would have double-checked the scan in the first place.'

'I can hardly destroy him for being a kind boss.'

'Why not? If he's a mediocrity, he deserves it.'

I know, of course, that to create buildings as perfect as Edward's requires a certain ruthlessness. He's told me how he once battled the planning authorities for six months to avoid putting a smoke alarm on a kitchen ceiling. The planning officer had a nervous breakdown, and Edward got away with no alarm. But I suppose I've never liked to think about that side of him.

Unbidden, I hear Carol Younson's voice. *All the traits of the narcissistic sociopath* . . .

'Tell me about Tessa,' Edward suggests, pouring himself some wine. He never fills the glass more than half full, I've noticed. He offers me some, but I shake my head.

'She sounds zealous,' he comments when I've finished my verbal portrait.

'She is. That is, she takes no shit from anybody. But she's got a sense of humour, too.'

'And what does *she* think about your Dr Gifford?'

'She thinks his speech was scripted,' I admit. *It's the difference between responsibility and liability, Jane, she'd told me afterwards, over cookies and lattes in Starbucks. Between one doctor's mistake and an organisation's institutional failures. They'll do anything they can to keep the Trust out of it.*

'So now you have to decide whether you want your dead daughter to become part of this woman's personal crusade,' Edward says thoughtfully.

I look at him, surprised. 'You think I should drop it?'

'Well, it's your decision, of course. But your friend certainly seems intent on fighting this battle at any cost.'

I consider. It's true – I'm fairly sure that, in Tessa, I *have* made a friend. I enjoy her company, but most of all I admire her toughness. I want her to like me back, and, of course, if I were to withdraw from the case I might forfeit that.

Separating Emma from her friends and family . . .

'You don't have a problem with that, do you?' I say.

'Of course not,' he says easily. 'I just want you to be happy, that's all. Incidentally, I'm going to change this sofa.'

'Why?' The sofa is beautiful – a long, low expanse of heavy cream linen.

'Now I'm living here I've noticed a few things that could be better, that's all. The cutlery, for example – I don't know what I was thinking of when I chose the Jean Nouvel. And the sofa invites us to slouch. Really, two armchairs would be better. Le Corbusier's LC3, perhaps. Or the Ghost chair by Philippe Starck. I'll give it some more thought.'

Already, in the short time since Edward has moved in, I've noticed a difference – not so much in my relationship with him, but my relationship with One Folgate Street. That feeling I used to have of playing to an invisible audience has been replaced by the consciousness, the ever-presence, of Edward's discerning eye, a sense that the house and I are now part of one indivisible mise-en-scène. I feel my life becoming more considered, more *beautiful*, knowing that he considers it. But for that very reason, it becomes increasingly hard to engage with the world beyond these walls, the world where chaos and ugliness reign. When choosing cutlery is this difficult, how will I ever decide whether to sue a hospital?

'Anything else?' I ask.

Edward thinks. 'We need to be more disciplined about putting away toiletries. This morning, for example, I noticed you left your conditioner out.'

'I know. I forgot.'

'Well, don't beat yourself up. It takes discipline to live like this. But I think you're already discovering that the rewards are worth it.'

Then: Emma

I'd been dreading the identification parade. I'd been imagining me and Deon Nelson eyeball to eyeball as I walked slowly along a line of men, like in the movies. But of course it's nothing like that these days.

This is VIPER, DI Clarke informs me genially as he puts two mugs of coffee down next to his laptop. Short for Video Identification Parade Electronic Recording, apparently, though if you ask me someone at the Home Office just figured a sexy acronym would help it catch on quicker. Basically, we put the suspect on film, then the system uses facial recognition software to find eight other people from its library who look quite similar. It used to take weeks to set up an ID before we had this. Let's crack on, shall we?

He takes some documents from a plastic sleeve.

Before we start, he says apologetically, you'll just need to sign some forms to say you've only ever seen the accused when the alleged offence was taking place.

Of course, I say airily. Do you have a pen?

The thing is, Emma, he says, looking a little uncomfortable, it's very important that you're absolutely certain you couldn't have caught sight of him at the bail hearing.

Not that I'm aware of, I say, then mentally kick myself. If I'm saying I remember Nelson from the assault well enough to make a positive ID, then of course I ought to know if I saw him anywhere else. But DI Clarke doesn't appear to have noticed my slip.

Of course, I believe you completely. But you should be aware, because it may come up at trial, that the defendant is alleging you and he exchanged a glance, as it were, outside the court.

Well, that's nonsense, I say.

Furthermore, his brief is saying he remarked on it at the time. She says she looked up and saw you passing within fifteen feet.

I frown. I don't think so, I say. At least, I never noticed him there.

Yes. Well, it's got the brief fairly agitated, anyway. A formal complaint, plus notification that, er, witness veracity will be an issue at the trial.

Witness veracity . . . I repeat. Whether I'm telling the truth, you mean?

I'm afraid so. She may try to put this together with the whole amnesia thing. I'll be frank with you, Emma, it's not the nicest experience when a tricky barrister tries to pick holes in your story. But that is her job. And forewarned is forearmed, yes? Just stick to exactly what happened and you'll be fine.

I sign the forms, identify Nelson and walk home seething. So now I'm going to be attacked in court by a lawyer bent on under-mining my story. I have a horrible feeling that by trying to make up for the police's failures, I may have just made things a whole lot worse.

I'm so wrapped up in my thoughts that at first I don't notice the kid on the BMX bike who's slowed to walking pace beside me. When I do become aware of him, I see it's a teenager, about thirteen or fourteen years old. Instinctively, I move to the far side of the pavement.

Effortlessly he rides the bike up over the kerb. I try to duck back the way I came but he's behind me, cutting me off. He leans forward. I tense for the assault, but instead he snarls at me.

Oi, you. You're a lying bitch. That's a message, cunt. You know who from.

Almost casually, he bumps down the kerb again, does a U-turn and pedals away. But not before he's made a stabbing gesture at me.

Bitch! he shouts again for good measure.

Edward finds me huddled in the bedroom, sobbing. Without saying anything he wraps me in his arms until I manage to tell him what happened.

He was probably just trying to frighten you, he says when I've finished. Have you told the police?

I nod tearfully. I'd phoned DI Clarke as soon as I got back, leaving out only the bit about being called a liar. He said he'd get me some pictures of Nelson's associates to look at, but they'd almost certainly have used someone who wasn't known to the police.

In the meantime, Emma, the DI had added, I'm giving you my private number. Text me any time you feel threatened. We'll blue-light a response, get someone out to you right away.

Edward listens as I relay all this. So the police think it's just an attempt to intimidate you? Meaning it would stop if you withdrew your evidence?

I stare at him. You mean – if I let Nelson get away with it?

I'm not necessarily suggesting that's what you should do. Just that it's an option. If you want to be free of all this stress. You can put it all behind you and never think about Deon Nelson again.

He strokes my hair tenderly, tucking a stray lock behind my ear. I'll make us something to eat, he says.

Now: Jane

I sit very still, my body turned to the window so that it catches the light.

The only sound is the soft scratch of Edward's pencil as he sketches me. He has a leather-bound notebook he carries at all times, along with a steel Rotring propelling pencil, as heavy as a bullet. Sketching is what he does to relax. Sometimes he shows me the drawings. More often, though, he tears the page out with a sigh and takes it to the recycling bin built into the refectory counter.

'What was wrong with that one?' I asked him once.

'Nothing. It's a good discipline, to throw away things you like but don't necessarily need. And a picture – any picture – left in view becomes invisible to the eye within minutes.'

Once, that would have seemed a strange, even faintly comic thing to say. But I'm coming to understand him better now. And, to some extent, I agree. So many things about this way of life that previously seemed onerous are now habitual. These days I slip my shoes off when I enter One Folgate Street's little hallway without a second thought. I arrange my spices in alphabetical order, just as he likes them, and find it no great hardship to put each one back in its rightful place after use. I fold my shirts and trousers according to the precise method of a Japanese guru who has written several books on the subject. Knowing Edward finds it hard to sleep if I use the bathroom after him, in case a towel has been left haphazardly on the floor, I spread them out after every shower and come back to deal with them when they're dry. Cups and plates are washed, dried and put away within minutes of being used. Everything has its allotted place, and anything that can't be found such a place is probably redundant and should be jettisoned in any case. Our life together has acquired an efficient, calm serenity: a series of quiet domestic rituals, soothing in and of themselves.

There are compromises on his part, too. There are no book-shelves in the house, but he tolerates a neat stack of hardbacks in the bedroom so long as the edges are perfectly aligned and the construction four-square. Only when the pile begins to tilt does he start frowning at it as he dresses.

'Too high?'

'Perhaps a little, yes.'

I still can't bring myself to throw books away, not even for recycling, but the charity shop on Hendon High Street is grateful for these pristine, almost unthumbed gifts.

Edward rarely reads for pleasure. Once, I asked him why, and he said it was to do with the words on facing pages not being symmetrical.

'Is that a joke? I can never tell when you're joking.'

'Perhaps ten per cent of a joke.'

Sometimes when he sketches he talks, or rather thinks out loud, and those are the most precious times of all. He doesn't like to be pressed about his past, but neither does he shy from it when it comes up in conversation. His mother was a dis-organised, chaotic woman, I learn – not exactly an alcoholic, not exactly addicted to prescription pills; another child might have had Edward's childhood and come out completely normal, but some sensitivity or contrary streak determined that he took a different path. I talk, in turn, about my own parents – their relentless high standards: the hard-to-impress father who exhorted me by corporate email to try harder, do better, win more prizes; the habits of conscientiousness and diligence that have stayed with me all my life. We're complementary, we decide; we could neither of us settle for a partner who was happy being average.

Now he finishes his sketch, studies it for a few moments, then turns the page without tearing it out.

'Am I a keeper this time?'

'For the time being.'

'Edward . . .' I say.

'Jane?'

'Some of the things we did in bed last night made me feel uncomfortable.'

He lines up another sketch, squinting at my legs over the point of the pencil. 'You seemed to enjoy them at the time,' he says at last.

'In the heat of the moment, perhaps. But afterwards . . . I just wouldn't want that kind of thing to become a regular feature, that's all.'

He starts to draw, the pencil sweeping effortlessly across the page. 'Why deny yourself something that gives you pleasure?'

'One can dislike something, even if doing it is a momentary

indulgence. If it feels wrong. You of all people should understand that.'

The pencil's soft back-and-forth doesn't hesitate, like the stylus of a seismograph on a calm, earthquake-free day. 'You're going to have to be more specific, Jane.'

'Rough stuff.'

'Go on.'

'Basically, anything that causes bruising. Force, restraint, skin marks or hair pulling, ditto. And while we're on the subject, you might as well know that I don't like the taste of come and anal is a complete no-no.'

The pencil stops. 'Are you making *rules* for me?'

'I suppose I am, yes. Boundaries, anyway. It goes two ways, of course,' I add. 'Anything you want to say to me, feel free.'

'Only that you're a very remarkable woman.' He returns to his sketch. 'Even if one of your ears *is* a little bigger than the other.'

'Did *she* go along with it?'

'Who?'

'Emma.' I know this is dangerous territory, but I can't help myself.

'"Go along with it",' he repeats. 'An interesting way of putting it. But I never discuss my previous partners. You know that.'

'I'll take that as a yes.'

'You can take it any way you like. So long as you stop tapping your foot like that.'

In my History of Art degree, we did a module on palimpsests – medieval sheets of parchment so costly that once the text was no longer needed, the sheets were simply scraped clean and reused, leaving the old writing faintly visible through the new. Later, Renaissance artists used the word 'pentimenti' – 'repentances' – to describe mistakes or alterations that were covered with new paint, only to be revealed after years or even centuries as the paint thinned with time, leaving both the original and the revision on view.

Sometimes I have a sense that this house – our relationship in it, with it, with each other – is like a palimpsest or a pentimento, that however much we try to overpaint Emma Matthews, she keeps tiptoeing back: a faint image, an enigmatic smile, stealing its way into the corner of the frame.

Then: Emma

Oh my God.

Smashed glass litters the stone floor. My clothes are ripped. The sheets have come loose from the bed and been kicked into a corner. There's blood smeared across my thigh, I don't know where from. In the corner of the room is a broken bottle and some trodden food.

Bits of me hurt that I don't even want to think about.

We stare at each other like the two survivors of an earthquake or an explosion. Like we've been unconscious and we're just coming round.

His eyes search my face. He looks appalled. He says, Emma, I . . . His voice tails off.

I lost control, he says quietly.

It's all right, I say. It's all right. I say it over and over, the way you'd soothe a runaway horse.

We clutch at each other, exhausted, as if the bed is a raft and we've found each other in a shipwreck.

It wasn't only you, I add.

It was such a small thing that prompted this. Since Edward moved in I've been trying to keep things tidy, but sometimes that's meant chucking things in cupboards just a few minutes before he gets back. He opened a drawer and found it full of, I don't know, dirty plates or something. I told him it didn't matter, tried to make him come to bed instead of dealing with them.

And then . . . Bam.

He got angry.

And I got the best sex I've ever had.

I crawl into the warm bit between his arm and his chest and repeat the words I screamed at him not so long before.

Yes, Daddy. Yes.

8. *I try to do things well even when others are not around to notice.*

Agree ☐☐☐☐☐ *Disagree*

Now: Jane

'I have to go away.'

'So soon?' It's only been a few weeks since Edward moved in. We've been happy together. I know it in my heart, but I also know it from the metrics, which Edward has been doing along with me. His aggregate is fifty-eight; mine a little higher at sixty-five, but still a big improvement on where I started.

He sighs. 'I'm needed on site. The planners are being difficult. They don't seem to understand we're not going to complete the buildings and just hand them over for people to do what they like with. This was never about bricks and mortar. This is about building a new kind of community – one where people have responsibilities as well as rights.'

This is the eco-town the Partnership is building in Cornwall. Edward rarely talks about his work, but from what little he's said, I've gathered New Austell has been a titanic struggle – not just because of the huge size of the commission, but because of all the fudges and shortcuts the developers have tried to force on him along the way. He suspects they only appointed him because of the lustre his name brought to a controversial planning application – suspects, too, that it's exactly the same people who are now orchestrating a PR campaign against him, trying to put pressure on him to cram in more units, water down the rules, and thus make the whole thing more profitable. In the press, the idea of 'Monktowns' – austere communities of monastic simplicity – has become a standing joke.

'Do you remember what you said when you interviewed me? That I should talk to your clients about what it's like to live this way? I'd be happy to, if it would help.'

'Thank you. But I already have your data.' He holds up a sheaf of papers. 'Incidentally, Jane, Housekeeper is showing that you've been looking for information about Emma Matthews.'

'Oh. Perhaps once or twice, yes.' In fact, most of my noseying has been done at work, or using the neighbours' Wi-Fi, but sometimes, late at night, I've got careless and used One Folgate Street's own internet. 'Is that a problem?'

'It's just that I don't think any good can come of it. The past is over; that's why it's the past. Let it go, will you?'

'If you like.'

'I need you to promise.' His tone is mild, but his eyes are steely.

'I promise.'

'Thank you.' He kisses my forehead. 'I'll be gone for a few weeks, maybe a little more. But I'll make it up to you when I'm back.'

Then: Emma

At work I look up 'Elizabeth Monkford' and save the images to my desktop. I'm not surprised to discover his wife looked a bit like me. Men often go for the same type. Women do too, of course. It's just that in our case, it isn't usually physical resemblance so much as personality.

Simon was an aberration, I now realise. The kind of men I'm really drawn to are men like Edward. Alpha men.

I study the photographs carefully. Elizabeth Monkford had shorter hair than me. It gives her a slightly French, boyish look.

I go into the Ladies and stand in front of the mirror, pulling my fringe up with one hand and holding the rest of my hair behind my neck with the other, so it's out of sight. I like it, I decide. A touch of Audrey Hepburn. And it will show off the necklace.

Wondering whether Edward will like it too makes me a little weak at the knees.

If he hates it – if he's angry – at least I'll have got a reaction.

And what if he's really *angry?* a voice inside my head whispers.

Yes please, Daddy.

I turn my head this way and that. I like the way this style makes my neck look more delicate. Edward can wrap one hand around it. I can still see the marks left by his fingers from the other night.

I'm still looking when Amanda comes in. She gives me a smile, but she looks tired and drawn. I let my hair fall back. Are you OK? I ask.

Not really, she goes. She splashes water on her face. The trouble with working at the same company as your husband, she says wearily, is that when it all goes tits up, there's no getting away from it.

What's happened?

Oh, the usual. He's been screwing around. Again.

She starts to cry, pulling paper towels out of the dispenser to dab at her eyes.

Has he said so?

She snorts. I don't need him to, she says. When I first slept with him, he was still married to Paula. I should have known he wasn't going to be faithful.

She looks at herself in the mirror and attempts to repair the damage. He's been going to clubs with Simon, she says. But I suppose you already knew that. Since you two broke up, Saul's been hankering for bachelor freedom. Funny really, as Simon only ever goes on and on about getting back with *you*.

She meets my eyes in the mirror. I don't suppose that's going to happen, is it?

I shake my head.

Shame. He adores you, you know.

The problem was, I say, I got fed up with being adored. At least, by someone as wet as Simon. What will you do about Saul?

She shrugs despondently. Nothing, I suppose. Not yet, anyway.

It's not like he's seeing someone. I'm pretty sure it's just one-night stands when he's had a few. Probably proving to Simon he can still pull too.

At the thought of Simon sleeping with other women I feel a sudden stab of jealousy. I push it away. He wasn't right for me.

When are we going to meet Edward, anyway? she goes on. I'm dying to see if he's everything you say he is.

Not for a while. He's going away tomorrow – there's this massive project he's got starting in Cornwall. Tonight's our last night.

Got anything special planned?

Sort of, I say. That is, I'm going to get my hair cut.

Now: Jane

It should feel different with Edward not here. But the truth is, the house is so much a part of him, I feel his presence even when he's away.

It's nice, though, to be able to lay a book down while I cook, then simply pick it up again and read as I eat. Nice to have a fruit bowl on the refectory counter to graze from. Nice, too, to slouch around in a T-shirt and no bra, unfettered by the need to keep either myself or One Folgate Street pristine every single moment.

He's left me three different cutlery sets to try out: the Piano 98, designed by Renzo Piano; the Citterio 98, by Antonio Citterio; and the Caccia, by Luigi Caccia Dominioni and the Castiglioni brothers. I suspect it's a kind of test, to see if my judgement coincides with his, but I also feel flattered to be involved.

Gradually, though, I become aware there's something niggling at me. Just as Edward finds himself unable to ignore a left-out teaspoon or a stack of books that isn't perfectly aligned, so my tidy, conscientious mind refuses to leave alone the mystery of Emma Matthews' death.

I do my best to resist it. After all, I promised him. But the mental jarring only becomes more insistent. And what the promise he extracted from me failed to take into account is that this particular mystery is a barrier to our intimacy, to the quiet perfection of our life together. Really, what's the point of choosing precisely the right fork – and at the moment I'm favouring the weighty, sensuous curves of the Piano – when there's this monstrous, messy shadow hanging over us from the past?

The house wants me to know, I'm sure of it. If walls could talk, One Folgate Street would tell me what happened here.

I will satisfy my curiosity, I decide, but secretly. And once I've laid those ghosts to rest, I will never awaken them again. I won't ever speak to him of what I've learned.

Carol Younson described Edward as a narcissistic sociopath, so my first step is to research what that actually means. According to various psychology sites, a sociopath displays *superficial charm, a sense of entitlement* and *pathological lying*. He or she is *easily bored, manipulative, remorseless* and *lacking in emotional range*. Individuals with Narcissistic Personality Disorder *believe themselves superior to others, insist on having the best of everything, are egocentric and boastful,* and *fall in love easily*. They *put the love object on a pedestal, then just as easily find fault.*

But this is all wrong, I think. Yes, Edward is different to other people, but from a sense of purpose, not superiority. His self-confidence is never boastful or attention-seeking. Nor do I think he ever lies. Integrity is very, very important to him.

The first list might be closer, but it still doesn't feel right. Edward's reserve, his unavailability, could certainly be taken as evidence that he's lacking in emotional range. But actually, I don't think he is. Having lived with him, if only for a short while, it's more that he's . . .

I think, searching for the right words.

It's more like he's closed off. Like he's been hurt in the past, and has reacted by retreating behind these self-erected barriers into a perfect, ordered world of his own devising.

Was it his childhood?

Was it the death of his wife and child?

Could it even have been the death of Emma Matthews?

Or was it something else entirely, something I haven't yet guessed at?

Whatever the reason, it seems strange that Carol should get Edward so wrong. Of course, she never met him, relying instead on what Emma told her.

Which, in turn, suggests that Emma was also mistaken about him. Or – another thought occurs to me – that Emma herself deliberately misled her therapist. But why should she do that?

There's one person who might be able to tell me, I realise. I get out my phone and find a number.

'Hampstead Homes and Properties,' Camilla's voice answers.

'Camilla, it's Jane Cavendish.'

A pause while she places me. 'Jane, of course. Is everything all right?'

'It's fine,' I assure her. 'It's just that I found some things in the attic here I think probably belonged to Emma Matthews. Would you have any contact details for the man she moved in here with – Simon Wakefield?'

'Ah.' Camilla sounds guarded. 'I take it you heard about Emma's . . . accident, then. That was when we took over, actually – the previous agents lost the contract after the inquest. So I wouldn't have details for any tenants before then.'

'Who was the previous agent?'

'Mark Howarth, of Howarth and Stubbs. I can text you his number, if you like.'

'Thanks.' Something makes me add, 'Camilla . . . You say your agency started letting One Folgate Street three years ago. How many tenants have lived there since then?'

'Besides you? Two.'

'But when you showed me round, you said it had been empty for almost a year.'

'That's right. The first tenant was a nurse – she only lasted two weeks. The second managed three months. I found a month's rent stuffed through our door one morning and a note saying if she stayed there a day longer she thought she'd go mad.'

'They were both women?' I say slowly.

'Yes. Why?'

'Doesn't that strike you as odd?'

'Not really. I mean, no more than anything else about that house. But I'm glad *you're* all right.' She leaves the words dangling, as if inviting me to contradict them. I don't say anything. 'Well, bye then, Jane.'

Then: Emma

He leaves reluctantly, the Swaine Adeney holdall waiting on the stone table while we have one last breakfast together.

It won't be for long, he says. And I'll come back for a night or two when I can.

He takes a final look around the house, at the pale open spaces. I'll be thinking of you, he says. He points at me. Wearing that. Living like this. The way the house was meant to be lived in.

I'm wearing one of his white Comme des Garçons shirts and a pair of his black boxers as I eat the toast he's made me. Though I say it myself, it works. Minimal house, minimal clothes.

I'm becoming a little bit obsessed with you, Emma, he adds.

Only a little?

Perhaps the break will do us good.

Why? Don't you want to be obsessed by me?

His eyes go to my neck, to my new shorter haircut, almost too short for his hands to get a grip in when he fucks me.

My obsessions are never healthy, he says quietly.

After he's gone, I open my computer.

Time to find out more about the mysterious Mr Monkford.

The fact is, the way he reacted last night when he saw my

haircut has given me an idea. An idea so crazy I can hardly believe it myself.

Mr Ellis? I call. Tom Ellis?

At the sound of my voice a man turns towards me. He's wearing a suit, a yellow hard hat and a frown of disapproval.

This is a construction site, he says. You can't come in here.

My name's Emma Matthews. Your office said you'd be here. I just want a quick word, that's all.

What about? Barry, I'll catch you later, he says to the man he was talking to. The man nods and heads back into one of the half-finished buildings.

Edward Monkford, I say.

He stiffens. What about him?

I'm trying to find out what happened to his wife. You see, I think it could happen to me as well.

That gets his attention all right. He takes me to a café near the site, an old-fashioned greasy spoon, where construction workers in hi-vis jackets tuck into plates of fried eggs and beans.

Tracking down the fourth member of the original Monkford Partnership hadn't been easy. Eventually I'd found an old cutting online from *Architects' Journal* announcing the Partnership's formation. Four fresh-faced graduates stared out confidently from a fuzzy black-and-white photograph. Even back then, it was clear Edward was their natural leader. Arms folded, face impassive, he was flanked by Elizabeth on one side and a pony-tailed, much slimmer David Thiel on the other. Tom Ellis was to the right of the picture, a little separate from the others, the only one smiling for the camera.

He brings us mugs of tea from the counter and spoons two sugars into his. Although I know the *Architects' Journal* photo was taken less than a decade ago, he looks quite different now: heavier, gone to fat, his hair thinning.

I don't normally talk about Edward Monkford, he says. Or the rest of the Partnership, for that matter.

I know, I say. I could hardly find anything online. That's why I phoned your office. Though I must admit, I hadn't expected to find you working for somewhere like Town and Vale Construction.

Tom Ellis's employer is a massive company that builds estates of near-identical houses for commuters.

Edward's trained you well, I see, he says drily.

What do you mean?

Town and Vale builds affordable homes for people who want to bring up families. They site them near good transport links, schools, doctors' surgeries and pubs. The houses have gardens for children to play in and insulation to keep fuel bills down. They might not win architectural prizes, but people are happy in them. What's wrong with that?

So you had a difference of opinion with Edward, I say. Was that why you left the Partnership?

After a moment, Tom Ellis shakes his head. He forced me out, he says.

How?

In a thousand different ways. Challenging everything I suggested. Ridiculing my ideas. It was bad enough before Elizabeth died, but after he came back from his sabbatical and she wasn't there to rein him in any more, he turned into a monster.

He was heartbroken, I say.

Heartbroken, Tom Ellis repeats. Of course. That's the great myth Edward Monkford's spun around himself, isn't it? The tormented genius who lost the love of his life and became an arch-minimalist as a result.

You don't think that's right?

I know it isn't.

Tom Ellis studies me as if trying to decide whether or not to go on. Edward would have designed his barren little cells right from the start if we'd let him, he says at last. It was Elizabeth who held him back, plus the fact that with her and me backing each other up, he was effectively outnumbered. There was David, of course, but he only cared about the engineering side. Elizabeth and I, though – we were close. We saw things the same way, and the Partnership's early designs reflected that.

How do you mean, 'close'?

Close enough. That is, I suppose I was in love with her.

Tom Ellis glances at me.

You look a bit like her, actually. But I suppose you already know that.

I nod.

I never told her how I felt, he says. At least, not until it was too late. I thought it might be difficult if she didn't feel the same way, given we were working together so closely. That didn't stop Edward, of course.

If Edward wanted her, he'd have told her so, I say.

The only reason he made a play for Elizabeth was to take her away from me, Tom Ellis says flatly. It was all about power and control, just as it always is with him. By making her fall in love with him, he gained an ally and I lost one.

I frown. You think it was about the *buildings*? You think he married her just to make sure the Partnership built the kind of houses he wanted?

I know it sounds mad, Tom Ellis says. But Edward Monkford *is* mad, in a way.

No one's that ruthless.

He laughs hollowly. You don't know the half of it.

But the first house the Partnership built – One Folgate Street – was originally going to be quite different, I object.

Yes. But only because Elizabeth got pregnant. That hadn't been part of Edward's plan at all. Suddenly she wanted a family home with two bedrooms and a garden. Doors to shut off rooms for privacy instead of flowing open-plan spaces. They argued about it – God, how they argued. To meet her, you'd think Elizabeth was a sweet, gentle soul, but she was just as stubborn as him in her own way. An extraordinary woman.

He hesitates.

One night, not long before Max was born, I found her in the office, crying. She told me she couldn't bear to go home to him, that they were so unhappy together. He was incapable of the smallest compromise, she said.

Tom Ellis's eyes drift away from me, unseeing.

I put my arms around her, he says. I kissed her. She stopped me – she was completely honourable, she'd never have done anything behind Edward's back. But she told me she had a decision to make.

Whether to leave him, you mean?

He shrugs. The next day, she said I should forget what had happened, that it was just the hormones making her upset. That

Edward might be difficult but she was committed to making their marriage work. She must have managed to get him to compromise to some extent, because the final designs were actually quite good. No, more than good. The house was brilliant. It made perfect use of the available space. It wouldn't have won any awards. It probably wouldn't even have put the Partnership on the international map. Comfortable, well-thought-out architecture never does. But the three of them would have been happy there.

He pauses. Edward had other ideas, though.

In what way?

Do you know how she died? he says quietly.

I shake my head.

Elizabeth and Max were killed when a parked digger rolled into a stack of concrete blocks near where they were standing. At the inquest, it was suggested the blocks hadn't been stacked correctly and the pile was unstable. Plus the digger might have been parked on a slope with its handbrake off. I spoke to the site foreman. He told me the stack was sound and the digger parked correctly when he left the site on Friday afternoon. The accident happened on the Saturday.

Where was Edward?

On the other side of the site, checking progress. Or so he said at the inquest.

And the foreman? Did he speak out?

He watered his evidence down. Said there'd been squatters sleeping rough on the site who might have broken into the digger. Edward was still employing him, after all.

Can you remember the man's name?

John Watts, of Watts and Sons. It's a family firm.

So let me be clear about this, I say. You believe Edward killed his family just because they were getting in the way of the kind of house he wanted to build.

I say it as if I think Tom Ellis is crazy, as if the idea is so preposterous I can't believe it. But actually I can. That is, I know Edward's capable of anything that he puts his mind to.

You say 'just', Tom Ellis says flatly. There is no 'just' with Edward Monkford. Nothing's more important to him than getting his own way. Oh, I don't doubt he loved Elizabeth, after his own fashion. But I don't think he cared for her, if you see what I mean. Did you know there's a species of shark so vicious their embryos actually eat each other in the womb? As soon as they develop their first teeth, they turn on each other until only the biggest one's left, and that's the one that gets born. Edward's like that. He simply can't help himself. To challenge him is to be destroyed by him.

Did you tell the police any of this?

Tom Ellis's eyes look haunted. No, he admits.

Why not?

After the inquest, Edward went away. Later, we heard he was living in Japan. He wasn't even working as an architect. David and I thought we'd seen the last of him.

But he came back, I say.

Eventually, yes. One day he walked into the office as though nothing had happened and announced that from now on the Partnership would be going in a new direction. He cleverly pitched it to David as a fusion of visual simplicity and new technology, and persuaded him that I was standing in the way. It was his revenge on me for taking Elizabeth's side against him.

So while he was away, I say, you didn't want any scandal because you thought the Partnership was all yours. That's why you kept quiet.

Tom Ellis shrugs. That's one interpretation.

It sounds to me as if you were trying to piggyback off his talent.

Think what you like. But I agreed to talk to you because you said you were scared.

I didn't say I was scared. I'm curious about him, that's all.

Christ. You're in love with him too, aren't you? Tom Ellis says sourly, staring at me. I don't know how he does it – how he mesmerises women like you. Even when I tell you he killed his own wife and child, you aren't disgusted. It's almost like it excites you – makes you think he really is some kind of genius. When all he really is, is a baby shark in the womb.

Now: Jane

It takes a bit more detective work to track down Simon Wakefield.
I manage to speak to Mark, the agent who dealt with One Folgate
Street before Camilla, but he doesn't know how to contact Emma's
former boyfriend either.

'If you do speak to him, though,' he says, 'give him my best,
will you? It was tough, what happened to him.'

'Emma's death, you mean?'

'That too. But even before then, with the break-in at their
previous flat, and so on.'

'They were burgled? I didn't know that.'

'That was why they wanted to live at One Folgate Street in the
first place – for the security.' He pauses. 'Ironic, when you think
about it. But Simon would have done anything for Emma. He
wasn't particularly keen on living there himself, but as soon as
she said she liked it, that was that. The police asked me if I'd ever
seen any evidence he could be violent towards her. I told them
no way. He adored her.'

It takes me a moment to understand what he's saying. 'Wait a
minute. They thought *Simon* might have killed her?'

'Well, they didn't say so explicitly. But I had to liaise with
them quite closely after she died, letting the forensic teams into

the house and so on, so I got to know the detective running the investigation quite well. He was the one who asked about Simon. Apparently, Emma had claimed he'd physically hurt her.' He lowers his voice. 'I was never really sure about Emma, to be honest. Everything was all about her, if you know what I mean. Bit of a drama queen. It seemed like Simon didn't get much say.'

Mark might not have his contact details, but he remembers where Simon used to work, and that's enough information for me to track him down on LinkedIn. The magazine he wrote for then has closed now, and like most freelancers he keeps his profile and CV publicly searchable. Even so, I hesitate before contacting him. Yes, he might have left flowers for Emma outside One Folgate Street, but, from what Mark just told me, Simon had also been a suspect in her death. How sensible is it, really, to start questioning him about what happened?

I will be careful, I decide, and make sure I don't press or threaten him in any way. So far as he's concerned, I'll simply be trying to make amends for taking his floral tributes.

I send a bland email, asking if we can meet for a chat. A reply comes back within minutes, suggesting Costa Coffee in Hendon.

I'm early, but he is too. He arrives dressed much as he was that time outside One Folgate Street: polo shirt, chinos, trendy shoes – the smart-casual uniform of the London media worker. He has a pleasant, open face, but his eyes are troubled as he takes a seat opposite me, as if he knows this is going to be difficult.

'So you got curious,' he says once we've introduced ourselves properly. 'I'm not surprised.'

'Confused, more like. Everyone I speak to seems to have a

different version of how Emma died. Her therapist, for example – she thinks Emma killed herself because she was suffering from depression.' I decide to come right out with it. 'And I also heard some story that the police questioned *you*, because of an allegation Emma had made. What was that all about?'

'I don't know. That is, I've no idea why she said it, or even if she really did. I would never, ever have hit her.' He looks me in the eye, emphasising every word. 'I worshipped the ground Emma walked on.'

I've come here today telling myself to be cautious, not to take everything this man says at face value, but even so I believe him. 'Tell me about her,' I suggest.

Simon exhales slowly. 'What can you say about someone you love? I was lucky to have her, I always knew that. She went to a posh girls' school, then a proper uni. And she was beautiful – really beautiful. She was always getting approached by scouts for model agencies.' He glances at me, a little sheepishly. 'You look a bit like her, by the way.'

'So I've been told.'

'But you don't have her . . .' He frowns, trying to find the right word, and I sense he's probably trying to be tactful. 'Her *vibrancy*. It caused her no end of problems, actually. She was so friendly, men always felt they could approach her without getting knocked back. I told the police, the only times Emma saw me so much as threaten violence was when some idiot wouldn't leave her alone. Then she'd give me a look and that was my signal to step in and tell the guy to back off.'

'So why would she say that you hit her?'

'I really don't know. At the time I thought the police made it up to rattle me, to make me think they had more on me than they really did. To be fair to them, they apologised and let me go quite quickly. I think they were just going through the motions, really. Most murders are committed by someone close to the victim, aren't they? So they bring in the ex-boyfriend as a matter of course.' He's silent for a moment. 'Except they got the wrong ex. I kept telling them it was Edward Monkford they should be looking at, not me.'

I feel the hairs on the back of my neck prickle at the mention of Edward's name. 'Why's that?'

'Conveniently enough, he wasn't around much in the aftermath of Emma's death – he was away, working on some big commission. But I'll never accept it wasn't him who killed her.'

'Why would he do that, though?'

'Because she'd broken up with him.' He leans forward, his gaze intense. 'About a week before she died, she told me she'd made a terrible mistake, that she'd realised he was just a manipulative bully, a control freak. She said – and I suppose this is ironic, really, given how much he hated her to have any possessions of her own – that he treated her like an accessory, just one more thing to make his house look pretty. He couldn't stand her having any thoughts or independence of her own.'

'But no one murders someone just for having their own thoughts,' I object.

'Emma said that over time, he changed completely. When she called it off, he became almost deranged.'

I try to imagine a deranged Edward. Yes, there have been times I've sensed passion underneath that preternatural calm; a maelstrom of emotions, tightly reined in. His anger with the fishmonger, for example. But it's only ever lasted a few moments. I just don't recognise the picture Simon's painting.

'And there's something else,' Simon's saying. 'Something that might be another reason for him to want Emma dead.'

I bring my attention back to him. 'Go on.'

'Emma found out that he murdered his wife and their baby son.'

'What!' I say, confused. 'How?'

'His wife stood up to him – made him compromise his plans for One Folgate Street. Defiance and independence again. For whatever reason, Edward Monkford seems pathologically unable to cope with either.'

'Did you tell the police all this?'

'Of course. They said there was insufficient evidence to reopen the investigation. They also warned me against repeating my accusations at Emma's inquest – they said it could be libel. In other words, they decided to ignore it.' He runs his hand through his hair. 'I've been doing a bit of digging myself, ever since – gathering what evidence I can. But even as a journalist, it's hard to get far without the kind of powers the police have.'

Just for a moment, I feel a wave of sympathy for Simon – a perfectly nice, solid, unexciting guy, unable to believe his luck when he'd pulled a girl a bit out of his league. And then a series of unforeseen events had taken place and suddenly she was faced with choosing between him and Edward Monkford. There really wouldn't have been any contest. No wonder he found it impossible to move on. No wonder he had to believe there was some hidden conspiracy or secret behind her death.

'We'd have got back together if she hadn't died,' he adds. 'I'm absolutely certain of it. Sure, the way we broke up was messy. There was this one time she wanted me to sign some papers; I went to the house to try and win her round, but I was a bit drunk and I didn't handle it very well. I think I was jealous of Monkford, even then. So I knew I had a lot of work to do to make it up to her. The first step was persuading her to move out of that horrible house. And she'd agreed – in principle, anyway; there were issues with the lease, some kind of cancellation penalty. If she'd only managed to leave I think she might be alive today.'

'The house isn't horrible. I'm sorry you lost Emma, but you really can't blame it on One Folgate Street.'

'One day, you'll see I'm right.' Simon looks directly at me. 'Has he made his move on *you* yet?'

'What do you mean?' I protest.

'Monkford. Sooner or later he'll make a pass at you – if he hasn't already. And then he'll brainwash you as well. That's what he does.'

Something – perhaps knowing that if I admit we're lovers it'll simply confirm Simon's belief that women fall over themselves for Edward – makes me say, 'What makes you think I'd say yes?'

He nods. 'Good. Well, if me talking about Emma's death saves just one person from that bastard's clutches, it'll have been worth it.'

The café's filling up. A man sits down at the next table, clutching a sausage-and-onion toastie. A pungent reek of cheap, dank dough and overcooked onions wafts towards us.

'God, that sandwich smells disgusting,' I say.

Simon frowns. 'I can't smell it. So, what are you going to do now?'

'Is there any chance Emma could have been exaggerating, do you think? It still seems odd to me that she made such bizarre claims to you about Edward Monkford, and equally bizarre claims to the police about *you*.' I hesitate. 'Someone I spoke to described her as a person who liked being the centre of attention. Sometimes, people like that need to feel they're important in some way. Even if it means making things up.'

He shakes his head intently. 'It's true Emma liked to feel a bit special. But then she *was* special. I think that was one reason she liked One Folgate Street – it wasn't just the security, it was because it was so different. But if you're saying that made her some kind of fantasist . . . No way.' He sounds annoyed.

'OK,' I say quickly. 'Forget it.'

'Is it all right if I sit here?' A woman holding a sub points to the empty chair next to us. Simon nods reluctantly – I get the impression he'd like to go on talking about Emma all day. As the woman sits down I catch the nauseating smell of fried mushrooms. It smells like wet dogs and dirty bed-sheets.

'The food here really is disgusting,' I say in an undertone. 'I don't know how anyone eats it.'

He gives me an irritated look. 'You'd rather have met somewhere more upmarket, I suppose. That's more your style.'

'It's not that.' I make a mental note that Simon Wakefield carries a bit of a chip on his shoulder. 'I like Costas, normally. This one seems unusually smelly, that's all.'

'It doesn't bother me.'

A little nauseous, I stand up, eager to get into the fresh air. 'Well, thanks for meeting me, Simon.'

He stands too. 'Likewise. Look, here's my card. Will you get in touch if you find out anything else? And give me your own number, just in case?'

'In case of what?'

'In case I finally get some evidence that Edward Monkford really is a killer,' he says evenly. 'If I do, I'd like to be able to let you know.'

Back at One Folgate Street, I go up to the bathroom and undress in front of the mirror. When I touch my breasts they feel sore and full. My nipples have darkened perceptibly, and there are little raised spots, like goose bumps, around each areola.

My period isn't due for a week, so a test won't be reliable. But I don't really need one. The heightened sensitivity to smells, the nausea, the darkened nipples, the little raised bumps my midwife told me were called Montgomery tubercles – it's exactly what happened the last time I was pregnant.

9. *I get upset when things don't go as planned.*

Agree ☐ ☐ ☐ ☐ ☐ *Disagree*

Then: Emma

It's been a while since I saw you, Emma, Carol says.

Yes, I've been busy, I say, pulling my legs up underneath me on her sofa.

When we last spoke, you'd recently asked Simon to leave the house you shared. And we talked about how survivors of sexual trauma often find themselves contemplating big changes as part of their process of recovery. How have those changes been working out for you?

Of course, she means, *Have you changed your mind about Simon yet?* For all she swears her job isn't to make judgements or direct our sessions towards any particular conclusion, I'm coming to realise Carol often does exactly that.

Well, I say, I'm in a new relationship.

A pause. And is that going well?

It's with the man who designed the house – One Folgate Street. He's a breath of fresh air after Simon, to be honest.

She raises her eyebrows. And why is that, do you think?

Simon's a boy. Edward's a man.

And you haven't had any of the sexual problems you experienced with Simon?

Definitely not.

I add, There is something I'd like to talk to you about, though. Something specific.

Of course, she says.

I must hesitate because she goes on, There's nothing you can tell me that I won't have heard many times before, Emma.

I find myself thinking about being overpowered, I say.

I see, she says carefully. And it excites you?

I suppose it does, yes.

But also troubles you?

I just find it . . . strange. After what happened. Shouldn't it be the opposite?

Well, the first thing to say is that there's no should or shouldn't, she begins. And it's actually not that uncommon. Amongst the general population, around a third of women say they regularly engage in fantasy scenarios involving power transference.

Plus there's a physical aspect too, she adds. What's sometimes called 'excitation transfer'. Once you've experienced adrenalin in a sexual situation, your brain may unconsciously seek more of it. The point is, it's nothing to be ashamed of. It doesn't mean you'd enjoy it in real life. Far from it.

I don't feel ashamed, I say. And I do enjoy it in real life.

Carol blinks. You've been acting out these ideas?

I nod.

With Edward?

I nod again.

Would you like to tell me about it?

Despite her claim about being non-judgemental, Carol looks so uncomfortable that I find myself embellishing a little, just to shock her.

It's a funny thing, I conclude, but making him angry makes me feel more powerful, somehow.

You certainly seem more assertive today, Emma. More confident in your choices. The question I'm asking myself is whether these are healthy choices for you just at the moment.

I pretend to consider. I think they probably are, I decide.

Clearly this isn't the answer Carol was hoping her carefully phrased question would receive.

The choice of partner when you're experimenting is very important, she says.

Actually I wouldn't call them experiments, I say. More like discoveries.

But if it's all so wonderful, Emma, she says quietly, why are you here?

Good question, I think.

We've talked before about how survivors of rape can sometimes, wrongly, blame themselves, she adds. How they can feel they're the ones who deserve to be punished, or that they're somehow worth less than other people. I can't help wondering if that's partly what's going on here.

She says it so sincerely that for a moment I almost crumble.

What if I was never raped, though? I say. What if it was all a kind of fantasy?

She frowns. I'm not following you, Emma.

Nothing. But suppose I found something out about somebody – about a crime they'd committed. If I told you, would you have to tell the police?

If the crime hadn't yet been reported, or if it was reported but your evidence might make a difference to the investigation, then the situation is complex, she says. As you know, therapists have a professional code of ethics that includes confidentiality. But we also have a duty to uphold the law. In a conflict between the two, the law takes priority.

I'm silent, thinking through the implications.

What's troubling you, Emma? she prompts gently.

Really, it's nothing, I say, flashing her a smile.

Now: Jane

A blood test at my GP's surgery confirms it. I tell no one yet but Mia, Beth and Tessa. Mia's first question, of course, is 'Was it planned?'

I shake my head. 'Edward got a bit . . . carried away one night.'

'Mister Control, carried away? I'm not sure whether I should be worried, or relieved he's human after all.'

'It was a one-off. We had words about it afterwards, actually.' I know Mia will think I mean about the lack of contraception. I don't go into details.

'Does he know?'

'Not yet.' The truth is, I'm not sure how Edward is going to feel about this.

Mia's ahead of me. 'Correct me if I'm wrong, but wasn't "No children" one of the rules?'

'The house rules, yes. But this is hardly the same.'

'Is it?' She raises an eyebrow. 'We all know how men love unplanned pregnancies.'

I don't say anything.

'And you?' she adds. 'How do *you* feel, J?'

'Scared,' I admit. 'Terrified.' Because despite the whirligig of emotions – disbelief, joy, anxiety, euphoria, amazement, renewed grief for Isabel, happiness – when it all comes to a stop the one I'm left with is sheer, naked fear. 'I couldn't go through that again. If something happened to this one. That . . . *misery*. I just couldn't. It would break me.'

'They said at the time there was no reason why your next baby shouldn't be perfectly healthy,' she reminds me.

'There was no reason last time, either. It still happened.'

'But you *are* going to keep it, right?'

There are very few people in the world who could ask me that question, and even fewer to whom I would give an honest answer: that there's a part of me that's been saying, *Don't*. You're back in the light after so long in a dark and lonely place. Why roll those dice again? It's the same part of my brain that looks around One Folgate Street and thinks, Why jeopardise all this?

But there's another part of me, the part that remembers holding a dead baby in my arms, that gazed down on her perfect face and felt the ecstatic joy of motherhood just the same, that knows I could never even consider terminating a healthy baby because of my own cowardice.

'Yes, I'm going to keep it,' I say. 'I'm going to have this baby. Edward's baby. I know he won't like the idea at first, but I'm hoping he'll get used to it.'

Then: Emma

When I haven't heard from Edward in two weeks, I send him a selfie.

I got a tattoo, Daddy. Do you like it?

The reaction is instant. *WHAT HAVE YOU DONE?*

I know I should have asked your permission first. But I wanted to see what would happen if I was really, really bad . . .

In truth, the tattoo is small, quite pretty, and invisible when wearing normal clothes – a stylised representation of a seagull's wings, just above the swell of the right buttock. But I know how much Edward loathes them.

PS it's quite sore.

The reply comes a few minutes later.

And going to get sorer. Tonight. I'm coming back to London. Angry.

It's the longest text he's ever sent me. I smile as I send my reply. *I'd better get ready then.*

I have a shower, drying myself carefully, dabbing the tiniest amount of perfume on my skin. I wear the dress and the pearl collar, but leave my feet bare. Already, my skin is tingling. The feeling of anticipation is delicious, but it's mingled with nervous excitement. Have I pushed him too far? Can I handle what he's going to do to me?

I arrange myself on the sofa. Eventually I hear the faint beep from Housekeeper as it senses someone at the front door, then a ping as it grants him access. He strides towards me, his face dark.

Show me, he snarls.

I barely have time to turn round before he's grabbed both my wrists with one hand and bent me over the sofa, almost ripping the dress as he pulls it up with the other.

He freezes. What the—?

I start to laugh uncontrollably.

He shakes my wrists angrily. What in God's name are you playing at?

It was Amanda's, I manage to gasp. She did it to celebrate splitting up with her husband. I went along to the tattooist's with her.

You sent me a picture of someone else's arse? he says slowly.

I nod, still helpless with laughter.

I cancelled a dinner with the mayor and the regional planning committee to come back here tonight, he growls.

Well, which is going to be more fun? I say, wiggling my buttocks at him invitingly.

He doesn't let go of my wrists. I'm furious with you, he says wonderingly. You've deliberately made me angry. You deserve every bit of what you're about to get.

I pull away to test his grip, but he's got me tightly.

Welcome home, Daddy, I sigh happily.

Later, much later, before he leaves, I give him a letter.

Don't read it now, I say. Read it when you're on your own. Think about it when you're in your boring planning meetings. You don't have to reply. But I wanted to explain myself to you.

Now: Jane

My first maternity appointment. Opposite me, across an ugly NHS desk, sits Dr Gifford.

A few days ago, I got a computer-generated letter explaining that, although there was no reason to be concerned, my medical history meant my pregnancy had automatically been graded as higher risk. I would therefore be under the care of a consultant, Dr Gifford.

Someone obviously realised their mistake, because later the same day I got a call saying they completely understood that I'd want to see a different consultant. I might in any case be aware that Dr Gifford had tendered his resignation.

They say pregnancy muddles your thinking. So far, I've found the opposite. Or perhaps it's simply that some decisions become easier to make.

Finally, I know what the right course of action is.

'The thing is,' I tell him, 'I don't think you should have to resign because of something that wasn't your fault. And we both know your replacement will be just as overworked as you are.'

He nods warily.

'So here's my proposal. I suggest we work together to put pressure on the Trust. I'll write to them saying I don't want them to make Isabel's death a formal SUI, but I do want reassurance that they're going to increase staffing levels and introduce more Doppler scans. If you tell them those are also your conditions for withdrawing your resignation, chances are they'll see the opportunity to make a deal. How does that sound?'

It hadn't sounded great to Tessa, who would rather I went for the formal investigation and the big solution. But I'd stood firm, and eventually she'd come round.

'Is she always like this?' she'd said to Mia ruefully.

'Before Isabel, she was,' Mia replied, smiling at me. 'The most organised, stubborn, think-through-every-last-detail person I know. I think we've finally got the old Jane back.'

Dr Gifford isn't totally convinced either, at first. 'At a time of scarce resources—' he begins cautiously.

'At a time of scarce resources, it's more important than ever to fight your corner,' I interrupt. 'You know as well as I do that scans and extra doctors will save more lives than some expensive new cancer drug. All I'm doing is helping your department get its voice heard.'

He nods. 'Thank you.'

'And now you'd better examine me,' I say. 'If I'm going to be under your care, I may as well make the most of it.'

The examination is thorough – much more thorough than the one I had at this stage with Isabel. I know I'm getting special treatment because of what Dr Gifford and I have been through together, but that's fine. I no longer consider myself one of the herd, an average person.

The size and position of the uterus are good. A Pap smear is taken to test for cervical cancer, and a tissue sample to test for STDs. I'm not concerned. There is absolutely no chance that the fanatically fastidious Edward could have an untreated STD. My blood pressure is good. Everything is in order. Dr Gifford says he's pleased.

'I've always been good at exams,' I joke.

While I'm lying there, I tell him about the birth I'd wanted with Isabel: a water birth with Diptyque candles and music. He tells me there's no medical reason why that shouldn't happen this time. Then we talk about supplements. Folic acid, obviously – he suggests eight hundred micrograms. Vitamin D is also advisable. Avoid multivitamins that might contain vitamin A, but consider vitamin C, calcium and iron.

Of course I will take those – all of them. I'm not the kind of person who can ignore a guideline or leave undone anything, however small, that might help. I get the necessary pills on the way back to the house, double-checking the labels to make sure no vitamin A has crept in by mistake. The first thing I do after hanging up my coat is to go to my laptop to see what other dietary changes I should be thinking about.

Jane, please score the following statements on a scale of 1–5, where 1 is Strongly Agree and 5 is Strongly Disagree.

Some house facilities have been disabled until the assessment is completed.

I stop dead. It seems to me these metric tests have been more frequent since Edward's been away. Almost as if he's checking up on me. Making sure I'm still calm and serene and living according to the rules, all the way from his distant site office.

More to the point, I would have typed *pregnancy recommended diet* into Housekeeper without thinking, if it hadn't been disabled. I must remember to use the neighbour's Wi-Fi for everything now. At least until I've told Edward.

And also, I think, until I know what really happened to Emma. Because the two – the revealing to Edward of my secret, and the prising open of his own secrets – are connected now, and it's a lot more urgent than it was. For my baby's sake, I have to know the truth.

Then: Emma

Detective Inspector Clarke calls me into the station for yet another chat. The process of the law is clearly speeding up because he takes me, not to his cubbyhole of an office, but to a large well-lit meeting room. There are five people ranged down one side of the table. One's in uniform – I get the impression he's quite high up. Next to him is a petite woman wearing a dark suit. Then comes John Broome, the CPS barrister from the bail hearing. And Sergeant Willan, my support officer, who sits with a space between her and the others, as if to indicate that she's not senior enough to take any real part in this.

DI Clarke, who up to now has been his usual avuncular self, indicates that I should sit opposite the petite woman and places himself on the far side of Sergeant Willan. There's a jug of water and a glass in front of me, but, I notice, no biscuits and no coffee. No Garfield mugs today.

Thank you for coming, Emma, the woman says. I'm Specialist Prosecutor Patricia Shapton, and this is Chief Superintendent Peter Robertson.

The big guns. Hello, I say, waving at them. I'm Emma.

Patricia Shapton smiles politely and continues, We're here to talk about Deon Nelson's defence to your allegations of rape and aggravated burglary. As you probably know, it's a requirement these days for the prosecution and defence to share information before the trial, to prevent cases coming to court unnecessarily.

I hadn't known, but I nod anyway.

Deon Nelson is claiming misidentification, she goes on. She takes a document from the pile in front of her and puts on some reading glasses. Then she looks at me over the top of the glasses, as if waiting for me to respond.

I didn't see him at the bail hearing, I say quickly.

There are several witnesses who say you did. But that's not the specific issue we're here to discuss.

For some reason, I'm not relieved to hear this. Something about her tone, and the silent, watchful faces of the others, is making me uneasy. The atmosphere has turned serious. Aggressive, even.

Deon Nelson has provided medical evidence – *intimate* medical evidence – that he cannot be the man who filmed himself receiving oral sex from you, Shapton says. The evidence is compelling. In fact, I'd go so far as to say it's incontrovertible.

I feel a sense of vertigo that swiftly turns to nausea. I don't understand, I say.

From a legal standpoint, of course, that's all his defence needed to do to secure an acquittal, she continues as if I hadn't spoken. She picks up some more documents. But in fact, they've gone considerably further. These are sworn statements from some of your colleagues at Flow Water Supplies. The most relevant for our purposes is the one from Mr Saul Aksoy, in which he describes a recent sexual relationship with you. During the course of which, he says, at your request, the two of you made a film fitting the description of the one Detective Inspector Clarke found on your phone.

There's that phrase *I wanted the ground to swallow me up*. It doesn't begin to describe what happens when your whole world implodes, when all the lies you've told suddenly come crashing down around your ears. There's a long, horrible pause. I can feel tears stinging my eyes. I fight them back. I know Patricia Shapton will think they're just a ruse to get sympathy.

I manage to say, What about the other phones you found? You said Deon Nelson had done this before. He's hardly innocent.

It's Chief Superintendent Robertson who answers. It used to be thought there was a link between committing burglary and watching hard-core pornography, he says. Because burglars often had unusually large collections of explicit DVDs. Then someone realised that burglars just hung on to the pornography they found in other people's houses. Deon Nelson did the same with phones. He kept the ones with sexual images on. That's all.

Patricia Shapton takes off her glasses and folds them up. Did Deon Nelson force you to give him oral sex, Emma?

There is a long, long silence. *No*, I whisper.

Why did you tell the police that he did?

You asked me in front of Simon! I explode. The tears do come now, tears of self-pity and anger, although I keep talking, desperate for them to understand, to see that this is their fault just as much as mine. I point at Sergeant Willan and DI Clarke. They said they'd found the film and it looked like Nelson, forcing me. They said you couldn't see his face or the knife. What was I supposed to do? Tell Simon I'd had sex with someone else?

You accused a man of raping you at knifepoint. And of

threatening to send obscene images of that attack to your family and friends. You kept up the deception when your story was challenged. You even read a Victim Personal Statement out in court.

DI Clarke made me do that, I say. I tried to back out but he wouldn't let me. Anyway, Nelson deserved it. He's a thief. He stole my stuff.

The words, so pathetic and petty, hang in the air. I catch sight of DI Clarke's face. Written across it is a whole library of emotions. Contempt. Pity. And anger – anger that he allowed himself to be deceived by me, that I've exploited his desire to protect me by piling lie on lie on lie.

There's another long silence. Patricia Shapton glances at Chief Superintendent Robertson. Clearly this is some pre-arranged signal because he says, Do you have a solicitor, Emma?

I shake my head. There's the lawyer who drew up the deed of variation when Simon moved out, but I don't think he'd be much use in this situation.

Emma, I'm going to arrest you now. It means you can have access to a duty solicitor later, when we interview you formally about this.

I stare at him. What do you mean?

We take cases of rape very seriously. That means assuming every woman who says she's been raped is telling the truth. The flipside of that is that we take false rape allegations equally seriously. On the basis of what we've heard today, we have enough evidence to arrest you on suspicion of wasting police time and attempting to pervert the course of justice.

You're going to arrest *me*? I go, disbelieving. What about Nelson? He's the criminal.

We'll have to drop the charges against Deon Nelson, Patricia Shapton says. All of them. Your evidence is totally discredited now.

But he stole my things. No one's disputing that, are they?

Yes, actually, Chief Superintendent Robertson says. Deon Nelson claims he bought the phones from a man in a pub. We may not believe him, but, in evidential terms, there's absolutely nothing tying him to you.

But you can't think—

Emma Matthews, I am arresting you on suspicion of attempting to pervert the course of justice and wasting police time contrary to section five point two of the Criminal Law Act 1967. You do not have to say anything, but it may harm your defence if you do not mention when questioned something which you later rely on in court. Anything you do say may be given in evidence. Do you understand?

I can't speak.

Emma, I need you to answer. Do you understand the nature of the allegations against you?

Yes, I whisper.

Good. Sergeant Willan will now take you to the custody suite.

After that there's a numb sense of having stepped through a looking glass. Suddenly I'm not the victim any more, to be treated with kid gloves and sympathy and brought mugs of coffee. Suddenly I'm in a different part of the station altogether, where the lights have metal cages over them and the floors stink of vomit and bleach. A custody sergeant looks down at me from a raised platform behind a desk and explains my rights. I empty my pockets. I'm handed a copy of the custody code of practice and told I'll be given a hot meal if I'm still here at supper time. My shoes are taken away and I'm escorted to a cell. There's a bed built into one wall and a short shelf on the opposite side. The walls are white, the floor grey, the light diffused through the ceiling. The thought occurs to me that Edward would be quite at home here, but of course he wouldn't really – it's grimy and smelly and uncomfortable and cheap.

I wait three hours for a duty solicitor. At some point the custody sergeant brings me a copy of my charge sheet. Written down, it looks even bleaker than it sounded upstairs.

I try not to think about the expression on DI Clarke's face as I left the room. The anger was gone, leaving only disgust. He'd believed in me and I'd let him down.

Eventually a plump young man with gelled hair and an over-large Windsor knot in his tie is shown in. He stands in the doorway and shakes my hand over an armful of files.

Er, Graham Keating, he says. I'm afraid the solicitors' rooms are all in use. We'll have to talk in here.

We sit side by side on the hard bed like two shy students who can't quite get it on, and he asks me to say in my own words what happened. Even to my ears it sounds feeble.

What will happen to me? I say when I'm done.

It really depends on whether they go down the time-wasting route or the perverting-the-course-of-justice route, he says. If it's the former, and you plead guilty, you could be looking at community service or a suspended sentence. If it's the latter . . . well, there's no limit on the sentence a judge can impose. The maximum is life imprisonment. Obviously, that's only for very extreme cases. But I should warn you, it's a crime judges do tend to take seriously.

I start to cry again. Graham delves into his briefcase and finds a pack of travel tissues. The gesture makes me think of Carol, which in turn reminds me of another problem.

They won't be able to question my therapist, will they? I say.

What sort of therapist are we talking about?

I started seeing a psychotherapist after I was burgled. It was the police who suggested her.

And you've told this therapist the truth?

No, I say miserably.

I see, he says, although he's plainly baffled. Well, so long as we don't introduce state of mind, there's no reason for them to involve her.

He's silent a moment. Which does rather bring us to what our defence *is* going to be. Or rather, our mitigation. I mean, you've already told the police what happened. But you haven't really said why.

What do you mean?

Context is everything in RASSOs – Rape and Serious Sexual Offences. And because these charges originated with an allegation of rape, they'll continue to be handled under RASSO regulations. In the past, I've acted for women who've felt pressured or bullied into making or withdrawing an allegation, for example. That helps a lot.

That didn't . . . I begin, then stop. You mean, being frightened of someone might get me off?

Not completely. But it might dramatically reduce the sentence.

But I *was* frightened, I say. I was frightened of telling Simon. He's violent sometimes.

Right, Graham says. He doesn't say, *Now we're in business*, but that's his body language as he flips open a yellow pad and prepares to make notes. What sort of violence?

Now: Jane

'DI Clarke?'

The man in the brown windcheater nursing a half of bitter looks up. 'That's me. Although I'm not a DI any more, just plain mister. James, if you prefer.' He stands up to shake my hand. At his feet is a Sainsbury's bag-for-life full of fruit and vegetables. He gestures at the bar. 'Can I get you a drink?'

'I'll get myself one. It's good of you to meet me.'

'Oh, it's no bother. I come into town anyway on a Wednesday, for the market.'

I get myself a ginger ale and go back to join him. I'm amazed by how easy it is to track people down these days. A phone call to Scotland Yard had established that DI Clarke had retired, which felt like a setback, but simply typing *How do I find a retired police officer?* into a search engine – not Housekeeper, of course – had thrown up an organisation called NARPO, the National Association of Retired Police Officers. There was a contact form, so I sent them my request. A reply came back the same day. They couldn't give out members' details, but they'd forward my question.

The man sitting opposite me doesn't look old enough to be retired. He must guess what I'm thinking because he says, 'I was twenty-five years in the police game. Long enough to take my pension, but I haven't stopped work completely. Me and another ex-copper have a little business installing security alarms. Nothing too pressured, but it's tidy money. You want to talk about Emma Matthews, I understand?'

I nod. 'Please.'

'Are you a relative?'

He's clearly noted the resemblance. 'Not exactly. I'm the current tenant at One Folgate Street.'

'Hmm.' At first glance James Clarke seems like a solid, ordinary bloke, the kind of working-man-made-comfortable who might own a small villa in Portugal beside a golf course. But now I see that his eyes are shrewd and confident. 'What exactly do you want to know?'

'I know Emma made some sort of allegation against her former boyfriend, Simon. Not long afterwards, she was dead. I've heard conflicting explanations as to who or what killed her – depression, Simon, even the man she went on to have a relationship with.' I deliberately don't mention Edward's name, in case Clarke picks up on my interest in him. 'I'm just trying to shed some light on what happened. Living there, it's hard not to be curious.'

'Emma Matthews pulled the wool over my eyes,' DI Clarke says flatly. 'That didn't happen to me often as a detective. Almost never, in fact. But there I was, faced with this plausible young woman who said she'd been too scared to report a really unpleasant sexual attack, because the attacker had filmed it on her phone and threatened to send it to all her contacts. I wanted to do something for her. Plus, we were under pressure at the time to get rape convictions up. I thought with the evidence we had, for once I'd actually be able to please my masters, get justice for a victim, and put a nasty piece of work called Deon Nelson away for a long time into the bargain. Triple whammy. Turned out I was wrong on all three counts. She'd told us a pack of lies from the start.'

'She was a good liar, then?'

'Or I was a middle-aged fool.' He shrugs ruefully. 'My Sue had passed away the year before. And this girl, who could have been my daughter . . . Perhaps I was too trusting. That's certainly how our internal inquiry saw it, afterwards. Officer coming up to retirement, pretty young woman, his judgement goes haywire. And there was some truth in that. Enough to make me take the retirement a bit early when they suggested it, anyway.'

He takes a long mouthful of his beer. I sip my ginger ale. To me the soft drink screams *I'm pregnant*, but if he's noticed, DI Clarke doesn't mention it. 'Looking back, there were things I should have spotted,' he continues. 'She ID'd Nelson far too confidently on VIPER, given that she said he'd been wearing a balaclava during the assault. As for the accusation against the ex-boyfriend . . .' He shrugs.

'You don't believe that either, in hindsight?'

'We didn't even believe it at the time. It was just her brief's way of getting her off. "I felt scared; I can't be held responsible for what I said." It worked, too. Plus, the CPS were none too keen to tell the world in open court what a fool she'd made of us. She had to accept a caution for wasting, but it was a slap on the wrist, nothing more.'

'But you still arrested Simon Wakefield after she died.'

'Yes. Well, that was more arse-covering, really. Suddenly, there was a possibility we might have got this all wrong. Young woman alleges rape, then admits lying but claims her boyfriend's a Jekyll-and-Hyde character who's violent towards her. Soon after, she's found dead. If it turns out he *did* kill her, we're stuffed. Even if it turns out to be suicide, it doesn't look like the police treated her very well, does it? Either way, it's better to be seen to have arrested someone.'

'So you were just going through the motions?'

'Oh, don't get me wrong. That might have been why the high-ups wanted the arrest, but my team did a proper job when we interviewed him. There was no evidence whatsoever to suggest Simon Wakefield had anything to do with Emma's death. His only mistake was getting involved with her in the first place. And I can hardly blame him for that. Like I said, older and wiser men than him had fallen for her charms.' He frowns. 'I'll tell you something that *was* unusual, though. When most people are caught lying to the police, they cave in pretty quickly. Emma's response was to tell another lie. It might have been planted in her head by her brief, but even so, that's not a common reaction.'

'How do *you* think she died?'

'Two possibilities. One, she killed herself. Out of depression?' He shakes his head. 'I don't think so. More likely, her lies had caught up with her somehow.'

'And the second?'

'The most obvious one.'

I frown. 'What's that?'

'You don't seem to have considered the possibility that it was Deon Nelson who killed her.'

It's true – I've been so focused on Edward and Simon, the

possibility of it being someone else altogether has hardly crossed my mind.

'Nelson was – probably still is, for all I know – a particularly unpleasant individual,' he continues. 'He's got convictions for violence dating back to when he was twelve. When Emma nearly got him sent down with a made-up story, he'd have wanted revenge.' He's silent for a moment. 'Emma said as much, actually. She told us Nelson was making threats against her.'

'Did you follow them up?'

'We logged them.'

'Is that the same thing?'

'She had a caution for wasting police time. You think checking out every allegation she made after that was a top priority? It already looked as if we'd been far too quick to charge Nelson with rape in the first place. What with his lawyer alleging racial harassment, there was no way we were going after him again without firm evidence.'

I think. 'Tell me about this video – the one on Emma's phone. How come you mistook it for rape when it was nothing of the sort?'

'Because it was brutal,' he says flatly. 'Maybe I'm old-fashioned. I just can't see how people can enjoy that kind of thing. But if there's one thing I learned in twenty-five years' policing, it's that you can never understand other people's sex lives. Young people now, they see this nasty, aggressive porn on the internet, they think it might be fun to make a video like that on their own phone. Men treating women as objects; women going along with it. Why? It baffles me, it really does. But in Emma Matthews' case, that's what happened. And with her boyfriend's best friend too.'

'Who was that?'

'A man called Saul Aksoy, who worked for the same company as Emma. Simon was best man at his wedding. Nelson's lawyer got a private investigator to track him down and persuaded him to make a statement. It was a pretty remarkable piece of detective work, actually. Of course, Aksoy hadn't broken any laws, but still. What a situation.'

'But if it was Deon Nelson who killed her,' I say, my mind still running on Clarke's theory, 'how did he get into the house?'

'That I don't know.' Clarke puts down his empty glass. 'My bus is in ten minutes. I should go soon.'

'One Folgate Street has a state-of-the-art security system. That was one of the things Emma liked about it.'

'State of the art?' Clarke snorts. 'Maybe ten years ago. These days, we don't consider anything connected to the internet high security. They're way too easy to hack.'

I suddenly hear Edward's voice in my head. *The shower was on when they found her. She must have been running downstairs with wet feet . . .*

'And why was the shower on?' I say.

Clarke looks confused. 'Sorry?'

'The shower – it's operated by a bangle.' I show him the one on my own wrist. 'It recognises you when you get in and adjusts the water to your personal settings. Then, when you get out, it switches itself off again.'

He shrugs. 'If you say so.'

'What about the other data from One Folgate Street? The entry-phone video, and so on? Did you examine that?'

He shakes his head. 'By the time she was found, forty-eight

hours had passed and the hard drive had wiped itself clean. A lot of security systems do that, to save on disk space. It's a shame, but there you are.'

'Something happened with the house. That's got to be part of it.'

'Perhaps. It's a mystery we'll never solve now, I suppose.' He stands up and reaches for his Sainsbury's bag. I stand too. I'm about to offer him my hand when he surprises me by kissing my cheek. His clothes smell slightly of beer. 'Nice to meet you, Jane. And good luck. Frankly, I doubt you'll come across anything we didn't, but if you do, will you let me know? It still bugs me, what happened to Emma. And there's not many cases do that.'

Then: Emma

There was a time when One Folgate Street seemed like a calm, serene haven. Now it doesn't. It feels claustrophobic and aggressive. Like the house is angry with me.

But of course I'm just putting my own feelings on to these blank walls. It's people who are angry with me, not the house.

That makes me think about Edward and I start to panic about the letter I gave him. What was I thinking? I send him a text. *Please don't read it. Just throw it away.* With most people that would be enough to make them read it for sure, but Edward isn't like most people.

That still doesn't solve the problem that sooner or later I'm going to have to tell him about Simon and Saul and Nelson and the police. And there's no way of doing that without admitting I've been lying to him. Even just thinking about it makes me want to cry.

I hear my mother's voice, that thing she always said when I was caught lying as a child: *Liars shouldn't be criers*.

There was the rhyme she used to recite, too, about a little girl called Matilda who called the fire brigade so often, they didn't believe her when there really was a fire.

For every time she shouted 'Fire!'
They only answered 'Little Liar!'
And therefore when her Aunt returned,
Matilda, and the House, were burned.

I got my own back on my mother, though. When I was fourteen I stopped eating. The doctors diagnosed anorexia but I knew I never really had an eating disorder. I was just proving that my willpower was stronger than hers. Soon the whole household was frantically worrying about *my* diet, *my* weight, *my* calorie intake, whether *I* was having a good or bad day, whether my periods had stopped or I was feeling faint or if I had pale furry hair called lanugo sprouting on my arms and cheeks. Mealtimes dragged on forever, with my parents trying to cajole or bribe or bully me into swallowing just one more forkful. I was allowed to devise ever more outlandish diets on the basis that if I found something I liked, I'd be more likely to eat it. For a week we all ate nothing but slices of fried apple sprinkled on avocado soup. Another time it was pear and watercress salad, three times a day. My father had been a distant, detached parent before but once I was ill I became his number-one priority. I was sent to various private clinics where they talked about low self-esteem and the need to feel successful at something. But of course I *was* successful at something: not eating. I learned to smile wearily but angelically and to say I was sure they were right and that from now on I would try, really try, to think more positive thoughts about myself.

I stopped when a tough female psychologist looked me in the eye and said she knew perfectly well I was just manipulating people, and that if I didn't start eating soon it would be too late. Anorexia changes the way your brain works, apparently. You get into patterns of thought, patterns that emerge when you least expect them. Stay that way for too long and you carry those patterns for the rest of your life. Like that old wives' tale about the wind changing when you frown.

I stopped being anorexic, but I did stay thin. People liked that, I discovered. Men in particular felt protective towards me. They thought I was fragile when actually I'm a person of iron determination.

But sometimes – when things are getting out of hand, like they are now – I remember the lovely, satisfying feeling it gave me not to eat. Knowing I was in control of my destiny after all.

I manage to resist the temptation to starve myself for now. But there's a sick, hollow feeling in my stomach whenever I think about what's happened. *These are sworn statements from some of your colleagues.* How many? Who else besides Saul? I suppose it doesn't even matter now. The news will be all round the building anyway.

And Amanda – one of my best friends – will know that her husband had sex with me.

I email HR to say I'm ill. I need to stay away from work until I can figure out what to do.

To keep myself busy I give the house a much-needed tidy. Not thinking, I leave the front door open while I deal with the rubbish. It's only when I hear a noise behind me that I whip round, my heart in my mouth.

A tiny, skeletal face, as wide-eyed as a baby monkey, stares up at me. It's a kitten – a little Siamese. Seeing me, it sits down on the stone floor expectantly, as if to say I'm responsible for finding its owner now.

Who are *you*? I ask. It only mews. Unconcerned, it allows me to pick it up. It's all skin and bones and soft, suede-like fur. The moment it's in my arms, it starts to purr noisily.

And what am I going to do with you? I say.

I go from house to house, taking the kitten with me. This is the kind of street where both partners need to work to afford the mortgage or the rent, and at most of the houses there's no answer. But at number three a woman with curly red hair and freckles comes to the door, wiping floury hands on an apron. Behind her I can see a kitchen and two red-haired children, a boy and a girl, also wearing aprons.

Hello, she says. Then she sees the kitten, still purring voluptuously in my arms. Oh, aren't you sweet? she tells it.

I don't suppose you know whose it is? I ask. It just came into my house.

She shakes her head. I've not heard of anyone round here getting a kitten. Which house are you?

Number one, I say, gesturing next door.

The Führer's bunker? she says disapprovingly. Well, I suppose someone's got to live there. I'm Maggie Evans, by the way. Do you want to come in? I'll make some calls to the other mums.

Already the children are clustering round, clamouring to be allowed to stroke the kitten. Their mother makes them wash their hands first. I wait while she phones some neighbours. Three builders in hard hats troop up through the kitchen from a base-ment, placing empty mugs politely in the sink.

Welcome to the madhouse, Maggie Evans says as she comes off the phone, although actually it doesn't seem very mad at all. Both the children and the builders are incredibly well mannered.

I'm drawing a blank, I'm afraid, she adds. Chloe and Tim, do you want to make some 'Found Kitten' posters?

The children agree enthusiastically. Chloe wants to know if they can keep the kitten if no one claims it. Maggie says firmly that the kitten will soon grow up into a great big cat, at which point it will eat Hector. Who Hector is, I never find out. While the children draw their posters Maggie makes tea and asks me how long I've been at One Folgate Street.

We weren't terribly keen on it being built in the first place, she confides. It's just so out of keeping. And the architect was so rude. There was a planning meeting for him to listen to our concerns. He just stood there without saying a word. Then he went away and he didn't change a thing. Not a single thing! I bet it's hell to live in.

Actually, it's lovely, I say.

I met a previous tenant who couldn't stand it. She only lasted a few weeks. She said it was like the place had turned against her. There are all these strange rules, aren't there?

A few. They're quite sensible really, I say.

Well, I couldn't live there. Timmy! she calls. Don't use the china plates for paint. What do you do, by the way? she says to me.

I work in marketing. But I'm off sick at the moment.

Oh, she goes. She looks sideways at me, puzzled. I clearly don't look very sick. Then she glances anxiously at the children.

Don't worry, it's nothing catching. I lower my voice. Just a course of chemotherapy. It wipes me out, that's all.

Instantly her eyes are full of concern. Oh, my dear, I'm so sorry.

Don't be. I'm fine, really. Tickety-boo, I say bravely.

By the time I leave, clutching a pile of home-made 'Is this your kitten?' posters as well as the kitten itself, Maggie Evans and I are firm friends.

Back in One Folgate Street the kitten explores with increasing confidence, making tiger-like little leaps up the stairs to the bedroom. When I go to look for it I find it spread out on my bed on its back, fast asleep, one paw stretched out to the air.

I realise I've come to a decision about work. I get out my phone and dial the main switchboard.

Flow Water Supplies. How may I help you? a voice says.

Can you put me through to Helen in HR, please?

There's a pause, then the head of HR comes on the line. Hello?

Helen, it's Emma, I say. Emma Matthews. I need to make a formal complaint about Saul Aksoy.

Now: Jane

If tracking down DI Clarke was straightforward, getting hold of Saul Aksoy's email address is even easier. Typing his name and *Flow Water Supplies* into Google reveals that he left the company three years ago and is now the founder and CEO of Volcayneau, a new brand of mineral water sourced – so a slick website informs me – from under a dormant volcano in Fiji. A picture shows a good-looking, dark-skinned man with a shaved head, very white teeth and a diamond stud in one ear. I send him my by-now-standard email.

> Dear Saul,
> I hope you don't mind me writing to you out of the blue like this. I'm doing some research about a former tenant of the house I live in, One Folgate Street . . .

We're all connected now, I think, as I send it off into cyber-space. Everyone and everything. But for the first time since I started this, I get knocked back. The answer comes back swiftly, but it's a no.

Thank you for your email. I don't discuss Emma Matthews. Not with
anyone.
Saul Aksoy.

I try again.

I'm actually going to be near your office tomorrow evening. Maybe we
could have a quick drink?

I attach my Messenger details. From the little I know about Saul
Aksoy, I can be reasonably sure he'll check me out on Facebook.
And, perhaps immodestly, I'm guessing he wouldn't mind having
a drink with me.

This time the answer's more positive.

OK. I can spare you half an hour. I'll meet you at the Zebra bar in
Dutton Street at eight.

I get there early and order a lime and soda. My breasts are bigger
now and I'm needing the loo more. Otherwise, you'd barely suspect I was pregnant, although Mia claims I'm looking unusually
well. Glowing, she says. It doesn't feel like that when I'm throwing
up in the mornings.

My first impression of Saul Aksoy is jewellery. In addition to
the ear stud, he wears a fine gold chain tucked into the V of his
open-collar shirt. Cufflinks are visible under the sleeves of his
suit, and there's a signet ring on his right hand as well as a fat
metal watch on his left. He seems upset that I've already got a
drink, particularly a soft one, and tries hard to press a glass of

champagne on me before giving up and ordering one for himself.

Saul is as different from Simon Wakefield as it's possible to get, I find myself thinking. And Edward Monkford is utterly different from both. Where Simon's eager to please, but also touchy and insecure, and Edward's calm and confident, Saul is pushy and brash and loud. He also has a habit of saying 'Yeah?' aggressively at the end of his sentences, as if trying to get me to agree with him. It seems incredible that Emma could have had relationships with all three men.

'Thank you for meeting me,' I say after some preliminary chat. 'I know it must look odd, given that I didn't even know Emma. But it seems to me that almost no one really knew her. Everyone I speak to has a different version of what she was like.'

He shrugs. 'I didn't really meet you for that, yeah? I still can't stand to talk about her.'

'Why's that?'

'Because she was a bunny-boiler,' he says frankly. 'And she cost me my job. Not that I miss the job, which was shit, but she lied about me and I don't take that from anyone.'

'What did she do, exactly?'

'Complained to HR that I'd got her drunk and pressured her into sex. Said, amongst other things, that I'd offered to help her move into marketing if she'd sleep with me. She claimed she'd said no and I couldn't handle the rejection. As it happens, I *did* have a word with the marketing director, tried to do her a favour, but that was before we slept together, not after. But she made this allegation before it all came out that she'd been done for crying rape, yeah? And it just so happened there were a few girls in that company who were a bit upset when they found out about each other, plus my wife Amanda – my now *ex*-wife – looking to stitch me up, so I was screwed. Best thing that ever happened to me, as it turned out, but she wasn't to know that at the time.'

'So you and Emma had – what? A fling? An affair?' There's a bowl of salted nuts on the bar and I'm finding it hard not to eat them all while he's talking. I push them away.

'We had sex a couple of times, that's all. A training awayday with an overnight in a hotel. Things got out of hand on the free booze.' He grimaces. 'Look, I'm not proud of it. Simon's my mate – or at least, he was before all this. But I've never been good at saying no and it was her who kept coming on to me, believe me. In fact, she wanted to go on with it even when I decided we'd had our fun and it was time to finish. I reckon the risk was a big part of it for her. She definitely liked the fact that we were doing it behind Simon's back. Amanda's too, for that matter. If you ask me, I ended up doing Simon a favour, although he never saw it that way.'

'Are you and Simon still in touch?'

He shakes his head. 'We haven't spoken in years.'

'I've got to ask you this . . . Someone who looked at the video on Emma's phone told me it was quite rough.'

He doesn't look embarrassed. 'Yeah. Well, she liked all that, didn't she? Most women do, when it comes down to it.' He gives me a direct look. 'And I like a woman who knows what she wants.'

I feel my skin crawl, although I try not to show it. 'But why make a video at all?'

He shrugs. 'Just fooling around. Everyone's done it, yeah? She told me later she'd deleted it but she must have kept it. That was Emma – she'd have enjoyed knowing she had something like that, something that could blow her whole fucking world and mine apart if it came out. Her little bit of power. I probably should have double-checked. But by then I'd moved on.'

'Did you ever notice her lying about other things? That seems to be something else people say about her – that she didn't always tell the truth.'

'Who does, yeah?' He leans back, more relaxed now. 'Though I did notice she'd say these stupid things sometimes. Like, Simon told me she'd almost been a model – some top agency had been desperate to sign her, but she'd decided modelling wasn't for her. Yeah, right – she was saving herself for a career as a PA in a water supplies company instead. Anyway, she told *me* a local photographer had approached her once in the street, but he seemed a bit pervy so she hadn't done anything about it. And it got me thinking: which version was the real one? Like, sometimes she just exaggerated a little bit for effect, and sometimes she went all the way and created this whole fantasy world for herself.

'Mind you,' he adds, 'to hear me talk to retailers, you'd probably think I've already got a million-pound turnover. Fake it till you make it, right?' He finishes his champagne. 'Hey, let's not talk about her any more. Let's get a bottle and talk about you. Has anyone told you you've got really beautiful eyes?'

'Thank you,' I say, already sliding off my stool. 'I've got to be somewhere else, but I do appreciate you meeting me.'

'What?' He affects to look shocked. 'Going already? Who are you meeting? Is it your boyfriend? We've only just started. Come on, sit down. We'll get cocktails, yeah?'

'No, really—'

'It's the least you can do. I've made time for you. You owe me now. Let's have a proper drink.' He's smiling, but there's a hardness and a desperation behind the eyes. An ageing lothario trying to bolster his fading self-esteem with sexual conquests.

'No, really,' I repeat firmly. As I leave the bar he's already scanning the room, looking for someone else to hit on.

Then: Emma

They say with alcoholics there's a moment when you finally hit rock bottom. Nobody can tell you when it's time to quit, nobody can persuade you. You have to get to that place by yourself and recognise it for what it is, and then, only then, do you have a chance of turning things around.

I've reached that place. Blaming Saul was at best a stopgap. There's no doubt he deserves it – he's been leching after girls in the office behind Amanda's back for ages; everyone knows what kind of person he is and it's time someone stopped him – but on the other hand, I have to face up to the fact that *I* let him get me legless, *I* let him do what he did. After Simon's neediness and his constant, irksome adoration, it was actually refreshing just to be wanted for selfish, uncomplicated sex. But that doesn't change the fact that what I did was stupid.

I have to change. I have to start being someone who sees things clearly. Not a victim.

Carol once told me that most people put all their energies into trying to change other people when the only person you can really change is yourself, and even that's incredibly difficult. I see what she means now. I think I'm ready to be someone different from the person who let all this shit happen to her.

I look for the card with Carol's number on it, meaning to call her, but I can't find it. It beats me how anything can go missing in One Folgate Street but it seems to happen all the time – everything from laundry to a bottle of cologne I could have sworn was in the bathroom. I no longer have the energy to track them down.

The kitten, though, I can't ignore. Despite the children's posters, there haven't been any calls about him – I've established he's a boy, now – while, for his part, he wanders round One Folgate Street as if he owns the place. He needs a name. Of course I think of calling him Cat, after the stray in *Breakfast at Tiffany's*, but then I have a better idea.

I'm like Cat, here: a no-name slob. We belong to nobody, and nobody belongs to us.

Slob it is. I go down to the corner shop and buy him some cat food and other supplies.

When I get back, there's someone outside the house – a kid on a bike. For a moment I think he must be here about Slob. Then I realise it's the same youth who swore at me after the bail hearing.

He grins and unhooks a bucket from his handlebars. No, not a bucket – a tin of paint, already open. He plants both feet on the ground, straddling the bike, and hurls the contents directly at the house, at the pristine pale stone, just missing me. A red gouge, like a giant bleeding cut, appears across One Folgate Street's front. The tin clatters to the ground and rolls away, still spiralling red.

Know where you live now, bitch, he shouts in my face as he pedals off.

My hands are shaking as I get out my phone and find the number DI Clarke gave me.

It's me, Emma, I gabble. You said to call you if it happened again and it has. He just threw paint all over the front of the house—

Emma Matthews, he says. It's almost like he's repeating my name for the benefit of other people in the room. Why are you calling this number?

You gave it to me, remember? You said to call you if there was any more intimidation—

This is my personal phone. If you want to report something, you should call the front desk. I'll give you the number. Do you have a pen?

You said you'd protect me, I say slowly.

The circumstances have changed, obviously. I'll text you the right number, he says. Then the line goes dead.

Bastard, I hiss. I'm crying again, tears of impotence and shame. I go and stare at the huge red smear. I have absolutely no idea how to get it cleaned off. It means I'm going to have to speak to Edward now.

10. *A new friend confides she was once sent to prison for shoplifting.*
    It was some time ago and she has turned her life around since.
    Do you:

    ☐ *Consider it irrelevant – everyone deserves a second chance*

    ☐ *Appreciate her honesty in sharing this with you*

    ☐ *Reciprocate by confiding a mistake of your own*

    ☐ *Feel sorry for her that she was ever in that situation*

    ☐ *Decide she's not really the kind of person you want as a friend*

Now: Jane

I come back from my meeting with Saul Aksoy by Tube, wishing I could afford a taxi; the overcrowding, the grime and the end-of-day smell of damp and dirty bodies are getting increasingly hard to take. No one offers me a seat – not that I'd really expect them to yet – but a woman with an eight-month-sized bump and a 'Baby on Board' badge gets on at King's Cross and somebody stands up for her. She sinks into the seat with an audible gasp. In a few months' time, I think, that'll be me.

One Folgate Street, though, is my haven, my cocoon. One reason I'm putting off telling Edward about the pregnancy, I've realised, is because a part of me is frightened Mia's right and he'll simply throw me out. I tell myself he'll be different when it's his own child, that our relationship is stronger than his precious rules, that he'll be fine with baby monitors and buggies and nursery friezes and play mats and all the other messy paraphernalia of parenthood. I've even been checking developmental milestones online. Given his parents' Type-A, disciplined personalities, our child could be sleeping through the night at three months, walking within a year, toilet trained by eighteen months. Surely it's not so very long to put up with a little chaos?

But somehow, I haven't been so confident that I actually call him.

And, of course, however serene my surroundings, there are still my own terrors to be faced. Isabel was born silent and still. This baby – pray God – will be different. Over and over, I imagine that moment: the waiting, the first snatch of breath, that exultant, mewling cry. What will I feel? Triumph? Or something more complicated? Sometimes I actually find myself apologising to Isabel in my head. *I promise I won't forget you. I promise no one can take your place. You'll always be my firstborn, my beloved, my precious girl. I will always grieve for you.* But now there will be another to love, and can there really be such an inexhaustible store of love in me that my feelings for Isabel remain undimmed?

I try to focus on the immediate issue: Edward. The more I tell myself I have to speak to him, the more a little voice reminds me that I don't really know this man, the father of my child, at all. All I know is that he's remarkable, which is another way of saying he's unusual and obsessive. I still don't even know what really happened between him and Emma: what responsibility, moral or otherwise, he might bear for her death, or whether both Simon and Carol, in their different ways, are wrong about that.

I am as methodical and efficient as ever. I buy three packets of fluorescent Post-it notes in different colours and turn one of the refectory walls into a giant mind map. On one side, I stick a Post-it labelled *ACCIDENT*, then, in a row, *SUICIDE, MURDERED – SIMON WAKEFIELD, MURDERED – DEON NELSON* and *MURDERED – PERSON UNKNOWN*. Finally, and somewhat reluctantly, I add a Post-it labelled *MURDERED – EDWARD MONKFORD*. Underneath each one, I put more Post-its for the evidence that supports it. Where I have no proof, I put question marks.

There are only a couple of notes, I'm pleased to see, underneath Edward's name. Simon, too, has fewer than the others, although following my conversation with Saul I have to add one that says *REVENGE FOR SEX WITH BEST FRIEND???*

After some thought I add another to the row. *MURDERED – DI CLARKE.* Because even the policeman had a motive. Being made a fool of by Emma had effectively cost him his job. Of course I don't actually believe he did it, any more than I think Edward did. But he'd clearly been a little bit smitten with Emma, and I don't want to rule out any possibilities prematurely.

Thinking about DI Clarke, I realise I forgot to ask him if the police knew about Edward's stalker. Jorgen something. I add another Post-it: *MURDERED – EDWARD'S STALKER.* Eight possibilities in all.

As I stare at the wall, it dawns on me that I've got precisely nowhere. As DI Clarke said, it's one thing to theorise, quite another to find proof. All I have here is a list of suppositions. No wonder the coroner reached an open verdict.

The bright colours of the Post-its are like a jangling piece of modern art on One Folgate Street's pristine stone. Sighing, I take them down and drop them in the bin.

The recycling's full now, so I carry it outside. One Folgate Street's wheelie bins are down the side of the house, next to the boundary with number three. As I tip everything in, it all comes out in reverse order – the most recent first and then the older stuff. I see yesterday's food packaging, a copy of last weekend's

Sunday Times magazine, an empty shampoo container from the week before. And a drawing.

I fish it out. It's the sketch Edward did of me before he went away, the one he said was fine, but didn't want to keep. It's as if he's drawn me not once, but twice. In the main drawing I have my head turned to the right. It's so detailed, you can see the tautness of my neck muscles and the arch of my clavicle. But underneath or over that there's a second drawing, barely more than a few jagged, suggestive lines, done with a surprising energy and violence: my head turned the other way, my mouth open in a kind of snarl. The two heads pointing in opposite directions give the drawing a disturbing sense of movement.

Which one's the pentimento, and which the finished thing? And why did Edward say there was nothing wrong with it? Did he not want me to see this double image for some reason?

'Hello there.'

I jump. A woman of about forty, with red curly hair, is standing just across the boundary with number three, emptying her own rubbish. 'Sorry – you startled me,' I say. 'Hello.'

She gestures at One Folgate Street. 'You're the latest tenant, are you? I'm Maggie.'

I shake her hand over the fence. 'Jane Cavendish.'

'Actually,' she confides, 'you gave *me* a bit of a shock too. I thought you were the other girl at first. Poor thing.'

I feel my spine tingle. 'You knew Emma?'

'To talk to, nothing more. She was lovely, though. So sweet. She came round once with a stray kitten she'd found and we got chatting.'

'When was this?'

Maggie makes a face. 'Just a few weeks before she ... you know.'

Maggie Evans. I remember now. She was quoted in the local paper after Emma died, saying how much the neighbours all hated One Folgate Street.

'I felt so sorry for her,' Maggie goes on. 'She mentioned she was off work because of cancer treatment. When they found her, I wondered if that was something to do with it – if the chemotherapy hadn't worked and perhaps she'd taken her own life. Obviously she told me in confidence, but I felt I had a duty to mention it to the police. But then they said there'd been a full post-mortem and she didn't have cancer. I remember thinking, How awful to have beaten such a terrible illness and still die like that.'

'Yes,' I say, but I'm thinking, *Cancer?* I'm fairly sure it must be yet another lie, but why?

'Mind you,' she adds, 'I told her to keep that kitten well hidden from the landlord. Anyone who can build a house like that ...' She tries to leave the words hanging, but anything more than a few moments' silence is beyond her, and pretty soon she's back on her favourite topic: One Folgate Street. Despite what she says, she clearly relishes living next to a building of such notoriety. 'Well, must get on,' she says at last. 'Got to get the kids' teas.'

I wonder how I'm going to cope with that side of being a mum: putting my own life on hold to make kids' meals and gossip with neighbours. There are worse things, I suppose.

I look down at the drawing in my hand. Another reference from my History of Art days springs into my head: Janus, the two-headed god. God of Deception.

Is the second image even me? Or is it – I suddenly think – Emma Matthews? And if so, why was Edward so angry with her?

I wait until Maggie's gone and then, discreetly, fish down through the layers of the wheelie bin until I find the Post-its again. They're all stuck together now, a millefeuille of bright green and red and yellow sheets. I take them back into the house. I'm not done with them after all.

Then: Emma

I put off going into work for as long as I can. But by Friday I know I need to get it over with. I leave Slob some cat food and a tray of litter and go.

At the office I feel eyes following me as I make my way to my desk. The only person who speaks to me is Brian.

Oh, Emma, he goes, feeling better? That's good. You can join us for the monthly catch-up at ten.

From his manner I gather no one's told him, but the women are another matter. No one meets my gaze. Heads studiously lower towards computer screens whenever I look round.

Then I see Amanda striding towards me. Quickly I get up and head for the loos. I know there's going to be a confrontation but it's marginally better we do it somewhere private than out here with everyone gawking. I just make it – the door hasn't even shut behind me before she's banged it open so hard it bounces off the little rubber stopper.

What the fuck? she shouts.

Amanda, I go, wait.

Don't fucking give me that, she yells. Don't tell me you're sorry or any of that bullshit. You were my friend and you screwed my husband. You even kept a video on your phone of you giving him a blow job. And now you have the fucking nerve to make a complaint about *him*. You evil, lying *bitch*.

She's waving her hands in my face and for a moment I think she's going to hit me.

And Simon, she continues. You lied to him, you lied to me, you lied to the police—

I didn't lie about Saul, I say.

Oh, I know he's no angel, but when women like you throw themselves at him—

It was Saul who raped me, I say.

That stops her. *What?* she goes.

This is going to sound really weird, I say urgently. But I promise you, this time it's the truth. And I know I'm partly to blame. Saul got me drunk – so drunk I could hardly stand. I shouldn't have let him do that – I knew why he was doing it but I didn't realise how far he was going to take it. I think he may even have spiked my drink. Then he said he'd walk me to my room. Next thing I knew, he was forcing himself on me. I tried to say no but he wouldn't listen.

She stares at me. You're lying, she says.

I'm not. I have told lies, I admit that. But I swear I'm not lying about this.

He wouldn't do that, she says. He's not been faithful, but there's no way he's a rapist.

But she doesn't sound quite so certain any more.

He didn't even seem to think it *was* rape, I say. Afterwards, he kept telling me how great it had been. And I was so confused, I wondered if I was somehow remembering it all wrong. But then he sent me the video. I hadn't even realised he was recording it

– that's how out of it I was. He said how much he'd been enjoying watching it back. It was like a reminder that he could tell Simon any time he liked. I didn't know what to do. I panicked.

Why didn't you tell anyone? she says suspiciously.

Who could I tell? You seemed so happy then, I didn't want to be the one to break up your marriage. And you know how Simon's in awe of Saul. I wasn't sure he'd believe me, let alone whether he'd be able to handle knowing his best friend had done that to me.

But you kept the video. Why would you do that?

As *evidence*, I say. I was trying to work up the courage to go to the police. Or to HR, at least. But the longer I left it, the harder it got. When I looked at the video, even I could see it was ambiguous. And I was ashamed to let anyone see it. I thought maybe it was all my fault. And then the police found it on my phone and assumed in front of Simon that it was Deon Nelson, and everything just got so complicated.

Jesus, she says disbelievingly. Jesus. You're making this up, Emma.

I'm not. I swear I'm not.

I add, Saul's a bastard, Amanda. I think deep down you know that. You know there've been other girls – girls in the office, girls in clubs, anyone he can get his hands on. If you support me he'll get what he deserves, maybe not all of it but at least he'll lose his job.

What about the police? she says, and I know she's starting to believe me.

The police won't get involved unless there's concrete evidence of a crime. This is just about him losing his job, not going to prison. After what he did to you, don't you think that's only fair?

At last she nods. There are at least two girls in this company I know he's slept with, she says. Michelle in Accounts and Leona in Marketing. I'll give HR their names.

Thank you, I say.

Have you told Simon any of this?

I shake my head.

You ought to.

At the thought of Simon – kind, adoring, trusting Simon – something strange happens. I no longer feel quite so contemptuous of him. I used to hate him for being Saul's poodle, for going on and on about what a great bloke Sauly was, when all the time Sauly was actually just a selfish, aggressive prick. But now I don't. Now there's a part of me that remembers how nice it felt to be forgiven.

To my surprise I find I'm crying. I wipe the tears away with a paper towel from the dispenser.

I can't go back, I say. Simon's over. When something's gone that wrong, you can't ever put it right.

Now: Jane

'Just some gel that may feel a bit cold,' the sonographer says kindly. I hear the ketchup squelch of K-Y jelly, then the gel gets smeared around my stomach by the probe. The feeling takes me back to Isabel's first scan: the stickiness on my skin that lasted all day, like a hidden secret beneath my clothes; the curl of printer paper in my bag that showed the ghostly, fern-like curve of a foetus.

I take a deep breath, ambushed by a sudden surge of emotion.

'Relax,' the sonographer murmurs, misunderstanding. She presses the probe hard against my midriff, angling it this way and that. 'There.'

I look up at the monitor. An outline emerges from the murk and I gasp out loud. She smiles at my reaction. 'How many children do you have?' she asks conversationally.

I must take a bit longer than most people to work out the proper answer to that, because she glances down at my notes. 'I'm sorry,' she adds quietly. 'I see you had a stillbirth.'

I nod. There doesn't seem to be anything else to say.

'Do you want to know the baby's sex?' she adds.

'Yes, please.'

'You're having a little boy.'

You're having a little boy. Just the simple confidence of that state-ment, the expectation that everything will be all right this time, overwhelms me with emotion – joy and grief colliding so that I burst into tears of both.

'Have one of these.' She hands me the box of tissues they use for wiping off the jelly. I snuffle into one while she gets on with her work. After a few minutes, she says, 'I'm just going to ask the consultant to pop in.'

'Why? Is something wrong?'

'I'd just like him to talk you through the results,' she says reassuringly. Then she's gone. I'm not overly concerned. This is happening because I'm technically a high-risk patient. Given that Isabel was fine until the very last week of pregnancy, there's no reason to think anything will be wrong now.

It seems an age before the door opens and Dr Gifford's face comes into view. 'Hello, Jane.'

'Hello.' I greet him like an old friend now.

'Jane, I just want to explain one of the main reasons we do this scan at around twelve weeks. It's so we can get an early steer on some of the more common problems.'

Oh no, I think. It can't be—

'The scan doesn't usually give us an exact indication, but it does highlight where there may be an increased risk. In your case, we're obviously looking for any issues with the placenta or umbilical cord, and I'm pleased to report that both of those seem to be working normally.'

I seize on the words. Thank God. Thank God—

'But we also measure what's called the nuchal translucency. That's the thickness of the fluid at the back of the baby's neck.

In your case, the NT does indicate a slightly increased risk of Down's syndrome. We class anything above a one in a hundred and fifty probability high risk. For you, it's currently about one in a hundred. That means, for every hundred mothers with this risk profile, one will give birth to a baby with Down's. Do you understand?'

'Yes,' I say. And I do – that is, I can follow what he's saying with my brain. I'm good with numbers. It's what I feel that I'm struggling to process. So many emotions, so overwhelming, that they almost cancel each other out, leaving me clear-headed but numb.

All my plans, my carefully laid plans, have fallen apart.

'The only way to know for certain is to do a test that involves putting a needle into your womb and drawing out some fluid,' Dr Gifford's saying. 'Unfortunately, that test itself carries a small risk of triggering a miscarriage.'

'How small?'

'About one in a hundred.' He smiles apologetically, as if to say he knows I'm bright enough to understand the irony of this. My risk of miscarriage with the test is exactly the same as the risk of my baby having Down's without it.

'There is a new, non-invasive test that can give a reasonably accurate result,' he adds. 'It measures tiny fragments of the baby's DNA in your blood. Unfortunately, it isn't currently available from this NHS Trust.'

I grasp at what he's saying. 'You mean I can have it privately?'

He nods. 'It costs around four hundred pounds.'

'I want it,' I say quickly. I'll find a way to pay for it somehow.

'I'll make a referral for you now. And we can give you some

leaflets to read. These days, many children with Down's live long and relatively normal lives. But there are no guarantees and it's a decision every parent has to make for themselves.'

By 'decision', I realise, he means whether or not to terminate.

I'm still numb as I leave the hospital. I'm going to have a baby. A little boy. Another chance at motherhood.

Or not.

Could I cope with a disabled child? Because I'm under no illusions – a child with Down's syndrome is just that. Yes, their prospects may be better than they once were, but these are children who still need more parenting, more help, more dedication, more love and support. I've seen mothers with disabled children in the street – endlessly patient, clearly exhausted – and thought to myself how amazing they are. Am I really one of them?

It's only when I get back to One Folgate Street that I realise I definitely can't put off talking to Edward now. It's one thing to pick my moment to tell him about being a father, quite another to conceal something like this. All the leaflets emphasise the importance of discussing the situation with your partner.

The first thing I do, though – inevitably – is a search on the internet for 'Down's syndrome'. Within minutes, I feel sick.

. . . Trisomy 21, as Down's syndrome is properly known, is associated with thyroid problems, sleep disorders, gastrointestinal complications, vision problems, heart defects, spinal and hip instability, low muscle tone and learning difficulties . . .

. . . What safety precautions can you take to reduce wandering? Install good locks on all internal doors, put STOP signs on outside doors, and think about fencing your yard completely . . .

. . . Potty training a child with low muscle tone is certainly extra challenging! We've had three years of accidents, but I'm glad to say we're getting there . . .

. . . We ate yoghurt in front of a mirror so our daughter could see why she was spilling it – that worked a treat! Hand–eye coordination remains a challenge . . .

Then, even more guiltily, I google 'Down's + termination'.

Of those couples who receive an antenatal diagnosis of DS in the UK, 92 per cent choose termination. Under the Abortion Act, termination of a baby with Down's is legal right up to the point of delivery.

. . . We realised it was better for my partner and I to suffer the guilt and grief of a termination than to let our daughter suffer all her life . . .

Oh God. Oh God oh God.

Isabel would be sleeping through the night by now. Isabel would be sitting up, grasping things, putting them in her mouth. She'd be crawling, perhaps even walking. She'd be clever and athletic and high-achieving, just like her mother. Instead of which, I have to decide whether or not to saddle myself with –

I stop. That's not the right way to think about this. Dr Gifford has made an appointment for me at the testing centre first thing tomorrow. They'll give me the results by phone within a couple of days, he promised. In the meantime, I must try not to let it hang over me. After all, the odds are still vastly in favour of everything being fine. Thousands of expectant mothers have a scare like this, only to discover that's all it ever was: a scare.

I call Mia and cry down the phone over her for what seems like hours.

Then: Emma

I sit on the train, wondering what I'm going to say to him. Power stations and fields flicker by. Commuter towns and rural stops come and go.

Every speech I prepare in my head sounds wrong. And I know the more I rehearse it, the more fake it'll get. Better to speak from the heart and hope he listens.

I don't text him until I'm off the train and waiting for a taxi. *Coming to see you. We have to talk.*

The taxi driver refuses to believe my destination even exists – There's nothing there, my love; the nearest house would be in Tregerry, five miles away – until we turn down a farm track to discover an encampment of Portakabins and chemical toilets surrounded by mud. All around us are open fields and woods, but across the valley lorries pass on a distant dual carriageway and I can see how this might indeed be a whole new town one day.

Edward strides from a Portakabin, his face dark with concern. Emma, he says. What's wrong? Why are you here?

I take a deep breath. There's something I need to explain, I say. It's really complicated. I had to tell you in person.

The Portakabins are full of surveyors and draughtsmen, so we walk beside the woods. I tell him what I told Amanda – that I was drugged and forced into sex by one of Simon's friends, that he sent me a phone video he'd made of it as a way of threatening me and the police assumed it was Deon Nelson, that I've had to accept a caution for wasting police time but really none of it was my fault. He listens carefully, his expression giving nothing away.

And then he tells me, very calmly, that it's over between us.

No matter whether I'm telling him the truth now or not, I've lied to him in the past.

He reminds me we agreed this would only continue for as long as it was perfect.

He says a relationship like this is like a building, that you have to get the foundations right or the whole thing falls apart. He thought our relationship was built on honesty when actually it was built on deceit.

He says that all *this* – he gestures at the fields – only came about because I told him I was attacked by Deon Nelson in my own home. He says this town is now being built on a lie as well. He'd been trying to design a community in which people looked out for and respected and helped one another. But such a community can only function on trust and now it's tainted for him.

He says goodbye, his voice empty of emotion.

But I know he loves me. I know he needs our games, that they answer some deep-seated hunger in him.

I was wrong, I say desperately. But think what you did. How much worse was that?

He frowns. What do you mean?

You killed your wife, I say. And your son. You killed them because you didn't want to compromise your building.

He stares at me. He denies it.

I spoke to Tom Ellis, I insist.

He makes a dismissive gesture. The man's a bitter, jealous failure.

But don't you see, I say, I don't care. I don't care what you've done or how bad you are. Edward, we belong together. We both know it. Now I know your worst secrets and you know mine. Isn't that what you've always wanted? For us to be completely honest with each other?

I sense he's torn, that he's weighing the decision in his mind, that he doesn't want to lose what we have.

You're quite mad, Emma, he says at last. You're fantasising. None of that happened. You should go back to London now.

Now: Jane

There are several reasons why I go back to see Carol Younson again.

'First,' I tell her, 'you and Simon are the only people Emma seems to have shared her fears of Edward Monkford with. Yet I now have proof that on at least one occasion, she effectively told lies to you, her own therapist. Second, you're the only person she spoke to who has a psychological background. I'm hoping you might be able to shed some light on her personality.'

I don't tell her the third reason yet.

She frowns. 'What lies?'

I tell her what I've learned – about Saul, and how Emma gave him oral sex after getting drunk.

'If you accept that she lied about being raped by Deon Nelson,' I say, 'do you accept she might have lied about Edward too?'

She considers for a moment. 'People do lie to their therapists sometimes – whether because they're in denial, or from simple embarrassment, it happens. But if what you're saying is correct, Emma didn't just tell one lie – she constructed an entire fantasy world, an alternative reality.'

'Meaning what?'

'Well, it's not strictly my area. But the clinical term for that kind of pathological lying is "pseudologia fantastica". It's associated with low self-esteem, attention-seeking and a deep-seated desire to present yourself in a more favourable light.'

'Being raped is hardly favourable.'

'No, but it does make you special. Male pseudologues tend to claim they're royalty or ex-special forces. Female pseudologues are more likely to pretend to be survivors of some terrible illness or disaster. There was a notorious example a couple of years ago: a woman who claimed to be a 9/11 survivor, who was so convincing she actually ended up running the survivors' support group. It turned out she wasn't even in New York on 9/11.' She thinks for a moment. 'Funnily enough, I do recall Emma saying something once along the lines of "How would you react if I told you I'd made it all up?" Almost as if she was playing with the idea of confession.'

'Might she have killed herself when her lies caught up with her?'

'It's possible, I suppose. If she couldn't construct a new narrative and use it to paint herself as a victim – at least in her own eyes – she might well have experienced what's called "narcissistic mortification". In plain English, she might have felt so ashamed she'd rather die than face up to it.'

'In which case,' I say, 'Edward's off the hook.'

'Well, perhaps,' she says cautiously.

'Why only "perhaps"?'

'I can't diagnose Emma as a pseudologue posthumously, just to make the facts fit a convenient theory. It's equally possible she told one perfectly logical lie, then told another to cover it up, and then another. The same goes for Edward Monkford. Yes, based on what you've told me, it seems Emma was the real narcissist, not him. But there's no doubting he's an extreme controller. What happens when a controller comes up against someone who's out of control? The combination could be explosive.'

'But there were other people who had far better reasons to be angry with Emma than Edward,' I point out. 'Deon Nelson narrowly escaped being sent to prison. Saul Aksoy lost his job. Detective Inspector Clarke was forced to take early retirement.'

'Possibly,' she says. But she still doesn't sound entirely convinced. 'Now that I think about it, there's another reason why Emma might have lied to me.'

'What's that?'

'She might have used me as a kind of sounding board. A dress rehearsal, if you like, before she tried her story on someone else.'

'Who?' But then I realise who it must have been. 'The only other person she told that story about Edward to was Simon.'

'Why would she do that, if she really wanted to be with Edward?'

'Because Edward had rejected her.' I feel a surge of satisfaction – not just because I think I've finally worked out what was behind Emma's bizarre accusations about Edward, but because I sense I'm catching up with her at last, hot on her heels, matching her every twist and change of direction. 'It's the only answer that makes sense. Simon was all Emma had left. So of course she told him it was her who'd broken up with Edward, when actually it was the other way round. Can I use your loo?'

Carol looks surprised, but directs me to a toilet.

'There's another reason I'm here today,' I say when I return. 'The most important one. I'm pregnant. It's Edward's.'

She stares at me, clearly shocked.

'And there's a chance – a very small chance, admittedly – it may have Down's syndrome,' I add. 'I'm waiting for the results of a test.'

She recovers quickly. 'And how do you feel about that, Jane?'

'Confused,' I admit. 'On the one hand, pleased to be pregnant. But on the other hand, terrified. And, on yet another hand, not sure when and what I should be telling Edward.'

'Well, let's start by unpicking those. Are you only pleased to be pregnant? Or has it renewed your grief for Isabel?'

'Both. Having another child feels so . . . final. As if I'm leaving her behind, somehow.'

'You're worried the new baby will replace her in your thoughts,' Carol says gently. 'And since your thoughts are the only place where Isabel now lives, you feel as if you're killing her all over again.'

I stare at her. 'Yes. That's it exactly.' Carol Younson, I realise, is a very good therapist indeed.

'Last time we met, we talked about repetition compulsion – the way some people get stuck in the past, acting out the same psychodrama again and again. But we're also given opportunities to break out of those cycles and move on.' Carol smiles. 'People like to talk about clean slates. But the only truly clean slate is a brand new one. The rest are grey from whatever's been written on them before. Perhaps this will be your chance for a truly new slate, Jane.'

'I'm worried I won't love this one as much,' I confess.

'That's understandable. The dead can seem impossibly perfect to us – an ideal no real person can ever live up to. Moving on from that isn't easy. But it can be done.'

307

I consider her words. They don't apply just to me, I realise, but to Edward, too. Elizabeth was his Isabel: the perfect, lost forerunner from whom he can never break free.

Carol and I talk for another forty minutes – about the pregnancy, about Down's, about the terrible, painful subject of termination. And by the end of it, I'm clear in my own mind what I'm going to do.

If the test does turn out to be positive, I'm going to terminate. It isn't an easy or a straightforward decision, and I'll bear the guilt of it for the rest of my life, but there it is.

And I won't tell Edward. He'll never even know I was pregnant. Some people might consider that moral cowardice. I just can't see the point of telling him there was a baby if there isn't any more.

If the test is negative, though, and the baby's all right – which, as both Dr Gifford and Carol have been at pains to point out, is still by far the most likely outcome – I'll go down to Cornwall straight away and tell Edward in person that he's going to be a father.

I'm just saying goodbye to Carol when my mobile rings.

'Is that Jane Cavendish?'

'Yes, speaking.'

'It's Karen Powers from the Foetal Testing Centre.'

I manage to reply, but my head's already swimming.

'I have the results of your cfDNA test here,' she continues. 'Is now a good time to discuss them?'

I'd been standing up, but now I sit down again. 'Yes. Please. Go ahead.'

'Can you give me the first line of your address?'

Impatiently, I go through the confidentiality preliminaries.

Carol has by now worked out who's calling and is also sitting down.

'I'm very pleased to tell you . . .' Karen Powers begins, and my heart soars. Good news. It's good news.

I start crying again and she has to repeat the results. They're negative. While only amniocentesis is an absolute guarantee, cfDNA is considerably more than 99 per cent accurate. There's no reason to think my baby will be anything other than healthy. I'm back on track. Now I just have to break the news to Edward.

Then: Emma

What follows is like the feeling after someone dies. I'm stunned and numb. It's not just losing Edward, it's the cold, almost clinical way he did it. One week I was his perfect woman, the next it was all over. From adoration to contempt in the blink of an eye. A part of me thinks he's refusing to admit how much he's into me, that he'll call any minute and say he's made a terrible mistake. But then I remember that Edward isn't Simon. I look at the pure, pristine walls, the uncompromising surfaces of One Folgate Street, and I can see his strength of will, his bloody-minded determination, in every square inch.

I stop eating. It makes me feel better, the hunger like a welcome old friend, the light-headedness an anaesthetic against the sense of loss.

I clutch Slob and use him as a tissue, teddy, comforter. Upset by my neediness, he struggles free and stalks upstairs, only for me to retrieve him from my bed when I crave the warmth of his soft fur.

When he goes missing I'm frantic with worry. Then I see that the door to the cleaner's cupboard is ajar. Sure enough, I find him in there, curled up on a can of polish in the dark, hiding from me.

That evening, while I'm having a shower, the lights suddenly go off and the water runs cold. It only lasts a few seconds, but it's long enough for me to yelp with alarm and fear. Maybe Slob just dislodged one of the cables inside the cupboard. But it feels more like the house itself is doing this: One Folgate Street turning cold on me just as Edward did, showing its master's displeasure.

Then the water flows hot again. It's just an outage, a momentary glitch. Nothing to get worked up about.

I let my head rest against the smooth wall of the shower, my tears tumbling with the water towards the drain.

Now: Jane

I return from my visit to Carol energised and happy. A corner has been turned. The future won't be easy, but at least it's clear.

As I walk into One Folgate Street I stop dead. By the stairs is a Swaine Adeney leather holdall.

'Edward?' I say tentatively.

He's in the refectory, staring at my mind map, the riot of Post-it notes plastered across the wall. In the middle, I've stuck the sketch: the double vision of me/Emma I retrieved from the recycling bin.

He turns his head towards me and I flinch from the icy anger of his gaze. 'I can explain,' I say quickly. 'I had to get things straight—'

'*Murdered – Edward Monkford*,' he says softly. 'Nice to see I'm only one of the suspects, Jane.'

'I know you didn't do it. I've just come from Emma's therapist. Emma lied to her and I think I understand why now. And I think I know why Emma killed herself.' I hesitate. 'She did it to punish you. A final, dramatic gesture to make you feel bad about breaking up with her. And I imagine, given what you'd already been through, that she succeeded.'

'I loved Emma.' The words, so flat and final, explode into

the air. 'But she lied to me. I thought perhaps I could have the love without the lies. With you, I mean. Do you remember your application letter? How you talked about integrity and honesty and trust? That was what made me think it might work, that it might be better this time. But I've never loved you the way I loved her.'

I stare at him, shocked.

'Why are you here?' I manage to say. I know it's hardly relevant, but I need time to process what he's just said.

'I had to come up to London to see the lawyers. The first resi- dents have moved in at New Austell, but they're being difficult. They seem to think if they get together, they can force me to change the rules. I'm going to serve them with eviction orders. All of them.' He shrugs. 'I brought us supper.'

On the counter are half a dozen paper bags from the kind of old-fashioned grocers Edward favours.

'It's actually a good thing you're here,' I say numbly. 'We need to talk.'

'Clearly.' His eyes go back to the mind map.

'Edward, I'm pregnant.' I say the words flatly, to a man who's just told me he doesn't love me. In my worst dreams, this isn't how I imagined it. 'You have a right to know.'

'Yes,' he says at last. 'How long have you been hiding this from me?'

It's tempting to lie, but I refuse to give myself that cop-out. 'I'm just over twelve weeks.'

'Do you intend to keep it?'

'They thought he might have Down's syndrome.' At this, Edward runs his hand over his face. 'Anyway, it turns out he doesn't. Yes, I am going to keep it. Him. I'm going to keep *him*. I know it's not what you'd choose, but there it is.'

He closes his eyes briefly, as if in pain.

'I assume, given what you've just said, that you don't want to be his father in any practical sense,' I go on. 'That's fine. I don't want anything from you, Edward. If you'd only told me you were still in love with Emma—'

'You don't understand,' he interrupts. 'It was like an illness. I hated myself every second I was with her.'

I don't know how to respond to that. 'The therapist I saw today . . . She talked about how we can get stuck inside a story, trying to re-enact our old relationships. I think somehow you're still stuck inside Emma's story. I can't help you get out of it. But I won't get stuck in there with you.'

He looks up at the walls, at the perfect, sterile spaces he's created. He seems to draw strength from them.

He says, 'Goodbye, Jane.' He picks up the Swaine Adeney bag and leaves.

11. Which relationship problem do you fear most?

☐ Getting bored

☐ Realising you could do better

☐ Growing apart

☐ Your partner becoming dependent on you

☐ Being deceived

Then: Emma

Sometimes it's as if I can shrink away to nothing. Sometimes I feel as pure and perfect as a ghost. The hunger, the headaches, the dizziness – these are the only things that are real.

Being good at not eating is the proof I'm still powerful. Sometimes I'm not so good and gobble a whole loaf of bread or a tub of coleslaw, but then I force my fingers down my throat and bring it up again. I can start over. Wipe the calorie slate clean.

I'm not sleeping. The same thing happened last time my eating disorder was bad. But this is worse. I wake abruptly in the night, convinced the house lights have flicked on and off or that I've heard someone moving about. After that, getting back to sleep is impossible.

I go to Carol and tell her that Edward is a vicious, bullying egomaniac. I tell her that he brutalises me, that he's controlling and obsessive and that's why I've left him. But although I want to believe what I'm telling her, longing for him permeates every cell of my body.

When I come back from seeing her, I notice something in the garden, what looks like a rag or a discarded toy. It takes my brain several moments to work out what it is and then I'm outside, hurrying across the pristine gravel.

Slob. At the front, he's upright, but the back half is lying sideways. He's dead. His left side has been staved in, a mess of bloodied fur. He looks as if he dragged himself here, away from the house, before collapsing. I look around. There's nothing to explain how he died. Hit by a car? Stamped on and then thrown over the fence? Or even trapped against the house and battered with a brick?

You poor thing, I say aloud, crouching down to stroke the side that isn't damaged. My tears fall on to his silky fur, so still and unresponsive now. You poor, poor thing. I say it to him, but really I mean me.

And then it hits me that this, just as much as the paint flung against the wall, is a message. *You're next.* Whoever is doing this wants me frightened as well as dead. And now I'm all alone, with no way of stopping them.

Except for Simon. I can still try Simon. There's no one else left.

Now: Jane

So here I am, come full circle. A bump and no man. Mia doesn't say, 'I told you so.' But I know she's thinking it.

There's one last piece of housekeeping I need to take care of. Edward might not have been interested in what I found out about Emma, but I think Simon deserves to know. I ask Mia to be there too, in case he takes it badly.

He arrives punctually, bringing a bottle of wine and a thick blue folder. 'I haven't been inside this place since it happened,' he says, looking around at the interior of One Folgate Street. 'I never liked it. I told Emma I did, but really it was her who wanted to live here. Even the tech stuff turned out to be less impressive than it first seemed. It was always going wrong.'

'Really?' I'm surprised. 'I haven't had any problems.'

He puts the folder on the counter. 'I brought you this. It's a copy of my research on Edward Monkford.'

'Thank you. But I don't need it now.'

He frowns. 'I thought you wanted to find out how Emma died.'

'Simon . . .' I make eye contact with Mia, who tactfully takes the wine away to open it. 'Emma lied about Edward. I can't be sure why, just as I can't be sure about the exact circumstances of her death. But there's no doubt that what she told you about him was wrong.' I leave a pause. 'She'd been caught out in another, bigger lie as well. It wasn't the burglar, Deon Nelson, in that video the police found on her phone. It was Saul Aksoy.'

'I know that,' he says angrily. 'That's got nothing to do with it.'

It takes me a moment to work out how he knows. 'Oh – Amanda told you.'

He shakes his head. 'Emma did. After she broke up with Edward, she told me everything.'

'Did she tell you how it happened?'

'Yes. Saul drugged her and forced himself on her.' He sees my expression. 'What? You've been playing detective and you didn't know that?'

'I spoke to Saul,' I say slowly. 'He told me it was Emma who initiated it.'

Simon snorts derisively. 'Well, he would, wouldn't he? I used to like Saul, but even before Emma told me what he'd done I knew there was a different side to him. We used to go out drinking sometimes after Em and I split up. He told Amanda I needed company, but the truth was he just wanted a free pass to go out on the pull. He always used the same technique. "Get them legless," he used to say. "What you want them for, you don't need the legs."'

I must look shocked, because he nods. 'Nice joke, right? But even then, I thought it was odd *how* drunk some of the girls got on just a couple of glasses. He makes a big thing of buying them champagne. It makes him look flash, but I read that the bubbles can also mask the taste of roofies.'

I stare at him. I'm remembering Saul Aksoy trying to press a glass of champagne on me. I'd thought he was a creep, but even so, I'd taken everything he'd told me at face value.

Just when I thought I had everything clear, it's spinning away from me again. Because if Saul did force himself on Emma, she wasn't a fantasist at all. She told a lie, certainly – perhaps several lies – but the essence of her story was true. She'd just shifted around the names of the actors, for reasons I can probably guess at.

As if reading my thoughts, Simon says, 'She was trying to protect me. She thought I wouldn't be able to handle knowing it was my best mate who'd done that to her. But even before the burglary I could tell something was wrong – she started getting angry with me for no reason, going off on one whenever I tried to be nice to her. And her eating disorder came back. It never really went away after that, although she didn't like to talk about it.'

'You spoke to her here?' I say, trying to get my head round all this new information.

He nods. 'She'd realised what a stupid mistake she'd made and she wanted to put things right. She was in a really bad way by then. There was a kitten – some stray she'd taken in. Someone had killed it.'

'A kitten?' I repeat. 'Here, in One Folgate Street?' Maggie Evans had mentioned a stray, but not that Emma had planned on keeping it.

'That's right. Why?'

Because it's against the rules, I think. No pets. And no children, for that matter.

Simon opens the folder and takes out a document. 'A solicitor gave her this. According to these plans, Monkford buried his wife and son here, right under this house. Look.' He shows me. There's an X and a handwritten notation, *Final resting place of Mrs Elizabeth Domenica Monkford and Maximilian Monkford*. 'What sort of weirdo does that?'

'You've had a lucky escape, J.' That's Mia, who has gradually been drawn back, ears flapping. I see Simon shoot me a curious look, but I choose not to explain.

'Emma's theory was that it was all part of some superstitious ritual,' he goes on. 'Almost like a sacrifice. I didn't think much of it at the time, but after she died I started looking at his other buildings. It turns out she was right. Someone has died in suspicious circumstances every time a Monkford Partnership building nears completion.'

He takes out some newspaper cuttings and lays them on the table for me to look at. Each is clipped to a map marking the location of the building and the location of the death. In Scotland, a young woman was killed by a hit-and-run driver a mile from the house Edward Monkford built near Inverness. In Menorca, a child was stolen from his parents two miles from the beach house Edward designed. In Bruges, a woman apparently threw herself off a railway bridge a few hundred metres from his chapel. During the fitting out of the Hive, an electrician's apprentice was found dead in a stairwell.

'But none of this even begins to prove he was responsible for those deaths,' I say gently. 'There are thousands of fatal accidents and disappearances every year. That some of them happened within a few miles of these particular buildings means nothing. You're seeing patterns and connections that aren't there.'

'Or there *is* a connection, and you're refusing to see it.' Simon's face is dark.

'Simon, the only thing this proves is how much you loved Emma. And that's admirable. But it's colouring your judgement—'

'Emma was taken from me twice,' he interrupts. 'Once when Edward Monkford muscled in on our relationship just when she was at her most vulnerable. And then a second time, when she was murdered. I'm certain that was to prevent me from having her. I want justice for Emma. And I won't stop till I get it.'

He goes soon after, leaving Mia still drinking his wine. 'He seems nice,' she comments.

'And somewhat obsessive?'

'He loved her. He can't let her go until he's found out what happened to her. That's almost heroic, isn't it?'

All these men who loved Emma, I think. For all her problems, men were fixated on her. Will anyone ever feel like that about me?

'Not that being loved did her much good in the end,' Mia adds. 'But for what it's worth, I think you'd be far better off with someone like him than with your crazy architect.'

'Me? With Simon?' I snort. 'Hardly.'

'He's solid and dependable and loyal. Don't knock it till you've tried it.'

I say nothing. My feelings about Edward are still too complicated to parcel up into a neat sentence or two for Mia's inspection. His cold contempt has made me feel vaguely ashamed of myself for ferreting away into Emma's death behind his back. But if he

323

could find a way to free himself from her, would he perhaps be able to see the situation with me more clearly?

I shake my head, as much in disagreement with myself as to get my mind empty of these thoughts. Wishful thinking.

Then: Emma

Bye then, Em, he says.

Bye, Si, I say.

Despite what he's just said, Simon lingers a bit longer at the door of One Folgate Street. I'm really glad we talked, he says.

Me too, I say. And I mean it. There are too many things I never said to him, too many things I kept locked up inside my head. Perhaps if we'd talked more when we were together, we might not have split up. There was a part of me that always wanted to kick Simon or push him away and I don't feel that any more. Now I'm just grateful for someone who doesn't judge me.

I'll stay if you want, he offers. If it makes you feel safer. If this Deon Nelson or whoever shows up, I can take care of him.

I know you can, I say. But honestly, you don't need to. This house is built like a fortress. Besides, one step at a time, yes?

OK, he says. He leans forward and kisses me, a little formally, on the cheek. Then he gives me a hug. The hug is nice.

When he's gone the house is silent again. I've promised him I'll eat something. I fill up a pan with water to boil an egg and wave my hand over the cooker.

Nothing happens.

I wave again. Same result. I look under the counter to see if there's some kind of override for the motion sensor. But there isn't.

Simon would know how to fix it and I almost reach for my phone to call him back. Then I stop myself. Being a frail female who depended on men to sort her problems out was partly what got me into this mess.

There are a couple of apples in the fridge so I get one of those instead. I'm just biting into it when I smell gas. Even though the cooker didn't light, the part that makes the gas come out is clearly working and now it's gushing its explosive fumes into the house. I look for a way to turn it off, waving my arms frantically over the counter. Suddenly there's a *click* and a ball of flame shoots into the air, blue and yellow, engulfing my arm. I drop the apple. There's a moment of shock – no pain yet, but I know that will come. Quickly I push my arm under the cold tap. It doesn't come on. I run upstairs to the bathroom. There, thank goodness, the water does work, cold on my burning skin. I let it run for a few minutes, then examine my arm. It's sore and red but the skin hasn't blistered.

This is not my imagination. It can't be. It's like the house didn't want Simon to come round for our talk and this is its way of punishing me.

It's a fortress, I'd said to Simon. But what if the house itself decides not to protect me? How safe am I really?

Suddenly I'm scared.

I go into the cleaner's cupboard and shut the door behind me. I could barricade myself in here if need be – the mops and brooms could be wedged against the door to keep it shut; from the outside, you wouldn't even know I was here. It's cramped, cluttered with tins and equipment, but I need a safe place and this is going to be it.

12. In a well-run society, there have to be consequences for those who break the rules.

    Agree ☐ ☐ ☐ ☐ ☐ Disagree

Now: Jane

I'm lying in bed, half asleep, when I feel it. As tentative and hesitant as a tap on the door, barely more than a flutter in my belly. I recognise it from Isabel. *The quickening.* Such a beautiful, biblical term.

I lie there, enjoying it, waiting for more kicks. A few come, then a tumbling movement that might or might not be a somersault. Maternal love and wonder wash over me, so much so that I start to cry. How could I ever have considered aborting this child? Looking back, it seems almost inconceivable. I smile through my tears at the pun.

Wide awake now, I swing my legs out of bed, looking down at my changing body. I'm still not at the stage where strangers make unprompted remarks – according to a chart I found at work, my baby is now roughly the size of an avocado – but naked, you couldn't miss that I'm pregnant. My breasts sag low and full, and my belly has taken on a comfortable roundness.

I walk towards the bathroom, amused to see I'm waddling slightly even though I surely don't need to yet – the muscle memory of motherhood settling around my body like a familiar coat. Something goes wrong with the shower – the warm water suddenly turns icy – but it's invigorating. Idly, I wonder if the house is having trouble recognising me now that I've got another person inside me. I don't think technology works like that, but I really don't know much about it.

I'm towelling myself dry when I feel a twinge of nausea. I sit down on the toilet seat, trying to breathe it away, but it comes back twice as bad. There's no time to do anything but plunge forward and aim my mouth in the direction of the shower. I turn on the taps to wash the vomit away.

The glass round the shower is flecked with water marks now, so I get down on my knees to polish it. I'm crouching down to clean the notch that runs along the base of the wall, my face almost at floor level, when I see something glint in there, catching the light. It's too far back for my fingers to reach, so I find a cotton bud and carefully prise it out.

At first I think I've just found a piece of grit, or perhaps a ball bearing. Then I see the tiny hole running through it. It's a pearl – quite small, an unusual pale cream colour. It must have come off my necklace.

I go to the bedroom and find the necklace in its case. The loose pearl looks the same as all the others, certainly. But the necklace isn't broken.

I can't see how the pearl escaped if the string isn't broken. It's impossible, like a logic puzzle, a riddle.

There's a jeweller's opposite Still Hope's offices. I decide to take it there and ask.

Then: Emma

I email the Monkford Partnership to complain about the problems with the house. There's no reply. I try phoning Mark, the letting agent, but he tells me anything technical should be referred direct to the Monkford Partnership. I end up shouting at him down the phone, which I suspect only makes things worse. I even text Edward. Of course he doesn't respond.

On top of everything else, I'm convinced the lighting has changed. When we moved in Mark said the house automatically added extra light to counter winter depression. If so, can it do the reverse? Not only am I not sleeping properly, I'm waking with dry, itchy eyes, feeling exhausted.

Simon phones and repeats his offer to come round. It would be so easy to say yes. I tell him I'll think about it. I can hear the elation in his voice, though he tries to hide it. Nice, safe, reliable Simon. My harbour in a storm.

And then Edward Monkford texts me back.

Now: Jane

'It's exceptional,' the jeweller says, rolling the pearl between finger and thumb as he examines it through an eyepiece. 'If it's what I think it is, it's very rare indeed.'

I produce the necklace in its clam case. 'Could it have come from this?'

He takes the case and nods approvingly at the Japanese characters. 'Kokichi Mikimoto. You don't see these very often.' Lifting out the necklace, he holds it up to the light and compares it with the loose one. 'Yes, it's a definite match. As I thought, they're keshi pearls.'

'"Keshi pearls"? What does that mean?'

'Saltwater keshi are the rarest pearls of all, particularly when they're almost round, like these. They come from oysters that had more than one pearl – twins, in other words. Because they have no nucleus, they acquire this unusual, glowing lustre. And, as I said, extremely rare. At some point, I imagine, the necklace snapped and the pearls came off. The owner had it restrung, but he or she missed one.'

'I see.' At least, I understand what the man's saying. But the implication – that Edward gave me a necklace he'd previously given to someone else – is going to take rather more digesting.

As I leave the shop, I reach for my mobile.

'Simon,' I say when he answers, 'do you happen to know if Edward Monkford gave Emma a pearl necklace? And if so, whether it ever got broken?'

Then: Emma

I need to see you. Edward.

I consider my reply before answering. *Are you still angry with me, Daddy?*

The response is swift. *No more than you deserve.*

Good. Does this mean you want me back?

We'll see after tonight.

Then I'd better be on my best behaviour. Already I'm weak at the knees.

7 p.m. Wear the pearls. Not much else.

Of course.

Two hours to get ready, to anticipate, to endure. I take my clothes off and get to work.

Now: Jane

'But don't you see?' Simon says urgently. 'This proves he was there when Emma died.'

We're sitting in the coffee shop, close to Still Hope, where Edward Monkford first made a pass at me. *Two people coming together with no agenda other than the present.* What a monstrous lie that turned out to be. No doubt he meant it at the time – thinking he could recapture just the parts of the relationship with Emma he liked, without the bits he didn't. But as Carol pointed out, you can't tell the same story twice and expect a different ending.

Simon's still speaking. 'Sorry,' I say. 'What was that?'

'I said, she only wore that necklace for him – she knew I hated it. She was meant to be seeing me that day. We'd half-made an arrangement. But then she cancelled. She said she wasn't feeling well. Even at the time, I wondered if she was actually seeing Monkford.'

I frown. 'You really can't read all that into a single pearl. It doesn't prove anything.'

'Think about it,' he says patiently. 'How did Monkford get hold of the necklace to give it to you? He must have been there when it got broken. But he knew if he left pearls scattered all over the floor it would look like a struggle, not suicide or an accident. So he cleared them up before he left – all except the one you found.'

'But she didn't die in the bathroom,' I object. 'She was found at the bottom of the stairs.'

'It's only a few steps from the bathroom to the stairs. He could easily have dragged her there and pushed her down.'

I don't believe Simon's overwrought suggestion for one minute, but even I have to admit that the pearl might be considered evidence. 'All right. I'll get hold of James Clarke – I know he comes into town on Wednesdays. You might as well come along too. Then you can hear him dismiss your theories at first hand.'

'Jane . . . would you like me to come and stay at One Folgate Street for a few days?' I must look surprised, because he adds, 'I offered to stay with Emma. She didn't want me to and I didn't like to push it. I'll always regret not having been more insistent. If I'd only been there . . .' He leaves the sentence hanging.

'Thank you, Simon. But we still can't even be sure Emma was murdered.'

'Every tiny piece of evidence points to the fact that Monkford killed her. You're refusing to admit it for reasons of your own. And I think we both know what they are.' His gaze goes down to my belly. I flush.

'*You've* got emotional reasons for wanting him to be guilty,' I counter. 'And for the record, Edward and I had a brief relationship, that's all. We're no longer together.'

He smiles, a little sadly. 'Of course not. You've broken the biggest rule of all. Just remember what happened to the cat.'

Then: Emma

I've tweaked and tweezed, depilated and buffed. Finally I put on the pearl necklace, tight against my throat like a lover's hand. My heart sings. Waves of anticipation wash over me.

There's still an hour before he gets here. I pour a large glass of wine and drink most of it. Then, still wearing the necklace, I head towards the shower.

There's a sound from downstairs. It's hard to identify, but it might be the squeak of a shoe. I stop.

Hello? Anyone there?

There's no reply. I grab a towel and go to the top of the stairs. Edward?

The silence drags on, thick and somehow meaningful. I feel the hairs on the back of my neck prickling. Hello? I say again.

I tiptoe halfway down the stairs. From there I can see into every corner of the house. There's no one here.

Unless they're directly below me, I think, hidden by the slabs of stone. I turn backwards, taking one step at a time, peering through the gaps.

No one.

Then I hear another sound, a kind of snort. It seems to come from above me this time. But as I turn towards it I become aware of a high-pitched whine – a frequency right at the edge of human hearing. It gets louder and louder, like a mosquito. I put my hands over my ears, but the noise penetrates right into my skull.

A light bulb pops in the ceiling, the glass blowing out and tinkling to the floor. The noise stops. In the living area, my laptop's rebooting. The house lights slowly fade down to nothing and then up again. Housekeeper's homepage appears on my laptop screen. It's as if the whole house has just reset itself.

Some malfunction of the house's technical systems, I decide. Whatever the glitch was, it's over now. And there's no one here. I pad back upstairs towards the shower.

Now: Jane

'Well, this is fascinating,' James Clarke says, looking from the necklace to the single pearl and back. 'Fascinating.'

'We can't decide what it means,' I say. Simon shoots me a look and I add, 'That is, we're split. Simon thinks it could be evidence that Edward killed her. I can't see how it makes any difference either way.'

'I'll tell you what it does make a difference to,' the retired policeman says thoughtfully. 'The case against Deon Nelson. If there was a pearl necklace lying around, broken or not, he wouldn't have left it there. He'd have taken it, in which case it wouldn't have been possible for Mr Monkford to restring it as a gift to you. So there's *my* pet theory out of the window.'

'Last time we met,' Simon says, 'after the inquest, you told me Monkford had an alibi.'

'Yes. Well, an alibi of sorts. To be honest, you seemed like you were going to have a hard time letting it go. And with a six-month police investigation finally tied up, the last thing we wanted was a heartbroken ex-boyfriend trying to get the coroner's verdict overturned. So I might have sounded more certain than I actually was. Mr Monkford said he was on site in Cornwall at the time of Emma's death. He was seen at his hotel in the morning and again in the early evening. There was nothing to indicate that he'd come back to London in between, so we were inclined to believe him.'

Simon stares at him. 'But you're saying he could have done it.'

'A million people *could* have done it,' Clarke says gently. 'That's not how we work. We look for signs someone *did* do it.'

'Monkford's mad,' Simon says urgently. 'Christ, just look at the houses he builds. He's a total perfectionist and if he thinks something isn't quite right, he doesn't just leave it. He destroys it and starts again. He told Emma that once in so many words – "This relationship will continue only for as long as it's absolutely perfect." What kind of person says that?'

Clarke replies, patiently explaining to Simon that amateur psychology and police work are two very different things. But I'm hardly listening.

Edward said the same thing to me, I realise. *This is perfect . . . Some of the most perfect relationships I've had lasted no more than a week . . . You appreciate the other person more, knowing it's not going to last . . .*

My baby puts out a foot and kicks me, just above the navel. I shudder. Are we in danger?

'Jane?'

They're looking at me curiously. I realise I've been asked a question. 'Sorry?'

James Clarke holds up the necklace. 'Could you put this on for us?'

The tiny clasp at the back is awkward to fasten blind and Simon jumps up to help. I hold my hair away from my neck so he can get at it. His fingers are clumsy as he touches me and I sense – to my surprise – that it might be because he's attracted to me.

When the necklace is on, Clarke examines it thoughtfully. 'May I?' he says politely. I nod, and he tries to slip a finger between the pearls and my skin. There isn't room.

'Hmm,' he says, sitting back. 'Well, I don't want to pour petrol on the fire, so to speak. But there is one thing that may be relevant.'

'What?' Simon says eagerly.

'When Emma was found, the first officer on the scene thought he saw a faint mark round her neck. He made a note of it, but by the time the pathologist arrived it had faded. There were just a couple of small scratches, here.' He points to where he tried to get his finger under the necklace. 'It was nothing, really – certainly not enough to kill her. And given the extent of her other injuries, we decided she was probably just flailing about as she fell.'

'But actually it was where someone had pulled the necklace off,' Simon says immediately.

'Well, that's your supposition,' Clarke says.

'There is another possibility,' I hear myself say.

'Yes?' Clarke says.

'Edward . . .' I find myself blushing. 'I have reason to think he and Emma liked rough sex.'

Simon stares at me. Clarke only nods. 'Indeed.'

'So if Edward *was* with her that day – which I still don't necessarily accept, by the way – it may just have been an accident that the necklace got broken.'

'Perhaps. I suppose we'll never know now,' Clarke says.

Something else occurs to me. 'Last time we met, you said there was no way of telling who'd entered the house immediately before Emma's death.'

'That's right. Why?'

'It just seems strange to me, that's all. The house is set up to capture and record data – that's the whole point of it.'

'You could raid their offices,' Simon says immediately. 'Take away their computers and see what's on them.'

Clarke holds up a warning hand. 'Hang on. *I* can't do anything, being retired. And what you're describing is an operation that would cost tens of thousands of pounds. It's highly unlikely you'd get a warrant after so long. Not without very strong corroborating evidence.'

Simon smacks his fist down on to the table. 'This is hopeless!'

'My advice to you is to try to put it behind you,' Clarke says gently. He looks at me. 'And my advice to *you* is to hurry up and find somewhere else to live. Somewhere with good locks and an alarm system. Just in case.'

Then: Emma

I step under the shower. For a moment nothing happens. Then water cascades like rain from the massive showerhead. I lift my face to it, exultant.

Everything's going to be all right.

I wash myself carefully for him, soaping all the intimate corners of my body that he might want to explore. Then, without warning, the water stutters and turns icy. I shriek and back away.

Emma, a voice says behind me.

I whirl round. What are you doing here? I say. I grab the towel off the rail and wrap it round me. And how did you get in?

Now: Jane

'Your budget is how much?' Camilla doesn't actually laugh, but she clearly thinks I'm deluded. 'While you've been at One Folgate Street, the rental market's gone crazy. Not enough houses, plus foreign investors piling into London property as a safe haven for their cash. You'd have to double that to get a two-bed now.' She gestures at the particulars in the agency's windows. 'Take a look.'

On the way back to One Folgate Street, I'd decided to take James Clarke's advice and start flat-hunting. Now, I rather wish I hadn't. 'A large one-bed would do. For the time being, anyway.'

'And you don't even have the budget for *that*. Unless you'd consider a houseboat?'

'I'm going to have a baby. Soon to be a toddler. I don't think a houseboat's a great solution, do you?' I hesitate. 'Are there other landlords who do what Edward does? Renting houses cheap to people who'll look after them?'

She shakes her head. 'The deal with Edward Monkford is unique.'

'Well, he can't evict me while I'm still paying the rent. And I'm not leaving until I've found somewhere else.' Something in Camilla's expression makes me stop. 'What?'

'There are over two hundred rules in that agreement you

signed,' she reminds me. 'I just hope you haven't broken any. Otherwise, you'll be in breach of contract.'

I feel an irrational burst of anger. 'Screw his rules. And screw Edward Monkford.' I'm so furious, I actually stamp my foot. Mother tiger hormones.

But for all my brave words, I know I won't fight Edward on this. Since the conversation with Simon and James Clarke, I'm starting to feel something about One Folgate Street I've never felt before. I'm starting to feel scared.

Then: Emma

I kept the keycode, he says.

He takes a step towards me. His eyes are red and slightly wild. He's been crying.

I told the estate agent I deleted it when I moved out, he says. But I didn't. Then I used it to hack the system here. It was easy. A child could have done it.

Oh, I say. I don't know what else to say.

I've been upstairs, he says. In the attic. I come in after you're asleep sometimes and sleep up there. So I can be near you.

He points suddenly at my throat and I step back, frightened. That's the necklace *he* gave you, isn't it? *Edward*.

Yes. Simon, you've got to go. I'm expecting someone.

I know. Simon pulls out a phone. Edward Monkford. Except you're not. *I* sent that message.

What? I say, bewildered.

I took your phone one night last week and put this number on your contacts under his name, he says, almost proudly. So when I text you, it looks like it's from him. I've deleted the messages now, of course. And this is a pay-as-you-go phone, so it can't be traced.

But . . . *why?*

Why? he repeats. Why? That's what I keep asking myself, Em. Why Monkford? Why Saul? Why any of them? None of them loved you the way I did. And you loved me back. I know you did. We were *happy*.

No. No, Simon, I say as firmly as I can. We wouldn't have been happy, not in the long run. I'm not right for you. You need someone kind and nice. Not someone like me.

Don't say that, Em. There are tears streaking his cheeks now. Don't, he repeats. I won't let you.

I try to take charge of the situation. You have to go, Simon. Right now. Or I'm calling the police.

He shakes his head. I can't do it, Em. Can't do it.

Can't do what?

Can't let it go, he whispers. Can't let you be that person who wants them but not me.

He looks at me with a strange, desperate expression and I realise he's steeling himself to do something awful. I make a sudden dash for it, trying to slip past him. He grabs my wrist, but his hand closes round my bangle which slides off and I'm free. But then he's blocking me with his body, his fingers scrabbling at my neck, at the necklace. I feel it snap, pearls bouncing like hail across the bathroom floor. He gets one arm round my neck, yanking me towards him, pulling me backwards out of the bathroom like a lifeguard in a pool. I'm rigid with fear but I have no option but to let him drag me with him.

Simon, I try to say, but his arm is too tight round my neck. And then we're at the top of the stairs and he twists me round so I'm facing down into the void. I love you, Em, he says into my ear. I love you. But he says it with a kind of fury, as if by *love* he really means *hate*, and as he simultaneously kisses me and pushes me away I know he means this to happen, that he wants me to die. Then I'm tumbling, my head cracking on the stone, stair after stair, pain and panic battering every part of me as my body gathers speed. Halfway down, I fall off the staircase and there's a moment of blessed relief mixed with terror before the pale stone floor comes up to meet me and my head explodes.

Now: Jane

I call Simon.

'I'm not in the habit of asking men I hardly know to dinner,' I tell him. 'But if you really meant what you said, I'd appreciate the company.'

'Of course. Do you want me to bring anything?'

'Well, I don't have any wine in the house. I won't be drinking, but you might want some. I do have steaks. None of your supermarket rubbish – these are from the smart butcher on the High Street. I warn you, though – I'll eat yours as well as mine if you're late. My appetite's ferocious at the moment.'

'Good.' He sounds amused. 'I'll come at seven. And I promise not to go on about Monkford killing my girlfriend this time, OK?'

'Thanks.' I'd been going to suggest we didn't discuss Emma and Edward tonight – I'm spooked enough as it is – but I couldn't think of a tactful way of saying it. Simon is a very considerate person, I'm coming to realise. I remember what Mia said. *For what it's worth, I think you'd be far better off with someone like him than with your crazy architect.*

I put the thought out of my mind. Even if I wasn't fat and pregnant with another man's child, that wouldn't happen.

When I open the door to him a couple of hours later, I see he's brought flowers as well as a bottle of wine. 'For you,' he says, handing me the bouquet. 'I always felt bad about being so rude the first time we met. It was hardly your fault that you didn't know who those flowers were for.' He kisses me on the cheek, and the kiss lingers just a little longer than it needs to. He *is* attracted to me; I'm pretty sure of that. But I don't think I could ever be attracted to him, whatever Mia says.

'They're lovely,' I say, taking the flowers to the sink. 'I'll put them in water.'

'And I'll open this. It's Pinot Grigio – Emma's favourite. Are you sure you won't have any? I checked online. Most people think a small amount of alcohol is all right at around fifteen weeks.'

'Maybe later. But you go ahead.' I arrange the flowers in a vase and put them on the table.

'Em, where have you put the corkscrew?' he calls.

'It's in the cupboard. The one on the right.' I do a double take. 'Did you just call me *Em*?'

'Did I?' He laughs. 'Sorry – I guess it's just such a familiar thing, being here with you and opening a bottle. I mean, not with *you*, obviously. With her. I won't do it again, I promise. Now, where do you keep the glasses?'

Then: Emma

Now: Jane

It feels strange to be cooking steaks for a man – any man – in One Folgate Street. Edward could never have let me – he'd have to have taken charge, tied on an apron, found the right pans and oils and implements, all the while explaining the different way steaks are cooked in Tuscany or Tokyo. Simon, though, is content just to watch me and chat – about the housing market, where to look for cheap flats, the pros and cons of the place he's currently renting. 'One of the best things about leaving this house was not having to worry about those stupid rules anymore,' he says as I automatically wipe the pan and put it away before we eat. 'After a while, you can't believe you ever lived like this.'

'Hmm,' I say. I know I'll soon be surrounded by all the clutter of babyhood, but a part of me will always miss the austere, disciplined beauty of One Folgate Street.

I take a few sips of wine, but find I've rather lost the taste for it.

'How's your pregnancy going?' he asks, and I find myself telling him about the Down's scare, which in turn leads to explaining about Isabel, and then I start crying and can't finish my steak. 'I'm sorry,' he says quietly when I've finished. 'You've had a horrible time.'

I shrug and wipe my eyes. 'Everyone has problems, don't they? It's the hormones – they make me weep at anything right now.'

'I wanted a family with Emma.' He's silent for a moment. 'I was going to propose to her. I've never told anyone that. Ironically, it was moving here that made me decide – being settled at last. I knew she'd been going through a tough time, but I put that down to the burglary.'

'Why didn't you? Propose, I mean?'

'Oh . . .' He shrugs. 'I wanted to do the most amazing proposal ever. Like those virals where the man gets a flash mob to sing the girl's favourite song, or spells out *Will you marry me?* in fireworks or something. I was just trying to come up with an idea that would really blow her away. And then, out of the blue, she ended it.'

Personally, I've always found those videos of over-the-top proposals a bit weird, even creepy, but I decide now isn't the time to say so. 'You'll find someone else, Simon. I know you will.'

'Will I?' He gives me a significant look. 'It's quite rare I meet someone I feel I've made a real connection with, actually.'

I decide this has got to be said. 'Simon . . . I hope you don't think this is presumptuous of me, but since we're talking so openly, I just want to make something clear. I like you, but I'm definitely not looking for a relationship at the moment. I've got enough on my plate.'

'Of course,' he says quickly. 'I never thought . . . But we're in a good place, right? As friends.'

'Yes.' I smile at him to show I appreciate his tact.

'Although you'll probably change your mind about being in

a relationship if Edward Monkford snaps his fingers at you,' he adds.

I frown. 'I really won't.'

'Only joking. In fact, there *is* a girl I've been seeing a bit of. She lives in Paris. I'm thinking of moving over there so I can see more of her.'

The conversation passes on to other things, pleasant and easy. I've missed this, I think: this niceness, this civilised give and take, so different from Edward's dominating presence.

Later, he says, 'Would you like me to stay tonight, Jane? On the sofa, obviously. But if it would make you feel safer . . .'

'That's kind. But we'll be fine.' I pat my belly. 'Me and my bump.'

'Sure. Another time, perhaps.'

13. *There is often a large gap between my goals and my outcomes.*

   Agree ☐ ☐ ☐ ☐ ☐ *Disagree*

Now: Jane

I wake up tired and lethargic. Probably the tiny amount of alcohol from the night before, I decide, now I'm so unused to it. Morning sickness clutches at my guts and I retch into the toilet. And then, just when I'm desperate for a shower, Housekeeper chooses its moment to turn everything off.

Jane, please score the following statements on a scale of 1–5, where 1 is Strongly Agree and 5 is Strongly Disagree.

Some house facilities have been disabled until the assessment is completed.

'Bugger,' I say wearily. I really don't have the energy for this. But I need that shower. I look at the first statement on the list.

If my children weren't successful at school, I'd rightly be labelled a bad parent.
         Agree ☐ ☐ ☐ ☐ ☐ *Disagree*

I choose *Slightly Agree*, then stop dead. I'm fairly sure there's never been a metric about parenting before.

357

Are these questions random? Or is this something more: some kind of subtle, coded dig on Housekeeper's part?

As I go on through the questionnaire, I notice something else. I *feel* different. Just answering these questions reminds me that living here is a privilege reserved for a select few, that leaving will be almost as great a wrench as losing Isabel . . .

I catch myself, appalled. How can I think such a thing, even for a moment?

I remember what the lecturer said when he took round that group of students. *You probably aren't aware of it, but you're currently swimming in a complex soup of ultrasonics – mood-enhancing waveforms* . . .

Are Housekeeper's questions somehow part of how One Folgate Street works?

I connect to the neighbour's Wi-Fi and type some of the questions I've just answered into Google. Immediately, there's a match. A scientific paper in an obscure-sounding magazine, the *Journal of Clinical Psychology*.

The questions in the Perfectionism Assessment Tool measure a variety of types of pathological over-perfectionism, including Personal Perfectionism, High Standards for Others, Need for Approval, Planfulness (obsessive neatness and organisation), Ruminance (obsessive over-thinking), Compulsive Behaviour and Moral Inflexibility . . .

I skim through, trying to get my brain round the technical language. It seems the questions were originally designed by psychologists as a way to diagnose unhealthy, obsessive perfectionism so that it could be treated. Just for a moment I wonder if that's what's been happening here: if the house is simply monitoring my psychological wellbeing, just as it checks my sleep patterns, weight, and so on.

But then I realise there's another explanation.

Edward isn't using the questionnaire to treat his tenants' perfectionism, but to make certain of it – to bolster it, even. He's trying to control not just our surroundings or the way we live in them, but our innermost thoughts and feelings.

This relationship will continue only for as long as it's absolutely perfect . . .

I shiver. Was it a poor score on a psychometric test that sealed Emma's fate?

I finish the questions, ticking whatever answers I think Housekeeper will score me highest on. When I'm done, my laptop reboots and the lights come back on.

I stand up, relieved to be finally heading for the shower. But as I'm going up the stairs, there's a glitch. The lights flicker. My laptop freezes, mid reboot. Everything hangs for a bit. And then—

Looking downstairs, I see something appear on my screen. Like a movie. Except this isn't a movie.

Puzzled, I go back for a closer look. It's an image of me, a live image, here in this very room. As I get closer, the figure on the screen moves further away.

The camera's *behind* me.

Picking my laptop up, I turn round. Now the screen shows my face instead of the back of my head. I scan the wall in front of me until the screen tells me I'm looking straight at the lens.

Except there's nothing there. Perhaps a tiny pinprick in the pale stone, no more.

I put the laptop down and click the window to close it. Behind it is another window. And another, and another. All showing different areas of One Folgate Street. I close each one, though not before I've registered where the cameras are. One shows the stone table from a different angle. Another is pointed at the front door. The next shows the bathroom—

The bathroom. Open plan, the shower completely exposed. If these are One Folgate Street's sensors, who else has access to them?

I click again. The final camera is mounted directly above the bed.

I feel sick. All those times it felt as if I was being watched . . . it's because I was.

And not just in bed either. When Edward took me over the kitchen counter, we'd have been in full view.

I shudder, revolted. And then, in a sudden sluicing cascade of hormones, my revulsion turns to rage.

Edward did this. He built these cameras into the very fabric of One Folgate Street. Why? Was it some voyeuristic thing? Or just another way of owning every moment of my life? I'm pretty sure it's not even legal – I seem to remember reading about a man who got sent to prison for something like this.

But then I realise Edward wouldn't have left a detail like that to chance. I go through my old emails until I find one from Camilla with One Folgate Street's terms and conditions attached. Eventually, buried deep in the small print, I find it.

. . . including, but not limited to, photographic and moving images . . .

Something else strikes me. Edward built the house, but the person who designed the technology was his partner, David Thiel.

And while I might have a hard time picturing Edward as a high-tech peeping Tom, Thiel's another matter.

I don't give my anger a chance to dissipate. I go and get my coat.

Now: Jane

I don't bother with an appointment. I simply wait on the ground floor of the Hive until a group of Monkford Partnership employees clutching lattes and wraps gather round one of the lifts, and follow them in. At the fourteenth floor, I follow them out again.

'Edward isn't here,' the impeccable brunette on reception says when she gets over her surprise.

'It's David Thiel I want to talk to.'

Now she looks even more surprised. 'I'll see if he's free.' She has to look up his extension number on her iPad. I get the impression the technologist doesn't get many visitors.

My rant at David Thiel is long, loud and liberally laced with swear words. I barely draw breath, but he simply waits for me to finish. I'm reminded of the way Edward listened to that client, the first time I came here, letting the man's anger wash over him.

'This is ludicrous,' Thiel says calmly when I'm finally done. 'I think your condition must be causing you to overreact.'

He could hardly have said anything more calculated to set me off again. 'First, I'm not *ill*, you cretin. And second, don't you dare patronise me. I know what I saw. You've been spying on me and you can't deny it. It's even in the bloody terms and conditions.'

He shakes his head. 'We ask you to sign a disclaimer. But that's just to cover ourselves. No one accesses those camera feeds apart from the automatic face-recognition software. It's so the house can track your movements, that's all.'

'And the shower?' I demand. 'Going hot and cold, trying to freak me out? You're not telling me that's something to do with face recognition?'

He frowns. 'I wasn't aware of any problems with the shower.'

'And then there's the really important thing. What were those cameras doing when Emma was killed? They must have recorded what happened.'

He hesitates. 'The FR feeds were offline that day. A technical problem. It was unfortunate timing, that's all.'

'You really can't expect me—' I begin, just as the door swings open, propelled with some force by Edward Monkford's arm as he strides into the room.

'What are you doing here?' he demands of me. I've never seen him so angry.

'She wants the data from One Folgate Street relating to the Matthews woman,' Thiel says.

Edward flushes with fury. 'This has gone far enough. I want you out, do you hear?' For a moment, I'm not sure if he means out of his office or One Folgate Street, but then he adds, 'We're invoking the penalty notice. You've got five days to leave the house.'

'You can't do that.'

'You're in breach of at least a dozen restrictive covenants. I think you'll find we can.'

'Edward . . . what are you so frightened of? What are you trying to hide?'

'I'm not *frightened* of anything. I'm just *pissed off* at constantly having my wishes ignored by you. To be honest, I actually find it amusing that you accuse *me* of being obsessed with Emma Matthews, when clearly you're the one who's fixated on her. Why couldn't you just leave it? Why do you care so much?'

'You gave me her necklace,' I say, equally angry. 'If you're so innocent, why did you have her necklace repaired and then give it to me?'

He looks at me as if I'm mad. 'I gave you both similar necklaces because I happen to like those particular pearls, that's all.'

'Did you kill her, Edward?' I hear myself asking. 'Because it certainly looks as if you did.'

'Where do you *get* this from?' he says incredulously. 'Who puts these crazy ideas in your head?'

'I want an answer.' I'm trying to sound calm, but my voice is shaking.

'Well, you're not going to get one. Now go.'

Thiel says nothing. Edward stares furiously at my bump as I get up to leave.

Now: Jane

I have nowhere to go except back to One Folgate Street. But I enter it with trepidation, like a bloodied fighter stepping back into the ring for yet another round.

The feeling of being watched is all-pervasive now. The feeling of being played with, too. Small things around the house randomly malfunction. Electric sockets choose not to work. Lights fade up and down. When I type *one-bed flats* into Housekeeper's search engine, it takes me to a site about women who lie to their partners. When I turn on the sound system, it selects Chopin's funeral march. The burglar alarm goes off, startling me.

'Stop being so fucking childish!' I shout at the ceiling.

The silence of the empty rooms is the only mocking reply.

I get my phone.

'Simon,' I say when he answers, 'if that offer still stands, I would quite like you to come round tonight after all.'

'Jane, what's wrong?' he says, instantly concerned. 'You sound frightened.'

'Not frightened exactly,' I lie. 'Just a little freaked out by this place. I'm sure it's nothing to worry about. But it would be good to see you anyway.'

Now: Jane

'I came as soon as I could,' Simon says, dumping a bag by the door. 'That's the advantage of being freelance, I guess. I can work from here just as easily as from a Starbucks.' He looks at my face and stops. 'Jane, are you sure you're all right? You look terrible.'

'Simon . . . I've got an apology to make. All this time, you've been telling me that Edward killed Emma and I've been dismissing it. But now I'm starting to think . . .' I hesitate, unwilling even to put this into words. 'I'm starting to think you may be right.'

'There's no need to apologise, Jane. But can I ask what's changed your mind?'

I tell him about the cameras and my confrontation with Thiel. 'And then I came straight out and accused Edward of giving me the same necklace as Emma,' I add.

Simon stares at me, suddenly tense. 'How did he take that?'

'He said they were two different necklaces.'

'Could he prove it?'

'He didn't even try to. He just threw me out.' I shrug resignedly. 'I've got five days to find somewhere else.'

'You can stay with me for a while, if you want.'

'Thank you. But really, I've imposed on you quite enough.'

'We will stay friends, though, Jane, won't we? Leaving here won't mean you just forget all about me?'

'Of course not,' I say, a little embarrassed by his neediness. 'Anyway, now I have a moral dilemma.' I gesture at the table, where my necklace lies in its clamshell case. 'All this stuff about necklaces made me look up how much it's worth. It turns out to be around three thousand pounds.'

He raises his eyebrows. 'Which would be a pretty hefty deposit on a flat.'

'Exactly. But I think I should give it back to Edward.'

'Why? If he chooses to give you something valuable, that's his lookout.'

'Yes, but . . .' I struggle to explain. 'I don't want him to think I only care about its financial value. The trouble is, I *do* need the money.' And I don't want to make him more contemptuous of me than he already is, I think but don't say out loud.

'It says so much about you that this is even a dilemma, Jane. Most people wouldn't hesitate for a moment.' Simon smiles. The tension he displayed just now when I talked about Edward and the pearls is gone. Why *was* he so tense? What did he think I was going to say?

Then something occurs to me – something tiny, but completely obvious.

If Simon's right and my necklace is the one Edward previously gave to Emma, one of the strings will have one less pearl than the others.

I run my fingers over the top string, counting quickly. Twenty-four pearls.

The second string also has twenty-four pearls.

So does the third.

Edward was telling the truth. The necklace he gave me wasn't the one he gave Emma, after all. The scenario Simon described, in which Edward killed Emma, then picked up all but one of the loose pearls, never happened.

Unless it was Simon.

The thought floats into my brain, fully formed. What if it all happened just as Simon said . . . but to him, not Edward?

You have no proof, I tell myself.

But suddenly I feel a whole lot less happy about having this man spend the night here.

Something else occurs to me. There have been no technical malfunctions at One Folgate Street when Simon's around. The water flows from the taps, the shower works, even Housekeeper stays unlocked. Why is that?

Unless he was somehow causing it all?

Thiel had looked shamefaced when I confronted him. But he'd also looked puzzled. And he'd said something about a problem on the day of Emma's death.

Was he embarrassed because he knew someone else had accessed One Folgate Street's systems?

Have I been getting this all wrong?

14. *I try not to let people know what I am really thinking.*

Agree ☐ ☐ ☐ ☐ ☐ *Disagree*

Now: Jane

'Jane? Are you all right?' Simon's watching me closely.

'Yes.' I shake myself and give him a little smile. 'It was sweet of you to come. Though actually there was no need to bring a bag. My friend Mia just texted. She's going to stay the night.'

'Doesn't Mia have kids? And a husband?' His tone is solicitous.

'Yes, but—'

'Well, there you go. They need her. And I'm here now. Besides, it'll be like old times.'

'Old times? How?' I say, confused.

He gestures. 'You and me. Here, together.'

'That's not old times, Simon.'

His smile doesn't waver. 'But not far off. For me, anyway.'

'Simon . . .' I don't know how to say this. 'I'm not Emma. I'm nothing like her.'

'Of course not. You're a better person than she was, for one thing.'

I pick up my phone from the table.

'What are you doing?' he asks.

'I should really put the necklace back upstairs,' I lie.

'I'll do it.' He holds out his hand. 'You're pregnant. You should be taking it easy.'

371

JP DELANEY

'Not that pregnant.' I suddenly think of something else. *Most people think a small amount of alcohol is all right at around fifteen weeks.* How does he know how many weeks I am?

I start to move past him. He keeps his hand out, but I ignore him.

'Careful on those stairs!' he calls, watching me. I force myself to slow down, acknowledging the comment with a wave.

Apart from the hall, the only place in One Folgate Street with a door is the cleaner's cupboard. I slip inside, then use the brooms and mops to wedge it shut.

I try Mia first. *Call Failed.*

'Shit,' I say aloud. 'Bloody shit.'

Edward Monkford. *Call Failed.*

999.

Call Failed.

Looking at the screen, I see there's no signal. With some difficulty, I hoist myself into the roof space and hold the phone up as high as I can. No signal here, either.

As I climb down again I hear Simon's voice, calling from downstairs. 'Jane? Jane, are you all right?'

'I need you to go away, Simon,' I shout back. 'I'm not feeling well.'

'I'm sorry to hear that. I'll call a doctor.'

'Please don't. I just need to rest.'

I hear his voice getting louder as he comes upstairs. 'Jane? Where are you? Are you in the bathroom?'

I don't reply.

'Knock knock . . . No, not in the bathroom. Are we playing hide and seek?'

372

The door of the cupboard creaks as he pushes at it from outside.

'Found you,' he says happily. 'Come on out now, babe.'

Now: Jane

'I'm not going to come out,' I say through the door.

'This is stupid. I can't talk to you in there.'

'Simon, I want you to go. Or I'll call the police.'

'How? I've got a gadget that blocks mobile-phone signals. Wi-Fi too.'

I don't reply. I'm slowly realising this is even worse than I thought. He's planned this.

'All I wanted was to be with you,' he adds. 'But you still prefer Monkford to me, don't you?'

'What's Edward got to do with it?'

'He doesn't deserve you. Just like he didn't deserve *her*. But nice guys don't get nice girls, do they? They lose them to pricks like him.'

'Simon, I've got a signal. I'm calling the police.' I raise my phone and say urgently, 'Police, please. The address is One Folgate Street, Hendon. There's a man in my house who's threatening me.'

'Not strictly true, babe. I haven't threatened anyone.'

'Please hurry. Yes, five minutes is fine. Thank you.'

'Very convincing. You're a good liar, Jane. Just like every other woman I've ever fucking met.' The sentence ends with a snarl as he unleashes a sudden barrage of kicks on the door.

The mops and brooms bend, but don't give way. I feel dizzy with terror.

'Doesn't bother me, Jane,' he says, panting. 'I've got all day.' I hear him going back downstairs. Long minutes pass. I catch the smell of frying bacon. Absurdly, it makes my mouth water.

I look around the cupboard, wondering if there's anything here I can use to defend myself. My eyes alight on the cables lining the wall: the veins and arteries of One Folgate Street. I start pulling them out at random. It must have some effect, because soon I hear him coming back up the stairs.

'Very clever, Jane. But a bit annoying too, actually. Come on out now. I've made you some food.'

'Go away, Simon. Don't you see? You've got to go. I mean it.'

'You sound just like Emma when you're angry.' There's the sound of a knife scraping across a plate. I picture him sitting cross-legged on the other side of the cupboard door, eating what he's cooked. 'I should have said no to her more often. I should have been more forceful. That was always my problem. Too reasonable. Too *nice*.' I hear a cork being pulled from a bottle. 'I thought maybe you were nice as well, so it would be different this time. But it wasn't.'

'DAVID THIEL,' I shout. 'EDWARD. HELP.'

I shout until my throat is sore and my voice hoarse.

'They can't hear you,' he says when I've finished.

'They can,' I insist. 'They're watching.'

'Is that what you thought? 'Fraid not. That was me. You remind me so much of her, you see. I've been in love with you for ages, Jane.'

'It's not love,' I say, horrified. 'Love can't be totally one-sided.'

'Love is always one-sided,' he says sadly.

I know I've got to stay calm. 'If you did love me, you'd want me to be happy. Not scared and trapped in here.'

'I do want you to be happy. With me. But if I can't have you, I certainly won't let that prick have you instead.'

'I told you. I broke up with him.'

'That's what *she* said.' He sounds weary. 'So I gave her a test. A simple test. And she wanted him back. Not me – him. I didn't want it to be like this, Jane. I wanted you to fall in love with me. But this is the next best thing.'

I hear the sound of a zipper as he opens his bag. Then a sloshing sound. A dark stain creeps under the cupboard door. Petrol.

'Simon!' I scream. 'For fuck's sake!'

'I can't, Em.' His voice sounds snotty and thick, like he's on the verge of crying. 'Can't let it go.'

'Please, Simon. Think of the baby. Even if you hate *me*, think of the baby.'

'Oh, I do. The bastard's little bastard. His cock in your cunt. His *child* in your belly. No fucking way.' Another slosh. 'I'm going to burn this place. He won't like that much, will he? And I'll be forced to burn you and the baby with it, if you don't come out. Don't make me do that to you, Jane.'

All these cleaning products will be flammable. One by one I throw them up into the roof space. Then I clamber up after them and check for phone signal again. Still nothing.

'Jane,' Simon calls through the door. 'Last chance. Come out and be nice to me. Pretend you love me, just for a little while. Just pretend, that's all I'm asking.'

I move along the crawl space, using my phone as a torch. There are wooden crossbeams and trusses everywhere. Once a fire gets hold up here, there'll be no stopping it. In any case, I seem to remember that in house fires, it's the smoke that kills you.

I step on something soft. The old sleeping bag. Something else clicks in my mind. It wasn't Emma who was sleeping up here in the days before she died. It was Simon. He had some of Emma's stuff and her therapist's card. Maybe he even thought about getting some help. If only he had.

'Jane?' he calls again. 'Jane?'

And then I see my suitcase, the one I put up here out of the way. Crouching down, I open it and take out Isabel's memory box. With trembling hands, I touch her things: the cloth she was swaddled in, the plaster casts of her tiny hands and feet.

All that's left of her.

I've let you down. Both of you.

I slump to my knees, my hands on my bump, and let the tears come.

15. *Your child has got into difficulty in the sea. As you go to rescue her, you realise she is only one of about ten children in the same predicament. You can either rescue your daughter immediately, or go and get help for the whole group, which may take some time. Which do you do?*

☐ *Save your own child*

☐ *Save ten other children*

Now: Jane

I don't know how long I cry for. But when I've finished, there's still no smell of fire. Only the acrid reek of petrol.

I think of Simon, somewhere below me, feeling sorry for himself too. His pathetic, needy snivelling.

And I think, *No*.

I am not Emma Matthews, disorganised and vulnerable. I am a mother who has buried one child and carries another inside me.

It would be so easy to stay here, luxuriating in the sweet passivity of grief. To lie down and wait for the smoke to seep up through the joists, wrapping itself around me, pulling me down.

But that is not what I do.

Some primeval instinct propels me to my feet. Almost before I'm aware of it, I'm lowering myself down through the hatch again. Quietly, I take the mops and brooms away from the cupboard door.

The necklace is still in my pocket. Pulling it out, I snap the strings, letting the pearls fall loose into my hand.

Softly, gently, I open the door.

One Folgate Street is unrecognisable. The walls are daubed with graffiti. Pillows and cushions have been ripped apart. Smashed crockery litters the floor. There's what looks like blood smeared across the plate-glass windows. As well as petrol, I catch the smell of gas from the cooker.

'Simon?' I say to the silent house.

As if from nowhere, he appears at the foot of the staircase. 'Jane. I'm so glad.'

'I can be her for you.' I haven't planned this, not in any detail, but now it seems obvious what I have to say and the words come out of my mouth without hesitation or tremors. 'Emma. Nice Emma – the one you loved. I'll be her for you, and then you'll let me go. Yes?'

He stares up at me without replying.

I imagine how Emma might have spoken, the rhythms of her voice. 'Wow,' I say, looking around. 'You've really done a number on this place, haven't you, babe? You must really love me, Si, to do all this. I never realised how passionate you were.'

Suspicion battles in his eyes with something else. Happiness? Love? I place a hand on my belly.

'Simon, there's something you should know. You're going to be a dad. Isn't that great?'

He flinches. *The bastard's little bastard.* 'Let's go and lie down, Si,' I say quickly, sensing I've taken it too far. 'Just for a few minutes. I'll rub your back and you can rub mine. That would be nice, wouldn't it? A cuddle would be nice.'

'Nice,' he repeats, coming up the stairs. His voice is hoarse. 'Yes.'

'Will you take a shower?'

He nods, then something hardens in his gaze. 'You too.'

'I'll just get a robe.'

I walk towards the bedroom, feeling his eyes follow me. I open the stone cupboard and slip a bathrobe from its hanger.

I catch the sound of water. He must have turned the shower on. But when I turn round he's back in the same spot, still watching me.

'I can't do it, Em,' he says.

For a moment, I think he means this charade. 'Can't do what, babe?'

'Can't lose you. Can't let you be that person who wants them but not me.' He says the words in a strange, sing-song way, like they're the lyrics of a song that's been going round and round in his head so long they've lost any meaning.

'But I *do* want you, babe. No one else. Come on, I'll show you.'

With a sudden gasping sob he buries his head in his hands and I seize my chance, dodging past him towards the stairs, the treacherous stairs where Emma died. I almost tumble on the top step, my heavy belly unbalancing me, but then I put a hand to the wall and manage to steady myself, my bare feet sure on the familiar slabs. With a roar of anger, he lunges after me. Somehow, he gets a hand into my hair and yanks me back. I fling the handful of pearls at his head. He barely flinches. But when he goes for the next step they're under his feet, lethal as ball bearings, and his arms flail wildly as his legs skate off in different directions. Surprise and shock are written across his face and then he's falling, falling into the void. His body hits the floor first, his head following with a sickening crack. Pearls patter down the stairs like a waterfall and tumble over the side after him, bouncing around his twisted, spreadeagled body. There's a moment when I'm sure he's still alive because his eyes look up at me, anguished, searching me out, reluctant to let go, and then the blood seeps from the back of his head and his gaze goes dead.

Now: Jane

I try again for phone signal, but Simon's jammer must still be working. I'll have to go next door to call an ambulance. Not that there's any great rush now. His eyes are open and unmoving and his head has a halo of dark red blood.

Carefully, I pick my way down the stairs and round the living room, skirting the pearls that still dangerously litter the floor, one hand curled protectively over my belly. My path brings me close to the big glass windows. Almost unconsciously, I wipe at the bloody graffiti with my sleeve. It comes off easily, revealing the reflection of my face against the darkness beyond.

It will all come off, I think. All this mess, this superficial disorder. The blood, and Simon's body, will soon be gone. The house will be pristine again. Like a living organism expelling a tiny splinter, One Folgate Street has healed itself.

I feel an overwhelming sense of serenity, of peace. I look at my reflection in the dark glass, feeling the house acknowledge me; both of us, in our different ways, ripe with possibility.

16. *A railway signalman is responsible for changing the points at a remote junction. Against regulations, he takes his son to work, but gives him strict instructions not to go near the line. Later, he sees a train approaching, but before he can change the points, he spots the boy playing on the track, too far away to hear him. Unless the points are changed, the train will almost certainly crash, causing multiple fatalities, but if he does change them, the train will almost certainly kill his son. If you were him, what would you do?*

☐ *Change the points*

☐ *Don't change the points*

Now: Jane

I never do get to have a water birth, with Diptyque candles per-
fuming the air and Jack Johnson playing on my iPad. Instead I
have a Caesarean, following the discovery during a routine scan of
a small blockage in my baby's stomach – nothing that immediate
post-natal surgery can't fix, thank heaven, but it tips the scales
from a natural to a medical birth.

Dr Gifford is careful to explain the implications, and I undergo
some further tests before it's all agreed. After the birth, I hold
Toby for just a few bittersweet, wonderful minutes, then they
whisk him away to theatre. But not before the midwife has put
him to my breast and I've felt his hard gums working at my
nipple, the deep pulling sensation reaching into my very core,
right down to my tender uterus, followed by the tingling euphoria
of let-down. Love flows from me into him, and his blue eyes
crinkle, huge and happy. Such a smiley baby. The midwife says it
can't be a real smile, not yet, just some passing gas or a random
quiver of his lip, but I know she's wrong.

Edward comes to visit us the day after. I've seen him quite a few
times during my final trimester, partly because of all the legal
bureaucracy that followed Simon's death, and partly because

Edward himself has had the grace to admit he should have realised how dangerous Simon was. We're in this for the long-term now, as co-parents; and if in the fullness of time we can be more than that ... well, that's a possibility, I sometimes think, that Edward no longer quite rules out.

I'm still sleepy when he arrives, so the nurse checks with me first, but of course I say to let him in. I want to show him our son.

'Here he is. Here's Toby.' I'm unable to stop myself from smiling. But I'm apprehensive too. The habit of being judged by Edward, of seeking his approval, is too recent to have altogether faded.

He lifts Toby high in his arms and examines his round, cheerful face. 'When did you know?' he says quietly.

'That he has Down's? After they found the blockage. Nearly a third of babies with duodenal atresia have it.' The cfDNA test, so much more than 99 per cent accurate, hadn't been infallible after all. But after the shock and grief of the initial confirmation, there's a part of me that's almost glad the test was wrong. If I'd known, I would have had a termination; and looking at Toby now – at the almond-shaped eyes, the snub nose, the gorgeous bow-shaped mouth – how could I possibly wish this life unlived?

Of course, there are worries. But every child with Down's is different and it looks as if we've been lucky. He's barely floppier than any other baby. His oral coordination, when he mouths at my nipple, seems good. He has no problems swallowing, no heart defects or kidney problems. And his nose, though stubby, is still recognisably Edward's; his eyes, though almond-shaped, not so dissimilar to my own.

He's beautiful.

'Jane,' Edward says urgently, 'this may not be the easiest time to hear this, but you have to give him up. There are people who adopt such babies. People who choose that to be their life. Not people like you.'

'I couldn't,' I say. 'Edward, I just couldn't.'

Just for a moment I see, deep in his eyes, a flash of anger. And something else too, perhaps: the tiniest glimmer of fear.

'We could try again,' he continues, as if I haven't spoken. 'You and me – a clean slate. We could make it work this time. I know we could.'

'If you'd been more honest with me about Emma,' I say, 'we might have made it work before.'

He looks at me sharply. I can see him wondering if this is what motherhood has done – if it has already somehow changed me, made me more assertive.

'I tried, believe me,' he says at last. 'But how could I talk to you about it, when I didn't even understand it myself? I'm an obsessive person. And she loved to provoke me. She found it exciting when she managed to make me lose control, even though I hated myself for it. In the end, I did break it off with her, but it was hard, very hard.' He hesitates. 'She gave me a letter, once. She said she wanted to explain herself. Later, she asked me not to read it. But by then, I already had.'

'Did you keep it?'

'Yes. Do you want to see it?'

'No,' I decide. I look down at Toby's face. 'It's the future we need to think about now.'

He seizes on that. 'So you *will* consider it? You'll think about giving this one up? I think I could be a father again, Jane. I think I'm ready for that. But let's have the child we want to have. A child that's been *planned*.'

And that, finally, is when I tell Edward the truth.

Then: Emma

I knew even before I met you, when the estate agent started talking about your rules. Some women, perhaps most women, want to be cherished and respected. They want a man who's sweet and kind, who whispers words of gentleness and love. I've tried to be that woman, and to love that man, but I can't.

As soon as I spilled the coffee on your plans, I was sure. Something I couldn't even put into words had happened. You were stern and powerful, but you forgave me. Simon could do the forgiveness, but it was out of weakness, not strength. In that moment, I became yours.

I don't want to be cherished. I want to be commanded. I want a monstrous man, a man other men hate and envy and who doesn't give a shit. A man made of stone.

Once or twice I thought I'd found that man, or at least someone with a small bit of his confidence and strength. And then I could never be the one to tear myself away. When those men used me and threw me aside, I accepted it as nothing more than the proof they really were who they claimed to be.

One of those men was Saul. I found him disgusting at first. An arrogant, loathsome creep. I thought because he was married to Amanda, his flirting didn't mean anything. So I let myself flirt back and that was my mistake. He got me drunk. I knew what he was doing, but I thought there was a *point where he'd stop. He didn't, and I suppose I didn't either. It felt like it was all happening to someone else. I know this will sound strange, but it felt like I was Audrey Hepburn dancing with Fred Astaire. Not a drunk PA giving a senior manager a seedy blow job at a corporate training day. And by the time I realised I didn't like what he was doing or the way he was doing it, it was far too late. The more I tried to stop him, the rougher he got.*

I hated myself after that. I thought it was my fault for letting him get me into that situation. And I hated Simon for always seeing the best in me when actually I'm not the person he thinks I am. It was just so much easier to lie to everyone than to tell the truth.

So you see, in you I thought I'd finally found someone who was kind as well as strong, Simon as well as Saul. And when I realised you had secrets too, I was glad. I thought we could be honest with each other. That we could finally rid ourselves of all the clutter from our past – not our possessions, but the stuff we carry around inside our heads. Because that's what I've realised, living in One Folgate Street. You can make your surroundings as polished and empty as you like, but it doesn't really matter if you're still messed up inside. And that's all anyone's looking for really, isn't it? Someone to take care of the mess inside our heads.

17. *It is better to tell a lie and remain in control of a situation than to tell the truth with unpredictable results.*

Agree ☐ ☐ ☐ ☐ ☐ *Disagree*

Now: Jane

'He *was* planned,' I say.

Edward frowns. 'Is that a joke?'

'Perhaps ten per cent of a joke.' He starts to relax, but then I add, 'That's to say, he was planned by *me*. Just not by you.'

I tuck Toby tighter into the crook of my arm. 'I knew the very first time I met you, actually, that time at your office. I knew you could be the father of my child. Good looking, intelligent, creative, driven . . . You were certainly the best I was likely to find.'

'You *lied* to me?' he says incredulously.

'Not really. There were a few things I didn't explain, that's all.' Not least when I answered the very first question on the application form, the one demanding a list of everything essential to my life. When you've lost the centre of your universe, there's only one thing that can possibly make you whole again.

I could never have done it anywhere but One Folgate Street. Second thoughts, self-doubts, moral qualms – in the ordinary world, they would have paralysed me. But in those stark, uncompromising spaces, my resolve only grew and grew. One Folgate Street colluded in my plans, and all my decisions had the clean simplicity of loss.

'I knew something was going on.' Edward has gone very pale.

'There were some anomalies with Housekeeper – data that didn't make sense. I put it down to your obsession with Emma's death, this ridiculous quest you were trying to keep secret—'

'I didn't care about Emma, not personally,' I interrupt. 'But I had to know if you could be a danger to our child.' Ironically, it was Simon's death that finally allowed me to resolve that question. In his blue folder, I found the name of the site foreman at One Folgate Street. Emma had been given it by Edward's former business partner, Tom Ellis, but in her usual chaotic way had never followed it up. The foreman confirmed what I was already almost certain of: that the deaths of Edward's wife and child were just a tragic accident.

'I don't feel sorry for you, Edward,' I add. 'You got exactly what you wanted – a brief, intense, perfect affair. Any man who sleeps with a woman under those conditions should know there may be consequences.'

Was what I did acceptable? Or, at the very least, understandable?

Can any woman say that, in my shoes, she wouldn't have done the same?

I feel no guilt about Simon, either. I knew when I closed the lid on Isabel's memory box that I'd kill him if I could. But by the time the police arrived I'd picked up all the loose pearls, and there was nothing to suggest I'd played any part in his sad, unfortunate death.

'Oh, Jane.' Edward shakes his head. 'Jane. How . . . magnificent. All the time I thought I was controlling you, you were actually controlling *me*. I should have known you had your own agenda.'

'Can you forgive me?'

He doesn't reply at first, letting the question hang in the air. Then, to my surprise, he slowly nods.

'Who knows better than me what it's like to lose a child?' he says quietly. 'How you'll do anything, however destructive or wrong, that seems to numb the pain? Perhaps we're more alike than either of us realised.'

For a long moment he's silent, lost in his own thoughts.

'After Max and Elizabeth died, I became quite deranged for a while – mad with guilt and grief and self-hatred,' he says. 'I went to Japan, to try to get away from myself, but nothing helped. And then, when I came back, I discovered Tom Ellis was planning to finish up One Folgate Street and put his own name to it. I couldn't bear to see the house Elizabeth and I had planned together come into existence like that. So I tore up the plans and started again. I didn't really care what kind of place I built instead, to be honest. I built something as sterile and empty as a mausoleum because that's how I felt at the time. But then I realised that, in my madness, I'd inadvertently created something extraordinary. A house that would demand a sacrifice from anyone who lived there, but repay that sacrifice a thousandfold in return. There are some, like Emma, it destroys. But others, like you, it makes stronger.'

He stares at me intently. 'Don't you see, Jane? You've shown you're worthy of it. That you're disciplined and ruthless enough to be One Folgate Street's mistress. So I'm making you an offer.'

His gaze never leaves me, his unblinking blue eyes boring into mine. 'If you'll give this baby up for adoption . . . I'll give you the house. *Your* house, now, to do with as you choose. But the longer you leave it, the harder the decision will become. What do you really want? A chance of perfection? Or a lifetime of trying to cope with . . . with . . .' He gestures wordlessly at Toby. 'The future you were always meant to have, Jane? Or this?'

18.

☐ *Give up the baby*

☐ *Don't give up the baby*

Now: Jane

'And if I say yes, we'll have another child?'

'You have my word on it.' He seizes on my hesitation. 'It wouldn't just be the right thing for us, Jane. It would be right for *Toby*. Better for a child like him to be adopted now, than to grow up without a father.'

'He *has* a father.'

'You know what I mean. He needs parents who can accept him for what he is. Not ones who grieve for the child who might have been, every time they look at him.'

'You're right,' I say quietly. 'He *does* need that.'

I think of One Folgate Street, the sense of belonging and calm I feel there. And I look at Toby, and think of what's to come. A single mother, alone with her disabled child, battling the system to get the therapies he needs. A life of turmoil and muddle and compromise.

Or a chance to try again, for something better and more beautiful.

For another Isabel.

There's a posset of regurgitated milk on Toby's shoulder. Carefully I wipe it away. There. All gone.

I make my decision.

I will take what I can from Edward. And then I will let them fade into history, all the characters in this drama. Emma Matthews and the men who loved her, who became obsessed with her. They're not important to us now. But one day, when Toby is old enough, I will take down a shoebox from the shelf where it is kept, and I will tell him again the story of his sister, Isabel Margaret Cavendish, the girl who came before.

Now: Astrid

'It's *extraordinary*,' I say, looking in disbelief at the pale stone walls, the space, the light. 'I've never seen such an amazing house. Not even in Denmark.'

'It *is* rather special,' Camilla agrees. 'The architect's actually rather famous. Do you remember the fuss last year about that eco-town in Cornwall?'

'It was something about the residents refusing to accept the terms of their leases, wasn't it? Didn't he get them all thrown out?'

'The lease here is quite complicated too,' Camilla says. 'If you want to take this any further, I should probably talk you through it.'

I look around me, at the soaring walls, the floating staircase, the incredible serenity and calm. In such a place, I think, I could be whole again, put all the bitterness and rage of the divorce behind me. 'I'm definitely interested,' I hear myself say.

'Good. Oh, and by the way . . .' Camilla's looking up at the roof void now, as if reluctant to meet my eye. 'I'm sure you'll google the address anyway, so there's no point in not telling you. The house does have a bit of history. A young couple who lived here . . . First she fell down the stairs and died, and then three

years later he died in exactly the same spot. They think he must
have thrown himself down deliberately, to be with her.'

'Well, it's certainly tragic,' I say. 'But as tragedies go, quite
romantic. If you're asking whether that would put me off . . . it
wouldn't. Is there anything else I should know?'

'Just that the owner can be a bit of a tyrant. I must have shown
dozens of prospective tenants round in the last few weeks, and
none of them have been accepted.'

'Believe me, I know how to deal with tyrants. I lived with one
for six years.'

And so, that evening, I find myself leafing through the endless
pages of the application form. So many rules to read! And so many
questions to answer! It's tempting to get myself a drink to help
me through it, but I haven't had one for almost three weeks now
and I'm trying to keep it that way.

*Please make a list of every possession you consider essential to
your life.*

I take a deep breath and pick up my pen.

ACKNOWLEDGEMENTS

Many, many people helped over the decade or so it took me to work out how to write this book. I'd particularly like to thank the producer Jill Green for her early encouragement; Laura Palmer for her typically insightful responses to an unfinished draft; Tina Sederholm for a poet's perspective; and Dr Emma Fergusson for advice on medical matters and much more.

At Penguin Random House, my deep gratitude goes to Kate Miciak, not only for buying the book and whisking a fifty-page sample almost overnight to her colleague Denise Cronin and her remarkable team at the Frankfurt Book Fair, but also for the months of stimulating debate, impeccable craftsmanship and editorial passion that followed.

My greatest debt, though, is to Caradoc King and his team at United Agents – Mildred Yuan, Millie Hoskins, Yasmin McDonald and Amy Mitchell – who read the initial pages when the story was barely more than a suggestion. Without their enthusiasm and belief, I doubt it would ever have been more than that.

This book is dedicated to my indomitable, unfailingly cheerful son, Ollie, one of the very few people in the world born with type-B Joubert's syndrome, and to the memory of his older brother, Nicholas, our boy before.

Read on for an exclusive extract from the
gripping new thriller by JP Delaney.

Coming August 2020

PLAYING
NICE

ONE

Pete

It was just an ordinary day.

If this were a colour piece or a feature, the kind of thing I used to write on a daily basis, the editor would have rejected it just for that opening sentence. *Openers need to hook people, Pete,* she'd tell me, tossing my pages back at me across my desk. *Paint a picture, set a scene. Be* dramatic. *In travel journalism especially, you need a sense of place. Take your readers on a* journey.

So: it was just an ordinary day in Willesden Green, north London.

Because the fact is, before that knock on my door, it *was* just an ordinary day. An unusually nice one, admittedly. The sun was shining, the air was crisp and blue. There was still some snow on the ground, hiding in corners, but it had that soft sugary look snow gets when it's all but melted, and none of the kids streaming into the Acol Road Nursery and Preschool could be bothered to get their mittens wet trying to scoop it up for snowballs.

Actually, there was one small thing out of the ordinary. As I took Theo into the nursery, or rather followed him in – we'd given him a scooter for his second birthday, a chunky three-wheeler he was now inseparable from – I noticed three people, a woman and two men, on the other side of the road, watching us. The younger man was roughly my age, thirty or so. The other was in his fifties. Both wore dark suits with dark woollen coats over them, and the woman, a blonde, was wrapped up in a kind of fake-fur parka, the sort of thing you might see on a fashionable ski slope. They looked too smart for our part of London. But then I saw that the older man was holding a document case in his gloved hand. An estate agent, I guessed, showing some prospective buyers the local childcare facilities. The Jubilee Line goes all the way from our Tube station to Canary Wharf, and even the bankers have been priced out of West Hampstead these days.

Something about the younger man seemed familiar. But then I was distracted by Jane Tigman, whose son Zack was already starting to thrash and scream in her arms at the prospect of being left. She hadn't realised that the trick is to make sure they walk into nursery on their own rather than being carried, which simply makes the moment of separation more final. Then there was a note about World Book Day on the nursery door that hadn't been there yesterday – God, yet another costume I'd have to organise – and after that I had to separate Theo from his helmet, gloves and coat, stuff the gloves deep enough into the coat pockets that they wouldn't fall out – I still hadn't got round to putting name tags on them – and help him hang the coat on his peg, deep among all the others, before crouching down to give him a final pep talk.

'OK, big man. You going to play nicely today?'

He nodded, wide-eyed with sincerity. 'Yef, Dad.'

'So no grabbing. And take turns. That's very important. Remember we said we'd take turns to choose lunch? So today it's your turn, and tomorrow it'll be mine. What do you want for lunch?'

'Booby smoovy,' he announced after a moment's thought.

'Blueberry smoothie,' I repeated clearly. 'OK. I'll make some before I pick you up. Have a good morning.'

I gave him a kiss and off he went, happy as Larry.

'Mr Riley?'

I turned. It was Susy, the woman who ran the nursery. It looked as if she'd been waiting for Theo to go. 'Can I have a word?' she added.

I snapped my fingers. 'The sippy cup. I forgot. I'll get another one today—'

'It isn't about the sippy cup,' she interrupted. 'Shall we talk in my office?'

'It's nothing to worry about,' she said as we sat down, which of course instantly made me aware that it was definitely something to worry about. 'It's just that there was another incident yesterday. Theo hit one of the other children again.'

'Ah,' I said defensively. That was the third time this month. 'OK. It's something we have been working on at home. According to the internet, it sometimes happens at this age if physical skills get ahead of verbal skills.' I smiled ruefully, to show that I wasn't stupid enough to believe every parenting theory I read on the internet, but neither was I one of those entitled middle-class dads who thought that, just because my son was now at nursery, I wasn't required to put any effort into being his parent anymore

– or, even worse, was blind to the possibility of my little darling having any faults in the first place. 'And, of course, his speech *is* a little delayed. But I'd welcome any suggestions.'

Susy visibly relaxed. 'Well, as you say, it is typical two-year-old stuff. I'm sure you know this, but it can help if you model the correct behaviour. If he sees you getting cross or aggressive, he'll come to believe that aggression is a legitimate response to stress. What about the TV programmes he watches? I'm afraid even *Tom and Jerry* may not be appropriate at this age, at least not until the hitting stage is over. And if you play any violent video games yourself—'

'I don't play video games,' I said firmly. 'Quite apart from anything else, I don't have the time.'

'I'm sure. It's just that we don't always think about the consequences of things like that.' She smiled, but I could almost see the thought process behind her eyes. *Stay-at-home dad equals aggressive kid.* She wouldn't have asked Jane Tigman if she played *Call of Duty*.

'And we're working on sharing, too,' I added. 'Taking turns who chooses what to have for lunch, that kind of thing.'

'Well, it certainly sounds as if you're on top of it.' Susy got to her feet to show the discussion was over. 'We'll keep a close watch here, and let's hope he grows out of it.'

Understandably, then, I wasn't thinking about the wealthy-looking couple and their estate agent as I left the nursery. I was worrying about Theo, and why he was taking so long to learn to play nicely with the other kids. But I'm pretty sure, looking back, that by the time I reached the street, the three of them were nowhere to be seen.

TWO

Case no. 12675/PU78B65: AFFIDAVIT UNDER OATH, by D. Maguire.

I, Donald Joseph Maguire, make oath and swear as follows:

1. I am the proprietor and chief investigator of Maguire Missing Persons, a London-based investigative agency which traces over two hundred individuals a year on behalf of our clients. We do not advertise. All our work comes by personal referral.

2. Prior to starting this business, I was a senior detective with the Metropolitan Police, a position I held for thirteen years, leaving with the rank of detective inspector.

3. Last August, I was approached by Mr Miles Lambert and Mrs Lucy Lambert, of 17 Haydon Gardens, Highgate, N19 3JZ. They wished me to act for them in the matter of tracing their son.

THREE

Pete

At home, I turned on the coffee machine and opened my laptop. The coffee machine is a Jura, the laptop a top-of-the-line MacBook. They were the only two bits of kit I insisted on when Maddie and I started having the difficult conversations about which of us was going to stay home to look after Theo once her maternity leave was over. The idea was that I'd work from home part-time, at least when Theo got a place at nursery. Having a really good computer and a bean-to-cup coffee maker made being a stay-at-home dad feel like a step up, a new opportunity, rather than a step down in my career.

Though actually I hate the phrase 'stay-at-home dad'. It's a negative, passive construction, the absence of something. No one calls women in my position 'stay-at-home mums', do they? They're 'full-time mums', which immediately sounds more positive. Total mums. Mums without compromise. 'Stay-at-home dad' sounds like you're too lazy or too agoraphobic to leave the house and get a proper job. Which is what many people secretly do think, actually. Or, in the case of Maddie's parents, not so secretly. Her father's an Australian businessman with political views slightly to the right of Genghis Khan, and he's made it clear he thinks I'm sponging off her. Though he'd probably phrase it, *The boy's a bloody bludger.*

There was breakfast to clear up, the recycling to sort and toys to tidy away, but while the Jura whirred and spluttered – grinding beans, frothing milk – I threw on a load of washing and logged on to DadStuff.

Just seen a poster for World Book Day at my DS's nursery. 7 March. Aargh! Ideas? Really don't want to buy a ready-made costume at Sainos or the motherhood will judge me even more.

Within moments I had a reply. There's a hard core of about a hundred of us who stay online pretty much throughout the day, coming back to the forum in between our parenting duties. Once you got used to the cliquey jargon – DS or DD means *darling son* or *darling daughter*, OP means *original poster*, while OH is *other half* and AIBU is *am I being unreasonable?* – it was reassuring to be able to throw questions out there and see what others thought.

The mouse from The Gruffalo, mate. Brown shirt, white vest, some ears on an Alice band. Sorted.

That was Honker6. I typed back:

Er, Alice band? Your DDs might go for it, but we don't even own one of those.

What about Peter Rabbit? Little blue jacket, paper ears on baseball hat, face-painted whiskers?

Greg being practical, as usual. *Nice one*, I replied, trying to remember if Peter Rabbit had ever been involved in any age-inappropriate violence that Susy the nursery manager might disapprove of. You had to be careful with those Beatrix Potter books.

Then the doorbell rang, so I put my cappuccino down and went to answer it.

On the step was the group I'd seen outside the nursery. My first thought was that they must have made a mistake, because our house wasn't for sale. My second was that it wasn't the group from the nursery, not quite; the woman was no longer with them. So maybe they weren't house buyers, after all – they could be political canvassers, or even journalists. And my third thought, the one that immediately crowded all the others out of my head, was that, now I saw him up close, I realised that the younger of the two men, the one roughly my age, was the spitting image of Theo.

He had dark hair that spilled over his forehead in an unruly comma, a prominent jaw and deep-set blue eyes – the kind of dark, boyish looks that in Theo look heart-stoppingly cute, but which in adults always make me think of the word *saturnine*, without really knowing why. He was almost six foot, chunky and broad-shouldered. An athlete's physique. There's a picture of the

417

writer Ted Hughes as a young man, glowering at the camera with the same lock of hair falling over his right eye. This guy reminded me of that. A chiselled, granite face, but not unfriendly.

'Hello,' he said, without ado. 'Can we come in? We need to speak to you.'

'Why?' I asked stupidly.

'I really think this would be better done inside,' he said patiently. 'It's about your son.'

'All right.' And his manner was so brisk and purposeful that I found myself stepping away from the door, even though I was now thinking, Was it *his* child Theo hit? Am I about to get shouted at?

'Er – coffee?' I said, leading the way into the lounge – which is to say, taking a few steps back. Like most people in our street, we've ripped out the walls downstairs to create one decent-sized room. The older man shook his head, but I saw the younger man glance at my cappuccino. 'I make them fresh,' I added, thinking a pause for coffee might defuse the coming row a bit.

'Go on, then.'

There was an awkward wait while I frothed more milk.

'I'm Miles Lambert, by the way,' he added, when I was done. 'And this gentleman is Don Maguire.' He took the cup I offered him. 'Thanks. Shall we sit down?'

I sat in the only armchair and Miles Lambert took the couch, carefully moving some toys out of the way as he did so. Don Maguire sat in my swivel desk chair. I saw him cast an admiring glance at my MacBook.

'There's no easy way to do this,' Miles said, when we were all seated. He leaned forward, lacing his fingers together like a rugby player about to take a penalty. 'Look, if it was me, I'd want to be told straight, with no bullshit, so that's what I'm going to do. But prepare yourself for a shock.' He took a deep breath. 'I'm sorry to have to tell you that Theo isn't your son. He's mine.'

I gaped at him. Thoughts crowded in on me. *That can't be right*, followed by, *So that's why this man looks like Theo*. Disbelief, shell shock, horror – all paralysed me. I'm not fast in a crisis, unfortunately; Maddie's the one who thinks on her feet.

Maddie. Oh my God. Was this man telling me they had an affair? Is that what this is? That I'm a—

The word *cuckold*, with all its medieval ugliness, crashed into my brain like a rock. Maddie and I have had our problems, we're like any couple in that regard, and there have been times over the last year or so when I've sensed her drawing away from me. But I've always put that down to the trauma of Theo's birth—

Theo's birth. Think straight, Pete. Theo was born just over two years ago. So it would have been almost three years ago when this supposed affair happened. Which was nigh on impossible. Maddie and I only came back from Australia, where we met, three years back.

I realised both Miles Lambert and Don Maguire were looking at me, waiting for me to react, and I still hadn't said anything. 'What are you trying to tell me?' I said numbly.

Miles Lambert simply repeated, 'Theo isn't your son. He's mine.' His blue eyes held mine, concerned. 'I'm sorry. I know it's a shock. Please, take your time.'

It was Don Maguire who coughed and added, 'You both have sons who were born prematurely, I understand, who were both separated from their mothers briefly when they were transferred

419

to the Neonatal Intensive Care Unit at St Alexander's. It's conceivable that, at some point during that process, the wrong tags were put on the wrong babies. That's our working theory, anyway.'

Double negative, the editor shouted at me. *The wrong tags got put on the right babies, you cretin.* Which only goes to show that, at moments of crisis, you think the most bizarre things.